John Bainbridge is the author of over thirty books and numerous articles for newspapers and magazines. He read literature and nineteenth century social history at the University of East Anglia and specialises in the history of the Victorian underworld.

First published in Great Britain in 2014 by Gaslight Crime

ISBN-13: 978-1496107619
ISBN-10: 1496107616

THE SHADOW OF WILLIAM QUEST

A William Quest Mystery Thriller

John Bainbridge

GASLIGHT CRIME

"Poverty is the parent of revolution and crime" Aristotle.

PROLOGUE

London 1853

Crowds jostled Henry Bartram as he left the noise of Mrs Bendig's night house behind and walked out into Leicester Square. A devil of an evening. He had lost at cards, a particular annoyance to someone who scarce ever yielded a hand. And now he was tipsy from too much drink. An alcoholic consolation for not finding the particular whore he had wanted.

Carlina, despite a tendency to talk too much, was a wonderful relaxation after the turmoil of a London day. Expensive but worth every last penny for her very adventurous spirit and even more vivid imagination. They had told him that she was busy elsewhere, at a house of assignation with a cabinet minister – a very rich one at that. Someone he knew. Information that one day might be profitable. But that was business for another time.

In Bartram's mind there was nothing worse than lust unsatisfied. The thought played on his mind as he walked down Shaftesbury Avenue. The theatres were turning out and he had to force himself between the crowds going home and the vast flocks of prostitutes seeking solitary gentlemen. He was approached, of course, being a well-dressed man of means. But he ignored the advances. His lusts had conjured up something special. And he knew just where he might find an object for them. Someone young and fresh. Someone inexperienced.

Bartram turned into one of the narrow sideways leading north to Oxford Street. In the days to come people would say that he had been journeying on foot to his home in Cavendish Square. And so he was. But he had another destination in mind long before he had travelled so far.

In this other trade, rare and expensive and so different from the bawdy openness of her night house, Mrs Bendig called herself Mrs Smythe. A procuress often had several names. Her talent was acquiring virgins, particularly very young virgins. These rare and expensive activities took place at a house in a quite respectable court not far west of Soho Square. Here, Mrs Bendig under the cover of her alias, posed as a lady, a little down on her fortunes, but still known for her charitable endeavours.

She was for ever making journeys into Seven Dials or the rookery surrounding St Giles church, distributing food and clothes. Occasionally bringing home young girls who might otherwise fall upon evil ways. They would stay with her for a few nights and then go on their way. Her neighbours were full of admiration, but believed that she was easily led. The girls, after all, presumably, drifted back to the slums that bred them.

Henry Bartram had visited the Smythe house on several occasions. An occasional virgin added to the delights of his night life in London. Whether they really were virgins didn't bother him terribly. Given the rookeries they came from, well, probably not. But they were very young and that was what mattered. Sometimes they would scream delightfully as he took them, in his usual forceful manner. Whether it was pretence didn't matter. And Bartram didn't subscribe to the belief that taking a virgin cured syphilis. He couldn't see how. It was just a fairy tale, a comfort for the afflicted.

His own health was good. He was sure of that. No symptoms despite his many amorous adventures. Only the week before he had walked speedily across London for the whole day inspecting the many properties he owned, enjoying the fearful looks on the faces of his tenants. Every property meant money. Lots of money in total. Money that paid for all of these pleasures and the fine house in Cavendish Square.

His elder brother, Charles, had inherited the family's country estate on the death of their father. Henry had been grateful to move away. Those broad Norfolk acres were boring compared to the delights of London life. Besides, he had never liked Charles, nor his brother's wife, nor their noisy little brats. Glad to see the back of them all, Charles in particular. His brother had always sneered at him.

Said he would never amount to anything. Well, I proved him wrong, Bartram considered. Buy him twice over, and the piddling little country house.

He thought of Charles so venomously that he almost forgot that the odious little man was no longer alive to annoy him. Come to a bad end. Found dead just a month before in a man trap set in his own pheasant covert. His head blown off with a shot from his own gun. Served him right. Man traps were illegal. Shouldn't have been set. There was some debate as to whether the death was an accident or a murder by an aggrieved poacher. Didn't matter. Charles was no more. Bartram wished his brother's dreadful wife and their spawn could be swallowed up in a whole forest of man traps.

The streets were quieter now, as he walked on into the heart of Soho. His thoughts turned again to what excitements lay ahead in Mrs Smythe's establishment. He could picture the room, furnished almost entirely in red. Windows shuttered to keep in the noise. A huge bed against the wall. Even the stout key in the door, which he always locked against interruption. He tried to picture the girl. Dark or fair? Didn't matter. It was just that look of innocence he craved, whether it was feigned or not. Just a hundred yards now, down the court. His lustful agony was almost unbearable.

Then he saw the man, well-dressed, standing on the corner under the gas lamp, his tall hat reflecting the light and a walking cane tapping the cobbles. He hoped that it was not another customer ahead of him. The procuress rarely had more than one virgin at a time and Henry didn't like to share. He touched his hat and mumbled an 'evening' to the man, attempting to walk past.

'Mr Henry Bartram.'

'I am he,' Henry replied, straining forward trying to see the man's face. 'I don't think we've met?'

'Oh, we have Mr Bartram. A very long time ago. In a different world to this. You would remember the circumstances even if you do not recognise me now.' The voice was refined, almost pleasant. Well bred. And yet...?

'I am at a loss?'

'I followed you tonight. Trod in your footsteps from the moment you left Cavendish Square. You may have seen me in the night house, but then again I've changed my appearance since then. I watched you fend off the women in Shaftesbury Avenue. You might have stayed safe if you had lingered there.'

'Safe?'

'Safe, Bartram,' replied the stranger, tapping his cane even louder on to the cobbles. 'Though in truth you haven't been safe for a long time. You signed your own death warrant an age ago. Now it is to be executed.'

'This is a strange attempt at humour...'

'No humour, Bartram. When has your life ever embraced humour? You showed none when you were young. Nor any now. I have followed your career with interest. I have seen the way you have made money. Talked to your many victims. Visited the hovels you own. Time to put a stop to it. That is one reason why I am going to kill you. There is another. Do you recall a hill on your father's estate in Norfolk? No? What a pity. Think of a name, Bartram. Think of a man called Marshall...'

'Now look...'

'No more words Bartram. It is time to die. I know you have a blade in that walking cane. Do you know how to use it?'

'This is absurd...'

'Whether you draw your blade or not, I will draw mine. You will die tonight.'

Bartram took a step backwards, breathing heavily. This stranger was a lunatic. He could be nothing else. He grasped the middle of his walking cane in one hand and drew out the blade with the other. He waved it towards the other man's face.

'Not good enough, Bartram. See you in hell.'

In his last moments Bartram puzzled at what happened next. He saw the stranger slightly raise his thin walking cane, caught a glimpse of a slender blade in the gaslight. He felt his own brushed aside very lightly, then a strange feeling in his chest. A sudden weakness as he fell forward on to his knees, all the strength gone from his body. He collapsed sidewards. He heard the hiss of the gas lamp and felt the damp of the cobbles as he died.

The man sighed as he wiped his blade on Bartram's coat, wondering vaguely what strange journey he had sent that pile of flesh on. Then he reached into his watch pocket, taking out what seemed to be a length of cord. He threw it down on to Bartram's body and walked away.

ONE

The streets of Bloomsbury were quiet as Mr William Quest made his way home to Tavistock Place. Drizzle had started and there were the first hints of a fog. Not a night to be out so late. There had been too many late nights in recent weeks. It had been a long and tiring day. He had been about at six that morning, spending much of his time tramping the streets of London.

Quest yearned for long hours by the fireside in his study, a glass of rum and an open book. He was past thirty now and found that he no longer had quite the staying power he had once enjoyed. London life made one lazy, he considered. Unfit for real existence. At his small house in the countryside he enjoyed long walks of five and twenty miles or more, an ideal way to keep up good health. He yearned for a break, but had such a lot of work to do. Sometimes he found himself craving domesticity, though he would have furiously repudiated the very concept of home life if any of his friends had made the suggestion.

But there was a comfort in seeing the lamplight glowing through his own windows as he stood outside the town house, searching a pocket for the key. The four-storeyed house was not that old, built by the Georgians in 1807 as they sprawled out across what had once been pleasant meadows surrounding the city. Quest had a very long lease on the property from the Bedford Estate. He liked being behind its doors. He enjoyed shutting himself in his study, giving himself time with his thoughts, his mementos and his books.

He let himself in and, after taking off his hat and long coat, climbed the stairs to the second-floor study, that sanctuary from the world. A fire was burning in the grate, the gaslight flickered as he closed the door. It was a small room, but crammed and untidy. There were a great many books lining most of the walls, tables of souvenirs, a rack of his favourite walking sticks. In all of London it was the place where he felt most at home. He took a book from the table and poured the rum. Then he counted up to ten and waited for the expected knock on the door. And there it was. A light tap and the door opened.

In formal terms Albert Sticks was his "man"; that strange mixture of valet, butler, footman, and master of all trades that single gentlemen with a small household were supposed to employ. But in the world of William Quest, Sticks, *he loathed the Albert*, was nothing like a servant. More like a father and fussy aunt rolled into one. He was one of the few real *confidantes* that Quest had in the world. The man was of indeterminate age, fifty at least, Quest guessed, though he had never dared to inquire, and of considerable build like the prize-fighter he once was. The face was battered, with cauliflower ears and a nose that had been broken on innumerable occasions. Quest's acquaintances in society were baffled as to just why anyone would employ Sticks as any sort of servant. Quest knew very well just why he did.

'Mr Borrow is it?' said Sticks, looking down at the first volume of *Lavengro* open on Quest's lap. 'Capital gentleman! Very good on prize fighting. Favourite of mine too.'

'Have you read all my books, Sticks?'

'Not all by any means. Some I can't get on with. Never warmed to Mr Thack'ray. But Mr Dickens, well, who can't enjoy him? Passed him in the street once. Stopped and complimented me on my bout agin Jem Ward, he did, though he said he didn't really approve. Not a man for the fancy, I think, though a gent for all that. Gave me a half sovereign. How can you not like a gent what gives you a half sov?'

Quest smiled as he pictured the encounter, which he had heard about on so many occasions. 'Like some rum, Sticks?' he asked, a challenging smile playing across his face.

'Now, Mr Quest, you know I don't drink! The route to ruin, that's what drink is. Haven't drunk for near twenty years, so don't think you can tempt me. But I'll pour you another before I says goodnight, if you care?'

'And send me on the route to ruin?'

'There's many a route to ruin, as it says in the Bible. We all have to find our own?'

~

Quest tried to read, but found himself nodding off from the heat of the fire. The sound of carriages out in the street broke through his consciousness for a while. The noise of people talking and laughing. The noises quietened. And then came the dream, the old familiar dream:

Running.

Running through the wood, the lowest boughs of the trees tearing at his head and shoulders. Running blindly. Not even knowing where he was running to. Only what he was running from. Fear heaving in his stomach and his chest tight. The ground uneven, the sound of many footsteps in his wake, with excited yells and people crashing through the brushwood. Then the dead stop in front of the great oak, which, even as he watched, transformed into a gallows. And the face of the hanged man, the poor pathetic face, lips blue and eyes bursting, first so high above and then seeming to come down and press against his own.

He woke with a start as the book slipped on to the floor, his breathing heavy and a touch of sweat on his forehead. The fire had died down and the street was quiet. Sticks was right not to drink, he considered.

The dream was always more vivid when aided by rum. But even when he was awake the dream was still there, at some place in his mind, waiting to be conjured up when other thoughts were absent. Always the need to keep busy, the need to keep the nightmare at bay.

He looked up at the little clock on the mantelpiece. Four in the morning. Better to sleep properly in a bed than try to rest like this. This sitting up into the small hours was a bad habit to have got into, indulgent, not the answer at all. Better to subdue the mind with proper rest. He picked up the book and put it back in the gap on the shelves, with its companion two volumes, before putting a guard in front of the fireside embers and going for a few hours to bed.

The walking cane he had used that night was no longer in the corner by the door, where it had been left. Sticks, as he always did after such outings, had taken it downstairs to clean and sharpen the blade within, always without a comment. A task performed too many times, thought Quest. And sometimes he could see a question in Sticks's eyes.

William Quest thought of the words of the man who had presented the sword stick to him. *Never take the blade out without honour, never put it back until justice has been done.* He thought of Bartram dying on those cobbles. Was that with honour and justice done? For the sake of his soul he hoped so.

TWO

'Henry Bartram!' said Abraham Anders, looking down at the corpse on the cobbles. 'Well, no great loss there, doctor. The same as the other two I suppose?'

Doctor Cooper looked up into the weary face of the detective inspector. 'One single stab wound to the chest, Bram,' he replied. 'Clear through the body. Slender blade from a sword stick, undoubtedly. Just like the others. The fact that the victim had his own swordstick blade out suggests that he tried to defend himself. It is possible of course that he was the assailant and the other man killed him in self-defence?'

'Possible but not probable.'

'Who are we to know? Was this Bartram a man with many enemies?'

'Half London! The poorer half, the people with little in life. This man Bartram owned many of their slums. Owned many of their lives. Not the kindest of landlords. He had, *methods* shall we say, in dealing with people. Unpleasant methods. Violence, rumours of perversion, unpleasant ways of bringing pressure to bear. Nothing we could do anything about. We sometimes accounted for those he employed in his businesses, but never the man himself.'

'Well,' said the young doctor as he looked thoughtfully at the body, 'he's just meat for the graveyard now. And you think it could not have been self-defence by the killer?'

'Bartram was a coward at heart. He would not have gone out to seek trouble, certainly not alone. He had associates who did that sort of thing for him. Did you find the cord?'

'Thrown down on the body, just like the others.' Cooper held up a stretch of tarred rope perhaps a foot long, tied to resemble a hangman's noose.

'Just like the others, then,' said Anders. 'Three men dead, all with the blade of a swordstick.'

'Three very unpleasant men.'

'Indeed. Write it up for me when you've done with him, Alexander. Bring it all round to my office and we'll digest the facts over some brandy. We won't tell the Commissioner until afterwards.'

'I'm sure Mayne will be delighted.'

'My dear Alexander. Our beloved Commissioner is never ever delighted!'

~

Sally felt the rough texture of the wall as the man pushed her harder against it. There was a time, when she was younger, when she had had a room in which to entertain her men. A time when she made real money. And now here she was up against a brick wall in a dark alley, her clothes pulled up, with this stranger grunting and groaning into her ear. All for

14

the sake of a shilling. He was young really, she considered, much younger than her. Perhaps a clerk in the city or an under-manager in a shop. One of those unfortunates who couldn't afford to marry and get to copulate behind closed doors. Sometimes these outdoor dealings made Sally feel like an animal in a barnyard. As he worked away she remembered those happier times when she was wined and dined before she had to entertain - in a luxurious room in Mrs Bendig's *salon*. But when her youth and looks began to go, she had to go too. Mrs Bendig liked her girls to be young and fresh.

She looked at the opposite wall, then raised her eyes to the sky, that narrow slit of grey above the alley. Despite the fact that it was mid-afternoon it gave very little light. It was brighter at night under the gaslight from the neighbouring street. She hated Seven Dials. When she was little her life had been all fields and woods in Essex. Now it was a world of slums and dingy courts, threats and noise, rookeries and crime. She wondered how this boy could tolerate the stench of the alley. He looked as though he might have been brought up for better things. But then, she thought, haven't we all?

He was just finishing when the light seemed to increase, the alley becoming brighter. Then they were both illuminated like actors upon a stage. The boy turned with a sudden gasp of fear, hurriedly pulling up his breeches. Sally saw the look of terror on his face as he turned.

The constable was a bulky man, his uniform from top hat down unbelievably smart. In his belt was a truncheon and his police rattle, that wooden device designed to summon up help. He was smiling, his fat face broken by the unfamiliar expression. He raised his bullseye lantern and shone the light full on to their faces. Sally pulled down her skirts and sighed. She knew what was coming next.

'Here we go again.' The constable looked at the boy. 'You don't want dealings with her, you know. You don't know what you might catch. Get lost before I take you in charge.' He flicked his large head sideways. As the boy ran the constable put out a foot to trip him into the alley filth. 'Go on. I said get lost!' he added, as the boy picked himself up and sped towards the street.

'You women never learn do you?' the policeman said. 'Human nature, I suppose. As long as there are brats like that with a bit of coin in their pocket to be used up. How much did you take from him?'

Sally held out the shilling.

'Just a shilling? You've fallen on hard times, haven't you? You're going down the scale, girl. It'll be tuppence next! Then you'll do it just for a penny ale. Then the river. How long before they fish you out of the Thames chewed up by rats?'

'Why don't you leave me alone, Johnson?'

'Oh, well, it's my duty you see. Keeping the vermin off the streets. What the Metropolitan Police pay me for. Not that they pay me very much, but that's by the by. You're a special case, as far as I'm concerned, that's why I take an interest in you. A bit prettier than the other scum what works the Dials. You get more men than the others. The money might be next to nothing but it mounts up.' He breathed his fetid breath over her face. 'You know what I want and what the alternative is?'

'Take the bloody shilling!' She held out the coin. 'And leave me alone.'

'Thank you,' said Johnson, taking the money. 'A good start. Now, how many men have you had today?'

'He's my first,' she muttered. 'It's early. I've only been out an hour. Honest.'

'Honest?' Johnson sucked in a noisy breath. 'Honest? What a word to hear anywhere 'round the Dials. Doubt you know what it means?' He looked into her eyes. 'I saw you out this morning. Standing around looking for gentlemen...'

He grabbed her by the wrist, twisting her arm back against the wall. 'How many, you lying little whore? You tell me now or I'll break your arm.'

'Three, only three, I swear it.' She cried out with the pain. 'I'll give you the other two bob. Just leave me alone.'

'Three? You should be doing better than that, a girl with your looks. Still, I'll have the money and take your word for it. This time. But you'll have to do longer hours, girl. We all have to keep in profit, don't we?'

She handed him the money. 'How am I s'posed to live?'

'Whores don't live,' said Johnson, shaking his head. 'Living isn't a word you use where whores is concerned. You just exist. As long as you can. Then it's the rats!'

~

Abraham Anders looked through the window at Scotland Yard, out across Whitehall Place. The late afternoon had turned dull and the first spots of rain spattered the glass. It had been a long day since the early call to see Bartram's body and not a lot had been achieved. He spent a moment studying his own reflection, the thick hair – too long the Commissioner always muttered, but then Mayne was losing his own. Anders was proud of his hair, though he despaired of how grey it had become in the past year. As grey as his long whiskers and moustache had been for a decade. The once jet-black hair had now followed their example.

'So,' he said, 'you've carved Bartram up have you, doctor?'

Cooper smiled at the very basic description of the *post mortem.*

'Not much to do. Nothing unusual except the hole left by a swordstick. He wasn't the healthiest of individuals, but he might have made another decade or two.'

'Exactly the same as the others?'

'Nothing different.'

'What I don't like about this,' said Anders, 'is that a pattern has developed. We have Bartram and the other two here in London. None of them worth worrying over, but murdered all the same. But for the fact that I am obliged to uphold the law and maintain the Queen's Peace, I wouldn't worry. Our killer had done the city a blessing.'

Anders watched as Sergeant Berry took the kettle from the fire and poured hot water into the tea pot. The tea would be strong. Too strong. Berry came from the North where they seemed to like it that way. The sergeant was a thick-set man who still enjoyed that jet-black hair and beard that Anders had once had himself.

'What do you think, Berry?'

'I think,' Berry replied, pouring the tea, 'that I've never known anything like it. As far as I can see none of the three dead men associated with each other. I've looked at them all. Different businesses, social circles not the same, different clubs. Nothing in common. Except that they're all dead by the same pair of hands. Three murdered men. Picked at random. No signs of robbery. Three dead mysteries.'

'Nearly right, Berry, nearly right. Only not three murders but four, and a connection between two of them.'

'I'm sorry,' said Cooper, 'but am I missing something here? Who is the fourth? I may be Scots and fond of a dram but my memory tells me I have only seen three dead at the police mortuary.'

'Ah, but the fourth was not killed in London. And killed in a different way. I've been reading accounts in *The Times* of the death of Charles Bartram, Henry's brother. He was found dead a month ago. In his pheasant preserves, caught up in a man trap. His head blown off with his own gun.'

'I thought man traps were illegal?' said Cooper.

'And so they are, but Charles Bartram was a landowner of the old school. A fanatical game preserver and a magistrate as well. I doubt the local constabulary were brave enough to question his preserving activities.'

'Just a coincidence,' said Sergeant Berry. 'Where I come from landowners were always shooting themselves. Or someone else on their shoot. An accident. At the very worst some poacher found him caught in the man trap and took the opportunity to top him.'

'Maybe, but I suspect not.'

'Did they find a noose by the body?' asked the doctor. 'If they did I might be convinced, Bram.'

'Nobody reported finding a noose.'

'Well, there you are then,' said Cooper. 'No noose and definitely not killed by a swordstick blade. Not the same killer.'

Anders looked out into the rain, which was falling heavily into the darkening streets of Whitehall. Pedestrians scuttled along seeking doorways or their carriages. The puddles reflected the first light of the gas lamps.

'But if it was his trial run, Angus?' he said thoughtfully. 'The first killing? He may not have thought up the idea of a noose a month ago. Perhaps that idea came later. There has to be some point to such a symbol of execution. And suppose, just suppose, he intended to use the swordstick but found Charles Bartram by that man trap. Perhaps he thought that a more appropriate end for the man?'

'We'll never know,' said Berry, supping the dregs of his tea.

'Well, not sitting here we won't. Tomorrow morning you and I will take the railway to Norwich. If I'm wrong, well, I'm wrong,' said Anders, swigging the awful tea back in one go.

THREE

It was still raining the next morning as Josef Critzman looked out at the busy crowds in Cheapside, wondering if any of them might come into his shop. Although his main trade was in walking sticks, he was promoting Mr Samuel Fox's new steel-ribbed umbrellas in the shop window. Perhaps the first flush of sales were done, though he could see few pedestrians with any sort of umbrella in the street. A marvellous improvement and yet still people didn't seem to mind getting wet. It was hard to understand. His shop always seemed to have more custom in drier weather. Perhaps people were inspired to take longer constitutional walks on better days and craved sticks as walking aids and for protection.

He stood in the doorway and watched as the rain came to a sudden halt. Then a burst of sunlight broke through the dark cloud and illuminated the scene in a way that was almost theatrical. It called for a player to stand out from the chorus, Josef thought, and sure enough there was one pedestrian with all the presence of a leading actor. A tall man, past thirty, with a slim pale face, locks of dark hair visible beneath the top hat, a horn-handled walking stick tapping down on to the pavement. He looked into the shop window for a moment and then noticed Josef by the door.

'I got your message, Josef,' said William Quest. 'Perhaps we had better go inside the shop.'

'Indeed we had,' Josef replied. 'These matters are better not discussed in such a busy street.' He locked the door behind them, pulling down the blind, as Quest took off his hat and placed it on the chair that Josef kept available for his more enfeebled customers.

He looked around the shop at the racks of walking canes and, more doubtfully, at the umbrellas. Josef's shop had fascinated him since the first time he ever saw it. He had spent many youthful hours examining the sticks, acquiring a passion for canes almost as great as that of the proprietor.

'I hear that the other Bartram brother is dead?' said Josef. 'Honour and justice done?'

'Not done yet,' Quest replied. 'Some accounts settled, but not all, before we can move on to wiser matters. Those in the shades may still wonder whether honour has been fulfilled and justice served.'

'You know my views, Will. I said at the beginning that executing the Bartram brothers was a dangerous obsession of yours. A distraction from our real work. Leave their associates alone!'

'Dear Josef, I know you don't approve, yet I can't continue without settling that outstanding debt.'

'But there is danger in it, Will. One of the strengths of our original idea was that it would *not* be personal. That we would fight our battles on behalf of those who could not.'

Quest looked at the thin little man, seeing the agitation in his face. Josef looked tired and every day of his sixty years. It was thirty years since he had arrived in London from Poland, escaping persecution and seeking a settled life. If Quest felt admiration for anyone it was for this brave and caring soul. He owed Josef his life in more ways than one.

'My concern,' said Josef, 'is that the authorities might try to seek out anyone who had a grudge against the Bartram brothers. An incident from their past. And who bears a greater grudge than you?'

Quest put a hand on the old man's shoulder. It was too thin. He could feel the bone quite clearly. The poor man hardly ate enough and what he did eat was soon burned off in nervous energy.

'But the man they would seek would not be William Quest.'

Josef frowned, tapping the counter in his usual nervous manner. Time and again he would look at the younger man and sense death. It had always been that way.

'Will, they are not fools, these policemen of yours. They are clever, determined men. It would be a terrible arrogance not to take them seriously.'

'My dear old friend, I take them most seriously.'

Josef smiled. 'I do hope so. Better men than we have fallen through being over-confident. Anyway, I expect you wish to know of our new task?'

'Isaac has found some work for me?'

'A simple one by comparison with the others. Someone that does *not* need to be killed. Just taught a lesson. A bully who needs to be brought down.'

'You intrigue me,' said Quest. 'Can you tell me more?'

'Better that Isaac does. You know the tavern in Queen Street? Near where they are building the new museum?'

'The Dog and Duck?'

'I think they do not call it that anymore,' Josef replied. 'Isaac will meet you there at one. He will not be alone, so better that you do not go as William Quest. You can change in the workshop and leave through the back door.'

~

Anders looked through the window of the closed compartment as the train sped through the Norfolk countryside. He was not in the best of moods. There had been a long delay on the journey. The train had stopped for a half hour, for no apparent reason, somewhere in Essex. Only Sergeant Berry had talked him out of clambering out to berate the engine driver, protesting that there had to be a good reason for the halt. Anders had sat down, looking out at a cow and tapping his foot impatiently until the train lurched back into life. All his life he had hated delays.

He looked across at Berry, asleep under his newspaper on the opposite seat, snoring heavily. Reaching out he tapped him with his walking cane. The sergeant crumpled up the newspaper and came back to life.

'I thought that we might review the victims of this killer, Berry,' he said. 'Apart from the Bartram brothers?'

Berry yawned and took out his notebook, opening it at the relevant page. 'Well, the first was James Osborne, well known around the town as a reprobate. Made a pretty penny from blackmail, though we could never find enough evidence to take him in charge. Drove at least three gentlemen and a lady to destroying themselves.'

'I met him once,' Anders nodded. 'At a function given by the Lord Mayor. A nasty character. Watched him work his way around the room, ears open for other people's conversations. There were many in society glad to see him turned off.'

'This killer did the world a favour then....?'

'We are not in employment as judges of morality. Our only task is to uphold the law, whatever our personal feelings. And the second?'

Berry turned over a few pages. 'Walter Jenkins. Started life running a workhouse but built himself into quite the civic figure, even becoming a borough mayor. Killed at least two honest shopkeepers, though we could never prove it. Burned down a number of business premises...'

'Only we could not prove that either?'

'Exactly, sir. He and his men would visit any number of small businesses, shops, workshops, whatever. They would collect a small amount of insurance the first weeks, amounts which increased as time went by. At first there would be some resistance, but it never lasted long. A face might be smashed here, a limb broken there. Occasionally they went too far, though never in front of witnesses. Jenkins's organisation died with him.'

'And they were found in different parts of London, Jenkins in Whitechapel and Osborne in the Borough. Both killed with the blade from a swordstick and with a cord like a hangman's noose across their body. Had he not slain them by such a method and left the cord we might have assumed a different killer was responsible for each.'

'I went back through their lives,' said Berry, 'and there was nothing to suggest any connection between them.'

'And no connection with the brothers Bartram,' remarked Anders. He rested his head back against the seat. He was still looking up at the top of the window twenty minutes later as the train entered Victoria Station in Norwich.

A few drinkers looked up as the rough-looking man entered the tavern in Queen Street. He was dressed in fustian, wore a canvas cap, and carried a heavy stick, more a club in fact, of blackthorn. He looked from his worn clothes as though he might be a workman on the museum building, but there was a dangerous look in his eyes that few exhausted working men bore. His face was stubbled with black hair and he bore a scar right down his left cheek. He looked with dark eyes through the smoky haze and noted the large man sitting in a corner with the woman.

Isaac Critzman was as fat as his brother was thin, and looked a great deal healthier. He dressed as something like a dandy, standing out against the poorer crowds in the tavern. The woman was clearly a tail, past the first flush of youth, but still pretty enough for her type. They both stood as the man approached.

'It is good to see you Bill,' Isaac said.

He spoke perfect English, without a trace of his brother's Polish accent. He poured three tankards of ale from a great jug on the table. 'Sit down and drink up, all of you. The jug is paid for.'

The woman looked nervously across at the newcomer. Those dark eyes seemed to be searching straight into her soul. She had to look down at the table.

'Seen you about,' the man said to her at last. 'In the Dials. You work the alleys off Monmouth Street.' The accent was deep cockney. Very deep and rough. 'Before that you were in a House. Mrs Bendig's was it? How is the old bitch?'

'Haven't seen her for a whiles,' Sally replied. 'We parted on bad terms.'

'Time she was strung,' Bill said. 'There'll be a crowd at Newgate when she's turned off. Does the old haybag still dish out poison? She doesn't let many of her girls walk. Wonder you're still here!'

'Bill knows everyone in the Dials, don't you Bill?' said Isaac. 'That's why I know he will help with your problem, Sally.'

'Always problems in the Dials. And this one is?'

'A fat constable, Bill. Fatter than me. Johnson.'

'I knows him. Want me to cut his throat for you?'

Isaac patted the table. 'Nothing so dramatic. Just a sharp lesson in good behaviour. You can do that for Sally, can't you Bill?'

FOUR

Sergeant Berry was never enthusiastic about the countryside. It was far too empty for his liking, too quiet, too open. It needed bricks. Lots of bricks, walls of them, making houses and factories, cluttering up all those wide spaces where the sky was visible. As the growler sped through the lanes out of Norwich, he looked with disfavour at the Norfolk landscape, feeling exposed in a way he never did in the darkest alleys of London. He watched as some peasant strolled across a bit of heathland. God or man could come for him and there would be no place to hide. No secret corner to crouch down in. He felt relief as the carriage entered dark woodland. It was good to feel the world closing in.

'Not far now,' said Inspector Gurney of the Norfolk Constabulary, a short stocky man with a permanent grin, who had met them at the railway station. 'Is this your first visit to Norfolk, Sergeant?'

Berry nodded. 'Yes, sir. Not often out of London and I hail from Manchester. Not familiar with many places in between.' First visit and the last was his silent afterthought.

'And you, Inspector Anders?'

'Been to Norwich once before,' Anders replied. 'I had a cousin in Yarmouth. Fisherman. We came for an outing when I was a boy. But I'm a Wiltshire man by birth. Liddington. Small place. Very open. Just like much of this county. Bit hillier.'

They watched for a moment as a pheasant ran into the fringe of the trees, beyond the *Keep Out* notices that lined a broken-down park wall.

'I confess to being puzzled as to your interest in the death of Mister Charles Bartram?' said Gurney at last. 'We considered it to be but a tragic accident?'

'As you know, Inspector, his brother was murdered in London the other day. We wish to be absolutely sure that there is no connection between the two deaths. And to appreciate something of Mr Henry Bartram's background in the county.'

'Mr Henry Bartram had not lived in the county for a considerable time as I understand it. His brother inherited the estate from their late father, leaving the younger son with a generous allowance.' Gurney grinned even more than usual. 'Like all families there were some frictions between the two, though they seemed to be closer when they were young.'

'So what caused the bother, sir?' asked Berry.

Gurney laughed. 'Ah, Sergeant, what indeed? Well, as is usual, a woman. Mrs Charles Bartram did not approve of her brother-in-law. Thought him wayward by all accounts. A bad influence on her husband.'

Anders nodded. 'There might be more than a grain of truth in that. Henry Bartram was a most unpleasant individual!'

31

'Then it ran in the family,' said Gurney. 'Charles Bartram was hated across much of Norfolk. Hence the man traps.'

'Tell me about the father?'

'Another Charles Bartram by name. A rake in his younger days. A man of promiscuity and violence. Vicious to his peasants. Heart failure took him some twelve years ago. No one mourned him very much. Ah, here we are at last.'

The growler pulled in from the lane and up a driveway between two stone lodges. The red-bricked house could be seen across the green acres of the parkland, a watery broad to one side of the wide valley. It was a much more modest dwelling than Anders had been expecting, suggesting that the Bartrams were not in the first rank of the gentry.

'The family are away,' said Gurney, as they alighted from the carriage. 'Mrs Bartram is taking the cure in Harrogate and the two boys are at school.'

'Do they inherit?' asked Anders. 'The boys?'

'I think the eldest does. The other gets an allowance. Mrs Bartram lives on the grace and favour of her sons, though she controls the estate until they are of age.'

'How old are they?'

'Twelve and ten.'

'The death of their father must have been quite an ordeal for such young chaps,' Berry remarked.

Gurney's smile was even wider. 'Well, I don't know about that sergeant. By all accounts they lived in some fear of their father. Too fond of flogging them, I believe. I talked to them both the day after the body was found. They seemed relieved.'

'I'd like to see where the death happened if I might?' said Anders. 'And perhaps talk to the servants?'

~

As the afternoon darkened over Seven Dials, the man with the blackthorn stick made his way back down Monmouth Street and into the narrow alley known as Neal's Yard. He looked around before opening a door leading on to a dimly lit flight of narrow stairs. He bolted the door, far more substantial on the inside than it looked from out, and climbed the steps. A tiny landing revealed a second door, adorned with a mighty lock. He reached inside the fustian jacket for a key and let himself in. The room beyond was barely furnished; a table and two chairs, a bed covered with some old blankets, and a wooden chest filled with a disreputable selection of clothes and rags. He lit a candle and looked at himself in the filthy mirror that hung crookedly on the wall.

'What a disreputable villain you are, William!' he said aloud. 'That it should come to this!'

Quest lay back on the bed and looked up at the stained, spider-haunted ceiling, contemplating the discussion with Critzman and the woman. Dealing with a rogue constable? A tad too easy, and surely not what was intended by their original enterprise. Easier to kill than to humiliate. Still, if that is what Isaac wishes, why not?

He knew Johnson very well. He had seen his bullying ways. On several occasions he had come near to knocking him down as he made his way through Seven Dials. He had resisted the temptation, not wishing his acquaintanceship with the area to be too widely recognised. He liked this lurk too much, this shabby disgusting room. It was his favourite of the several similar lurks he used across London and the most convenient. He thought it better that the police didn't look too closely into the activities of the man in fustian with the scar and the blackthorn cudgel.

~

The boy watched as the gentleman made his way through Clerkenwell on a cold winter afternoon. It had been a bloody useless day so far. The worst since the end of the hot weather. There were so many crushers about with their sticks and rattles, just hoping to haul a lad in front of the beaks. The deep frost had made people wrap up in too many clothes. It was harder to get at their pockets. But this man obviously didn't feel the cold and his pocket was broad. The boy needed an easy one. His fingers ached with the cold and his knuckles were battered

34

from the fight the day before when two other lads in St Giles had jumped him for his tin.

But here was a street empty of crushers and with enough of a bustling crowd to hide the activities of a young buzzer like himself. The gentleman seemed to be distracted as he walked along the street leading to Clerkenwell Green. In a world of his own. He looked rich enough, the boy considered. Should be more careful of his possessions, he really should. In a darker alley he might have come to a cruel end.

The gentleman accidentally bumped into a lady coming in the opposite direction, so away was he with his thoughts. He raised his hat and mumbled an apology. That momentary distraction was all the boy needed. His fingers dipped into the pocket and came away with two loose coins, before the hat was replaced. The boy eased back into the crowd and then walked smartly into the nearby churchyard so that he might examine his find. A half sovereign and a shilling. The boy whistled, shaking with excitement. Then he came to his senses and had a good look around. Nobody in sight.

It had been a good day after all.

~

Sergeant Berry wondered how on earth anyone could find his way through what seemed to be an endless forest. Every glade and ride looked the same to him. Yet Gurney seemed to know just where all the faint tracks in the pheasant coverts of the Bartram estate led. The first leaves of autumn tumbled silently on to them as the three men made their way deeper into the trees.

'And here is the spot,' said Gurney. 'We've taken away the man trap. He was lying with what was left of his head towards the trees. A real mess.'

Anders looked around at what seemed to be identical to a thousand places they had passed before. It was the edge of a grassy ride, where a side path joined it from between the trees.

'Where does this path go?'

'A direct route to the village, through a gap in the park wall. Probably why he had the man trap set there. Troubled by poachers.'

'Landowners always seem to be obsessed with the notion that someone is stealing something from them. I got a good thrashing in Burderop Wood when I was a lad. Near where I grew up. Keeper with an ash-plant.'

'Been poaching had you sir?' grinned Berry.

'Certainly not! Looking for nuts. All the lads did it.'

'Did it put you off trespassing, Inspector Anders?' Gurney asked.

'If anything it made me more determined, if a trifle cannier about the way I did it. And whoever came into this wood would have to be canny. Why was he not prosecuted for setting man traps?'

'We didn't know. Certainly nobody reported being caught in one. It may well be that just the notion of there being traps kept poachers away.'

'Perhaps,' said Anders, wandering around. 'Very grassy here. Nowhere for anyone to leave footprints. Was anything found by the body?'

'Only the gun lying two feet away, about there on the edge of the ride. Perfectly consistent with the man having accidentally shot himself.'

'And the gamekeeper found the body?'

'The head keeper, a man named Walsham. I've asked him to meet us at the house.'

Anders paced up and down for a few moments, looking in every direction as though trying to permanently fix the scene in his memory. 'Well, I think we've seen enough. Nothing here to suggest that anything but a tragic accident befell Mr Bartram.'

'So we have convinced you that it was an accident?'

Anders looked up at the clouding sky above the ash trees. He smiled at the Norfolk Inspector.

'No,' he said at last. 'I remain convinced that Charles Bartram was murdered.'

~

It was, the boy thought, the most awful place on earth, those few acres around St Giles church. Its bells rang over this Holy Land, as some wag had named it, a cramped collection of old houses and courts, falling in on each other, packed with the detritus of human existence. The worst criminal rookery in London. Being a boy from the country, he was puzzled that the old church had retained its title of St Giles-in-the-Fields. The only fields now were fields of misery, of death and despair, of stench and decay. A place where only the hardened survived at all, and then not for very long. The weakest only came here to spend a few miserable days or weeks before they died.

He walked down from the church and into the rookery along a narrow lane as dark as any cave, crammed with many people, some living on its cobbles, some dying there. Many were drunk, and as many again diseased. Some of them glanced up at the boy with dead, apathetic eyes, a few with hostility, some envious that he still had the strength to walk. He stepped sideways to avoid the corpse rotting in the middle of the lane, stinking and almost concealed in the darkness. He could not tell if it was a man or a woman. Only that it was near-naked and face down. Beyond that, it was too far gone.

He lived in what had once been a nethersken, a low lodging house of the worst kind though, since the landlord had died of the cholera, nobody had come to take the pennies of the tenants. Three families lived in the downstairs room, though the faces changed as one and then another family member died.

Here they existed, fought, intermingled and copulated with each other, abused their children, found escape only in drink and demise. A flight of broken steps led to the upper room, twelve foot square, and the home of twenty boys and girls. A great hole in the wall led into the next building of the lane, one of the many tunnels leading from house to house, enabling escape if the crushers came looking for anyone in particular, though Bow Street had mostly given up its forays into the rookery, leaving the Holy Landers to their own devices.

~

Walsham, the gamekeeper, was exactly what Anders expected; a muscular dark man of about fifty, with cruelty and contempt written on his face. Having seen the portrait of Charles Bartram inside the house, Anders had noted a similar cruelty in the face of Walsham's deceased master, clearly caught by the painter. Or perhaps that was just fancy, a projection from Anders' own mind. No, he suspected he was right. Cruelty in the faces of both of them. Anders held a lot of store in what he could read in the face of the people he met. Experience had taught him that first reactions were often correct.

'Heard the shot,' the gamekeeper mumbled. 'Went runnin'. He were dead.'

'How long did it take you to get there after you heard the shot?'

'I were down by the river, long ways away. Took me a time. Hard to say,' said Walsham.

'Why run at all?' Anders asked. 'Wasn't Mr Bartram out shooting?'

'Told me he were going after the ducks in the broad. Not much to shoot on the rise, where he were. Had a feelin' that's all. Thought he might have shot a poacher. Bastards comes in that way'.

'And you found him in the man trap?'

'Ah,' Walsham spat a plug of tobacco on to the ground.

'Did Mr Bartram know where you'd put the man trap?'

'Did show him, but it were a week or more afore.'

'Was there any sign of there being a poacher?'

The gamekeeper shook his head, 'Didn't see, but that don't mean there weren't. Never catch the bastards. We keeps most of 'em out but there's a few. I knows they come in here.'

'Local men?'

Walsham gave a violent nod of his head.

'Apart from the gun, did you find anything near to the body?'

The man looked quizzically at Anders. 'Just the gun, lying there on the grass. Nothin' else,' he said

A sudden idea came into Anders' mind. He turned to Gurney. 'What happened to the clothes Bartram was wearing?'

'We have them in the police mortuary,' Gurney replied. 'Covered in blood. Went through the pockets, but nothing unexpected. A brandy flask and a pocket knife. A few coins maybe. I believe that is all I recall.'

'And his game bag?'

'Game bag?'

'When I was a boy in Wiltshire, the gentlemen would usually carry a game bag when they went shooting. For their shot and to put in any birds they might bring down'.

'There was no game bag,' said Gurney.

Anders turned back to the keeper. 'Did Mr Bartram have a game bag?'

'Course he had a game bag. I picked it up off the grass and brought it back to the house.'

Gurney groaned, slapping his hands against his forehead. 'Then why the hell didn't you tell us? Give it to us at the time?' he yelled at the keeper.

'Didn't see no importance in it,' Walsham's voice was raised in retaliation. 'Picked it up without thinking, I s'pose. I was the one that carried it when most we went shootin' together.'

'Where is it now?' Anders asked quietly.

'In the gun room,' said Walsham. 'We keep such things in the gun room.'

The gamekeeper led them into the rear of the house, into a room filled with gun racks and hunting trophies. He threw out his arm to indicate the game bag lying on the table. Anders unfastened the flap and held the opening wide. Reaching in he pulled out a powder flask and some shot, a fierce looking knife, no doubt used for cutting up game, and a cord tied like an hangman's noose.

FIVE

Quest put on his jacket and looked into the hall mirror as he adjusted his hat. He had already selected the horn handled malacca walking cane from the rack in his study. He turned to find Sticks hovering behind him.

'Business or pleasure, sir?'

'I suspect it is both, Sticks. But nothing unpleasant. At least not tonight. I shall be out until the morning though.'

'Do give my regards to Miss Rosa.'

'If I ever dismiss you, Sticks, don't expect a reference!' Quest scowled.

'I should write my own anyways. Lovely girl, Miss Rosa. Always so polite to me...unlike some.'

'Ah, well, you'll have the joy of seeing her tomorrow afternoon. I need your help, both of you. We are going to correct the very bad behaviour of a police constable.'

'A permanent arrangement?'

'Not this time,' Quest replied. 'Just a sharp lesson. You may know the man. Johnson?'

'Big fat crusher? Has a beat in the Dials?'

'That is the man. I want you to meet me at three tomorrow afternoon at The Five Grenadiers. I'll explain then what we are going to do.'

'I'll bring the neddy then, shall I?' asked Sticks. 'Just in case...'

Quest frowned. 'If you have to cosh him do it gently please. I don't want to see you at Newgate at the hangings.'

'Nothing wrong with a good hanging!'

'I didn't mean in the crowds,' Quest replied, opening the door. 'Which of my books will you be reading tonight?'

'Mr Samuel Richardson, sir. *Clarissa.*'

'All of it? Heaven help you!'

~

Anders and Berry walked back across London, having caught the last train from Norwich. A fog was slinking in from the Thames and their progress through the streets was very slow.

'Shall I tell you what I always think when we are after a killer, Berry?'

'Sir?'

'I always think that perhaps I'm close to him in these streets, that he may have walked past me an hour before. I may have seen him in a shop or a bank. And I don't know who he is, and he doesn't appreciate that I'm the detective policeman who is pursuing him.'

'It's a big city, sir. Hard to find one man. But I see what you mean. Never thought of it like that. Possible. He could even have been on the train from Norwich. Steady there!' he yelled, as a carriage nearly ran them down as they crossed into Whitehall.

'There has to be some connection between our killer and the Bartram brothers. But what is it? What can it be? Something so personal that he tops the pair of them?'

'And then there's the other two victims. They have no connection with either brother or each other come to that? At least not one we know. And what is the point of the cord, the noose? It's a puzzlement to me, sir.'

Anders paused as they turned into Whitehall Place. A gas lamp flared and the street beyond became eerily silent. Berry stood quietly by. He knew well enough not to interrupt *this* man when he was deep in thought. In the quiet he heard a ship's bell ring from the Thames and a burst of laughter from someone in a room above.

'I think,' Anders spoke at last, 'we must go back to all the basics of detection to solve this mystery. I want you to get out into the streets and talk to your informants in the underworld. This man cannot have appeared from nowhere. He knows the streets as well as we do. He must have left a trail to follow. Someone must have had dealings with him.'

'I'll be out first thing,' said Berry. 'Can I use a little bribery? Loosen some tongues?'

Anders nodded. 'Whatever you judge to be necessary. And while you are doing that, I intend to look right back into the history of the Bartram family. He'll be there somewhere. I know it! We'll have him at Newgate on a hanging day yet!'

~

The boy sat in a corner of the cramped room, watching his friend Ned coughing his life away. He had seen a lot of deaths since arriving in London. As he looked around he noticed a great number of new faces, replacing the boys and girls who had been there when he arrived. Some had died in front of him, only to have their miserable wasted bodies put out into the alley. Others had been taken up by the crushers, never to be seen again. Most had simply disappeared, to be absorbed into the criminal underworld of St Giles and the sinister Seven Dials beyond. The boys for thieving, the girls, however young, to sell themselves on the streets. Every now and again the full figure of the dreaded Mrs Bendig would fill the doorway looking for virgins. She always found a girl or two willing to go with her.

He shuffled across to Ned and looked at the lad's pale face.

'Ned, Got somethin' for you.'

Ned looked up with eyes that already seemed to be dead. The boy slipped a piece of old cloth into his friend's cold white hand and closed his fingers round it.

'Money, Ned. Enough for a few good meals and a way out of here for a whiley. You go this evenin'. Move on from here before the rats get you...'

Ned's lips moved but there were no words.

'You see, I'm leavin' today, Ned. Done with this place, done with buzzin'. No more pocket pickin'. Not enough in it! Done with bloody London, but I can't move on just yet from that! Got to find richer pickin's.'

Ned looked across at him but there was little reaction.

'Don't you bloody die on me, Ned!' He paused for a moment, working out what to do for the best. 'All right, we go together then. For a little whiles at least. Come on! On yer feet!'

The boy lifted the wasted body of his friend and carried him towards the stairs.

~

'Are you really a parson's daughter?' Quest yawned, as the woman nuzzled her head against his shoulder. 'Because if you are I doubt if his parishioners will welcome you back.'

Rosa smiled, her dark hair falling across his bare chest. It was nearly morning, the first light was penetrating the curtains, along with the noise of the milk sellers in the street outside. The house was a modest building in a quiet *cul-de-sac,* close to where Bloomsbury met the road from Tottenham Court.

The room was cluttered with a great many theatrical costumes.

'Of course I am, my sweetheart,' she replied. 'Where do you think I got my taste for theatrical performing? Sitting in the pews watching my beloved father. He was by far the best actor I've ever seen.'

'These skills will serve you well now you are reduced to doing turns in the penny gaffs.'

She thumped her fist quite heavily into his stomach. 'I have never, *never ever*, played a turn in a penny gaff. Only proper theatres - both here and in the provinces. I have quite a reputation. I was quite the favourite of Madame Vestris at the Lyceum. Quite the leading lady in her *Extravaganzas*. She was sorry to see me go.'

'There was a rumour that you helped yourself to some of the takings?'

Rosa sat up in the bed, turning away from him. 'That's a bloody lie! I left the Lyceum in good faith. Just wanted to seek new opportunities. Madame Vestris and Mr Matthews said that they would welcome me back on any future occasion. I had made more than enough money in my profession.'

'I seem to recall that we met when you tried to pick my pocket in Shaftesbury Avenue. Had you depleted your funds by that point?'

'I've told you before. It was a lark. A preparation for Mr Jolys revival of *The Beggar's Opera*.'

'You take your preparation very seriously,' said Quest. 'You were disguised as a boy. I don't recall Mr Gay writing such a role in his masterpiece?'

'Sometimes, Quest, you are bloody impossible!'

'An opinion that many share,' said Quest, stretching out his arms and pulling her backwards towards him. 'Oh, by the way, Sticks sends his felicitations.'

'Now there is a gentleman! Such a rare being in these parts. Give him my love.'

'You can do that yourself, later today. We have a little enterprise afoot. In the Dials. We're going to bear up a crusher and I need someone to play the whore.'

She studied his face for a moment.

'Sometimes,' she said at last, 'I do wonder if that is all I am to you, Quest.'

'Far more than that, my love,' he replied.

'I hope so.'

'Anyway. An hour to full dawn. Plenty of time for another performance.'

'What sort of performance?'

His hands began to explore her body.

'This sort,' he said, drawing her towards him.

~

Old Josiah, the gravediggers called him. Old Josiah who sat on the bench most afternoons on the edge of the new cemetery at Kensal Green, where fresh planted trees were growing amongst the spreading tombs. He was a stocky man who must have been handsome in his youth. Now he was old, or seemed old, or grey from the cares of life. A figure always dressed in black, with a tall black hat and an ebony black walking cane, its silver top the same colour as his hair. He would sit on the bench for a good hour looking out across the tombs and the graves, regardless of the weather. When the sun shone he would seem to doze on the bench. In the rain or the snow he would just sit there, gripping the walking cane almost in a fierce manner, staring ahead. He would always wish a "Good Day" to the gravediggers, and tip them a coin, but he would never say more than that, either to them or any passers-by. People would touch their caps and hats to him, wish him well and pass on, not wishing to intrude on an old man's grief.

SIX

Jasper Feedle had lost his leg at Waterloo.

Or so he said, as he begged on the street corner at the lower end of Monmouth Street. He was a withered old man of nearly sixty years old and still wore the dark jacket of the Rifles, the 95th Regiment of Foot, which was, as he told anyone who might be interested, the uniform of his regiment. A brave rifleman who had come to hard times. He was certainly an educated man, who could read and write, though his contributions towards literature seemed to stop at gallows ballads and chap-books.

He had a reputation as a screever, a writer of fake testimonials which facilitated the activities of other beggars. If you wanted a letter purporting to be from a coastal magistrate, confirming how you had lost your livelihood in some shipping disaster, then Jasper was the man you came to. Or if you were a servant fallen on hard times, dismissed without a reference, then Jasper would provide you with one.

Jasper could often be seen at the front of the crowds on execution days at Newgate, reciting a verse he had made up about the activities of the man or woman about to be so publicly topped. If you admired his work he would sell you a printed version, beautifully illustrated with his own sketches. Jasper Feedle was a man of many talents.

Sergeant Berry was inclined to believe that Jasper had been at Waterloo. His own father had fought with Wellington both in Spain and at that battle. The beggar's tales had the ring of truth for him. And Jasper had another talent as far as Berry was concerned. He was the most reliable informant in London. Always there with a ready ear in the taverns around the rookeries. Never missing the scraps of gossip that floated down the filthy streets north of the river. Sergeant Berry found Jasper indispensable and dreaded the day that some villain might cut his throat.

He slipped a shilling across the table in the quiet corner of the tavern. Jasper admired it for a moment before concealing it in the hidden depths of his military tunic.

'And there is another like that if you can tell me more?' said Berry.

'Young lad! Young lad! I'll tell yer all I knows. Mayn't I have another tankard of the ale first?' the old man said, tapping the table. Berry poured out two more helpings.

'Here's to the blessed memory of yer father!' Jasper raised the tankard. 'A sergeant too weren't he? Only a proper one, with red coat. Not a crusher.'

'He was!' said Berry. 'And at Waterloo like you!'

'I remember those brave boys at Hoogymont. Their jackets all the redder with their own blood. And those that formed Square as Boney's cavalry charged. I looked down at 'em and felt a tear in my eye. Pride, yer know?'

'I'm not here to fight old battles, Jasper, but new ones. You said you knew about the killings.'

'Bartram!' the old man spat on the floor. 'The world won't weep for 'im. Burning in hell, he'll be. Good riddance! And the others like as not.'

'Tell me everything you know, Jasper,' said Berry, 'and I might make it three shillings.'

The old man looked around the tavern, taking in the noisy drunks at the counter, and the secretive groups clustered in the dark and dirty cubbyholes around the walls. He leaned forward towards Berry.

'Word has it there's a man about,' he tapped the side of his nose. 'A man what takes the part of the poor and desperate. Someone yer can go to if ye're in a bit of trouble. A gentleman who'll fight battles for yer.'

'A gentleman?'

'Well, so they say,' said Jasper. 'But he's only a part of it. There's others who works with 'im. People known in the Dials.' Jasper looked anguished. 'Yer must understand, Mr Berry, people are desperate. They'll turn to anyone when they're 'feared.'

Berry slid another shilling halfway across the grimy table.

'And if you are in trouble?' he asked. 'If you are desperate, Jasper? Who do you go to? How do you find this gentleman?'

The old man reached across the table and pulled the shilling towards him. His watery eyes looked across at the detective. He nodded slowly and supped some more ale.

'They comes to see yer,' he said at last. 'Yer see, if someone has trouble in the Dials, it's not hard to find out. Everyone here has troubles. Some of us shares our troubles. Some has worse troubles than others. It's a small world, Mr Berry. Word gets round.'

Berry held another shilling against the table, tapping it gently on the wood. 'Need a name Jasper? Just a name to be going on with? I'm sure you can help me with a name?'

The old soldier looked around the smoke-filled room, his eyes watering more than ever. He leaned his chin on to his crutch. He mouth opened in a toothless grin.

'Not that I don't want to, Mr Berry. This crutch...' he said, stroking its wood, 'helps me to walk. Been me companion for near forty years. Couldn't manage without it. And the folks round here. These poor, desperate folks. Well, they need their help, don't yer see. They need a friend to support them.'

Berry held the shilling in front of the old man's eyes. 'A shilling, Jasper? A shilling for one name. Five then if you name this gentleman?'

'I wouldn't do it, Mr Berry, no, not for thirty pieces of silver, neither. Napoleon took me leg. He never took me soul. And if I knew a name I wouldn't let on. Not for all the shillings and ale in the world.' A tear made its way down the old man's cheek.

'You must know more than you're saying?'

'I said I'd tell yer all I know. I have. Now leave me alone. Leave me alone.'

Berry stood, pulled on his hat and began to walk away. But before he left the cubbyhole he turned once more reaching out to shake the old soldier's hand.

'You know where I am, Jasper, should you hear more,' he said as he left the man to the rest of the ale.

When Berry had gone, Jasper turned over his hand to find the shiny shilling that Berry had pressed into his palm. He finished the last of the ale, looking thoughtfully at the coin before secreting it inside his tunic.

~

Constable Johnson had been following the girl for much of the afternoon, as she worked her way up Monmouth Street and into the very heart of the Dials. A pretty one, she was. Too good for the streets, though her face was over-painted and she had a smudge of dirt on her forehead. Her dark hair was piled up when it should have been running free. Choosy she was. He watched as she rejected several men who approached her. Worth more than a shilling, Johnson thought. A girl like her should be working in one of the night houses. She was too young and comely to be held up and poked against an alley wall. She'd find someone with money, no doubt about that! Johnson could almost feel the coins in his grasp.

And there he was, walking up the street and obviously looking around for tail. He was dressed in quite expensive clothes, though not of the very best. Perhaps the young owner of a shop or a manager in a factory. He was moustached with a few strands of beard adorning his chin. He looked an innocent, Johnson thought, with an expression of gullibility. He was clearly nervous of his surroundings, clutching his walking stick as though his life depended on it. In Seven Dials it may well have done.

He watched as the girl seemed to notice the man. Saw the hurry with which she crossed the street, putting herself in a position where their paths would have to cross. The little whore was obviously a skilled practitioner.

'She can smell his money, too.' Johnson muttered to himself, as he kept apace with them, watching their conversation. He saw the young man nod a few times and look all around. The girl walked away down the street and into the dark opening of an alley. The man looked around once more before he followed her.

~

Jasper Feedle stood in the passageway that led out of the back of the tavern and into the maze of alleyways that facilitated an easy escape for the villains who so often congregated there. He looked at the shillings in his palm. A rewarding day for a hero of the wars, he thought. He rested his head back against the dirty brown wall and thought of other shillings. Those given to him courtesy of King George. For a moment his mind wondered, filled with memories of Corunna and Talevera, the screams and powder smoke of Waterloo. They had been the best days of his life, well worth the loss of a leg and most of his friends. Better than this rat-ridden hell hole, anyways.

'I see that Sergeant Berry was generous,' Isaac Critzman whispered into his ear. 'More money than many a folk see in a long day.'

Jasper turned and smiled. 'Yer were right, Mister C. Yer said they'd seek me out. They always comes to me first. Three shillings for an old soldier.'

'You only told him what I suggested?' Isaac asked. 'Nothing more?'

'No more nor less. He was...intrigued.'

Isaac took the old man's hand and counted into his palm a further three shillings to join the other coins already there. He patted Jasper on the shoulder and walked back into the tavern.

~

Johnson gave the man and the girl a couple of minutes before he crept into the alley. The tall walls of London brick rose towards an almost indefinable slit of blue sky. It was a beautiful afternoon, the early autumn warmth even infiltrating the lowest depths of Seven Dials. The alley was extremely narrow, scarcely wide enough for two people walking side by side. It was not straight but had a long curve hiding its furthest portions from the sight of anyone in the street. It was an alley almost designed for illicit copulation. The police constable knew it well. It was one of his most productive hunting grounds.

And there they were: the young man already pressing the girl against the grimy wall, his hands impatiently lifting her skirts, his mouth against her cheek, muttering and moaning with excitement. The girl looking up at the distant stretch of sky with the usual detachment of her kind. It was a scene that Johnson had witnessed so many times before. Always to his profit.

He reached out and pulled on the young man's shoulder, seeing the fear on the man's pale face as he turned. Then the look of horror as he saw the police uniform. His mouth opened but he seemed not able to speak.

'Now then,' Johnson said. 'Come a-whoring have you sir?'

'I...'

Johnson sucked in a breath. 'Shouldn't have come a-whoring in the Dials. Not the place someone like you should come at all, *Sir*. Can get to be expensive, a-whoring on my beat.' He looked at the girl. 'How much did he give you?'

The girl looked down at the ground but said nothing.

'Well, we'll discuss that later.' He turned back to the young man, who was adjusting his clothing. 'Got a sovereign on you, have you sir?'

The man looked nervously across at the constable. 'I wasn't going to give her a sovereign. Just a bob or two. When we'd finished.'

'But have you got a sovereign? Important that you always carries enough to clear your debts.'

The young man nodded. 'Yes, I've got a sovereign. Only the one...and some change. I was going to pay her. Honest I was...'

Johnson smiled and shook his head. 'I can see that you're a bright young man. Made a mistake let's say. First time out? Yes, I thought so! No need to take you in charge then.'

'Then I –I can go?' the young man stuttered.

'Of course you can,' said Johnson. 'Not your fault you was so easily lured. Shouldn't come to these parts, young men like you. So, you see, on my beat I delivers a certain kind of personal justice. Stop it getting official. So I'll take your sovereign and we'll say no more about it.'

'What about me?' asked the girl.

'You got any money at all?' asked Johnson.

The girl shook her head, looking nervously at the constable.

'Then it'll have to be payment in kind, don't you see,' Johnson said, enjoying the look of disgust that crept over the girl's face. 'Just as soon as this young gent has paid up and gone on his way. And then you and I...'

A moment later he was falling to the floor as Sticks brought the lead-weighted life preserver crashing against the back of his neck.

'Hope I didn't keep you waiting?' said Sticks. 'Wanted to hear what he had to say for himself.' He stroked the life preserver with something approaching affection. 'Good old neddy...'

Quest smiled at Rosa. 'An admirable performance, though I felt that your flights of passion were a trifle restrained. You get well away from here now. We'll prepare Constable Johnson for his audience.'

~

Berry had had an unproductive afternoon in Seven Dials. He had had high hopes of Jasper Feedle, his best informant. But he obviously and truthfully knew very little. After leaving the old soldier he had spent an hour seeking out everyone he knew who might be bought, or bribed, or threatened. All to no avail. For while they all knew that something was afoot nobody knew what. Who was this gentleman who championed the poor? And how many more killings were there to be? What a waste of an afternoon!

He walked back down Monmouth Street in the direction of Whitehall, dreading the report he had to make. He knew Anders would be sympathetic. He always was. Nobody knew better than he how this secretive little world could close ranks when it wanted to. But their investigation seemed very little further forward. Police Commissioner Mayne would be making their lives a misery before long.

He was almost at the end of the street when he heard a sound that always made his heart beat faster. A crackling noise that he remembered from his own long hours on the beat through these very rookeries. The sound of a policeman's rattle being whirled as a constable summoned help and assistance. Then the confirming sound of a second rattle as some constable rushed to the assistance of the first. The old bloodlust for the hunt stirred in Berry's chest and he rushed back up Monmouth Street to give his own assistance.

He had not run a couple of hundred yards before he saw the crowd gathered at the mouth of an alley, two constables trying unsuccessfully to drive them back along the street. Berry forced his way through the throng, catching the questioning look in one constable's eye. For there, propped against the wall where the alley began, was the naked form of Constable Johnson, tied like a hog, groaning and spitting past the handle of the police rattle that was rammed into his mouth. And across the man's fat thighs was thrown, as though casually, a piece of tarred cord tied like a noose.

~

Old Josiah sat for longer than usual that cold afternoon. He had decided that he would not visit the cemetery at Kensal Green so often. After all, it was a place for the dead not the living and he thought that he might use his time more productively. For the greater benefit of society, perhaps. His son would understand, he knew that. The boy had always been a most compassionate little soul. More people were coming to the cemetery now. There were more tombs and gravestones. More people came and never left. Josiah thought it was long past the time to move on. He leaned on his stick and stood for a moment before walking down to the long triangular stone that marked that last resting place of someone so dear to him. He knelt for a moment and drew his hand along the carved inscription of the name. It was the tomb of his son. It was the grave of William Quest.

SEVEN

Lizzie Paynter thought that the library at Hope Down was the best of all the rooms, its walls lined with books and with comfortable armchairs in front of the fireplace. A long oak table of incredible age filled much of the centre of the room, leading across to the two windows with their lovely views over green pastures, and a tree-lined river just in sight.

Lizzie loved its quiet atmosphere, seeing books that were obviously cared for and read. She enjoyed looking out at that splendid view. She liked to spend time there, stretching out her cleaning work for as long as possible.

She would have liked to stay all day in the master's library if she could; not that difficult for the master was not there. Above the fireplace was a portrait of an old gentleman, dressed in black and with grey hair. A fine looking man, she always thought, with a kindly expression on his face. He seemed to smile down upon the room as though giving anyone within a sort of blessing. Lizzie could not look at his face without smiling back.

She had been the maid at Hope Down for barely a month. She had loved the old house from the first day and never wanted to leave. In all her sixteen years she had never known such peace and joy. Within a few days of her employment she had almost forgotten the horrors of the church paupers school where she was as much slave as pupil. They had taught her to read and to sew and that was about all.

In all the other hours she had shivered in the cold, when she was not scrubbing the floors and walls. As a child she had picked oakum in the workhouse, where she had been deposited at the age of six after her mother and father had died of the cholera. Her hands had been painful for years afterwards, from unravelling the tarred rope. She could still conjure up the stink of it.

Hope Down, for her, was like dying and going to Heaven. The work was not onerous, for it was a small property. Apart from Mrs Vellaby the housekeeper, there were only the Brewers, a married couple who lived over the stables. Tom Brewer served as gardener and groundsman and Mrs Brewer (nobody ever referred to her as anything but "Mrs" Brewer) served as cook. A girl came in from the village to lend a hand whenever the master was at home, but Lizzie had not yet met her.

But she soon would, for the master was coming down from London for a week. Lizzie could not imagine what he would be like, for there was no picture of him in the house. Mrs Vellaby had told her to just be polite and keep out of his way as much as possible, for the master cherished peace and quiet when he came to his country retreat.

'You won't see much of him,' the old lady had said. 'He's a caution! When he's not reading quietly in his library he's out on long tramps across the countryside. Dawn to dusk he's often away. Over the hills and along the lanes. And if you watch him, he never seems to walk very fast, but he can walk thirty miles in a day with no effort. Always been the same since the day he first came down to Hope.'

'And will his family be visiting him?' Lizzie had asked.

A look of concern crossed Mrs Vellaby's face. 'Oh, that's the tragedy of it! He has no family, not since the old master died.'

'The nice gentleman in the library?'

'Aye, that's him, as good and kind a soul as you could wish to meet. And his son every bit as pleasant and gentle. He ought to marry and settle down here. London's an evil place, you know girl. Too many distractions for a young man.'

'Has the master never thought of marrying?'

'There's been those around here who've tried to net him. But he's never round long enough. Miss Groves, the vicar's sister, pursued him like a huntress when he was here last summer. Like he was one of the foxes she chases. But every time she got near he went to earth.' Mrs Vellaby laughed at the memory. 'Anyway, I can't be standing here gossiping! Run along girl or he'll find the place a heap of dust.'

Lizzie picked up a broom and wandered out from the kitchen to attack the steps by the front door. A curlew cried from down by the river as she brushed away some stray autumn leaves.

~

'Mayne is spitting blood!' Anders said to Berry as he returned from the Commissioner's office. 'A constable stripped and hog-tied in broad daylight. Humiliated. And by a killer he thinks we should have accounted for a good while ago'

'Does he know that Constable Johnson has a reputation?'

'The world knows it now,' Anders said. 'Our killer sent this letter to *The Times* and a half dozen other sheets.' He threw the note down on to the desk. Berry noted the sketch drawing of a hangman's noose before reading the quite beautiful copperplate handwriting:

We have, on behalf of the residents of Seven Dials, made an example of Johnson, who is not worthy to hold the high office of constable. This despicable creature abused his responsibilities by acts of exploitation, extortion, rape, blackmail and cruel violence. He robbed common prostitutes of their earnings and forced himself on those who had no money. We have dealt with others in a similar or graver manner. In the name of Justice we shall

*continue our campaign against the wrongs that
plague this land. There will be no further warnings,
so wrongdoers take heed!*

'And do the newspapers intend to publish this?' Berry asked, passing the note back to the Inspector.

'They already have! The morning editions carry the story quite prominently. And I am given to understand from the beat constables that posters bearing much the same message have been posted all over London.'

'And Johnson? Does Mayne intend any action to be taken against him?'

'Johnson has left London,' Anders replied. 'Nobody knows where he has gone. But, yes, we would have had to seek his prosecution.'

'He described the circumstances of his assault?'

'No more than he told you when you took the rattle out of his mouth. A whore and her customer. A blow from behind from a third party. We do not know if the first two are part of this conspiracy, though I suspect so, given that Johnson said that he had not seen the woman before. We must assume they are. Three of them then. Our killer does not work alone.'

'In my experience that makes finding him easier,' Berry replied. 'The more the merrier, as they say. Easier to track down a group than a solitary individual. Harder for them all to keep quiet and evade notice.'

Anders nudged back a lump of coal that was threatening to fall from the small fireplace. It had suddenly become a colder afternoon. He put up the guard against the fire and reached his coat from the hook by the door.

'Come on then,' he said. 'Let us get out there and hunt them down.'

~

Cold weather always reminded Josef Critzman of his boyhood in Poland, in those heady days before the persecutions started. His abiding memory was of chopping logs for the fire in the great forest that had surrounded their home. It had been a lovely house, built of stone and rough timber with beautiful views across the river. Although he had now spent most of his life in London he yearned for the tranquillity of that valley. Much more than his brother Isaac who had become an Englishman in every word and gesture.

Isaac was waiting for him on the steps of his office in Albemarle Street. He had been polishing the plaque to one side of the door, which read: *The Metropolitan Society For The Alleviation Of Pauperism.* Lister, his clerk, offered to polish the plaque on an almost daily basis, but Isaac took a great pride in doing the task himself.

'You will wear that plaque away, Isaac,' Josef said. 'Once a week would be enough.'

'It needs to be polished,' Isaac frowned at his brother. 'And I need to be seen polishing it. There are many who seek the help of our Society who would be nervous of ringing the bell. If they see me here on the doorstep they feel easier about approaching me.'

Josef smiled at his brother. He had always been a kindly child, no more than a boy when they had fled Poland. Isaac had a way of putting himself in the shoes of others. Josef, who had shielded his brother so often from persecution, found it much more difficult.

'And have there been many approaches of late?'

'Our Society cannot fund all London. I wish it could!' said Isaac. 'Yes, there have been many approaches. Too many for our funds to cope with. We really must seek out some more benefactors. My factories and your walking stick shop cannot provide all that is needed. Nor can we give employment to all of those who are desperate for work.'

'I think I meant approaches of the other kind?'

'You saw the posters and the piece in *The Times*?' Isaac whispered.

Now Josef frowned. 'I do wonder if that altogether wise? A shade too early to put our cards on the table.'

Isaac raised his hands to the heavens. 'William is a young man and young men are impatient. Besides, he didn't want the assault on Johnson to be interpreted as just some brutal street attack on a constable. There could have been a danger of others getting the blame.'

'I do hope Feedle disguised his handwriting sufficiently?'

'I stood over Jasper as he wrote the letters to my dictation. He is the best screever in London and he only tells the police what I want him to. Have no fear Josef. We are safe enough. This is not Poland.'

Josef shook his head. 'No, it is not Poland. The police are much cleverer here than their more vicious counterparts at home. Cleverer than our young friend might appreciate. Anyway, it is too cold to stand here shivering on a doorstep. Might I come in and see the accounts? Do you have a fire lit? Have you any muffins?'

~

The little church was the destination for many of Quest's tramps from Hope Down. He might come to it by different routes but he usually ended up there. There was nothing exceptional about the building, except a kind of artless simplicity. For Quest that was the attraction. A few cottages backed on to the churchyard, but he seldom saw the cottagers who were probably out working in the fields most of the day. Gently sloping hills rose up from the valley and a river could be heard murmuring a hundred yards away. It was always a place of perfect peace, a setting where a man might rest, even slumber, without the invasion of nightmares.

Quest would sit against the churchyard wall, under the shade of a yew tree, and find a kind of mental freedom that he did not often experience. He liked the spot so much that he had bought the plot, as a place to be buried when his time should come, there being no church nearer to Hope Down. Assuming he might avoid the rope outside Newgate and burial in a common pit filled with lime.

It had been a wonderful walk on that clear autumn day, through deep forests and over wide and open ridges, with views of many miles. Tramping through such wild countryside he had seen few people, just distant impressions of men and women in fields far away. He had started his day cold, but the first rise on the walk had warmed him up, causing him to take off his coat and sling it through the straps of his knapsack. Skylarks still sang, near invisible against the blue sky and he disturbed many a pheasant as he kicked through the fallen leaves of the forest.

As he leaned back against the old stone wall he felt that delicious tiredness that comes only from pleasant exercise in peaceful surroundings. It had been a good walk, one of the very best. He was at peace, at home, and dazed with the joy of it.

~

Jacob Raikes sat in his rooms in Whitehall and read, once again, the piece in *The Times*. After some consideration he snipped out the account, read it again and tucked it away between the pages of his commonplace book. On an adjoining page he scribbled a few notes on the same subject, detailing the discussions he had had that morning with the prime minister. Raikes did not like Lord Aberdeen and the feeling was mutual. Raikes's hatred and distrust of Peelites was well known throughout Westminster. But they needed him and Raikes, being a practical man, relied on the support of the government.

Raikes was a tall man of five and forty, with green eyes that had a particular stare to them. His subordinates said that those eyes penetrated into their souls and consciences like daggers. Nothing could be hidden from their prolonged gaze for very long. It was, they said, what made Raikes so very efficient at his job.

In his earlier days, as a lawyer, witnesses at the Old Bailey had wilted under the power of those eyes. People who met Raikes, but once, saw little beyond his eyes. for the pale face and cropped dark hair of the man were unexceptional. Raikes could sit in a room with his eyes closed and scarcely be noticed. It was how he obtained a great deal of his information. Then when the eyes opened, and he brought that knowledge into use, all his victims trembled. It was an admirable skill, one that served his immediate master, the Home Secretary, Lord Palmerston, very well indeed.

He rang the little bell on his desk and sat back in the winged chair. After a moment a little man, almost a dwarf, looked nervously around the door.

'Sir?'

'Barker, which detective officer at Scotland Yard is dealing with the recent killings?'

'I – um, understand it to be Inspector Anders, sir.'

'Very well. Please take a message to Inspector Anders and ask if he would be so good as to come here at three this afternoon. Please ask him to bring with him any documents relating to the killings and the assault on the police constable.'

'Very good, sir.'

'Oh, and Barker?'

'Sir?'

'When you have done that, please bring me any information we have on Russians living in London, particularly any who are wealthy and might have influence with the Tsar.'

'Very good, sir.' The little man pulled the door to and breathed a sigh of relief. The tasks Raikes assigned to him were usually much more unpleasant.

After Barker had left the room, Raikes rested his head back against the hard wood of the chair, contemplating the long wall of books and the oak panelled walls. He tapped his fingers on the desk, a habit he had picked up during long and dull sessions at the Bailey. He was a man who was not happy unless something was happening and there was an immediate challenge to be countered.

He thought for a moment of those who worked under him, trying to decide who might be best placed to seek out the motives behind the recent killings, someone who could work outside the knowledge of Scotland Yard. A procession of faces floated in the air, almost as though he could see them parading in front of his dangerous green eyes. He stopped this examination as the very man came to mind. He pictured one particular face. The face of a man who might fit in anywhere, a man with all the appearance of a fat country businessman; an individual that people never saw any harm in confiding in. An ideal candidate for this kind of work, Raikes considered. Perhaps the best of all of the men who worked behind the scenes for Raikes, in his position as Queen Victoria's spymaster.

~

The fire in the library at Hope Down was burning low as the mantelpiece clock, sounding ten, brought Lizzie Paynter out of the world of Miss Jane Austen's *Persuasion*. It was a house where people retired early, and she cherished these peaceful moments when, under the guise of checking that the windows were locked, she might turn a few pages of one of the master's books. In the small time she had worked at the house she had read several of the leather-bound volumes, giving at least one blessing to the church pauper school where she had learned to read.

Mr Quest and his man, Mr Sticks, had arrived the previous day. She had liked Mr Sticks from the first. He had taken a great interest in her, told her jokes, and ordered Mrs Vellaby not to give her too much work to do. Mr Quest was different. He had smiled very nicely as the housekeeper introduced her, but seemed terribly shy. He had asked if she liked living at Hope Down and seemed pleased when she said yes. Lizzie hadn't seen either of the two men that day. Mr Quest had gone off on one of his long country tramps, and Mr Sticks had left for the nearest town to watch some horses being raced.

A strange one, Mr Quest, she considered. Almost like one of Miss Austen's gentlemen heroes. The thought brought her back to *Persuasion*. Perhaps she could just finish the novel before retiring to her room in the attic. She read on for the last few pages and smiled at the conclusion. She looked up, still smiling, into the questioning face of Mr Quest. She jumped to her feet, clutching the book as though it was the most valuable thing in the world.

Quest was still dusty from his long walk and he looked tired. The knapsack was slung loosely across one shoulder with the heavy walking stick placed like a rifle across the other.

'I am so very...' she began.

'Sorry?'

'Yes!'

He smiled. 'You should never be sorry if you have enjoyed a book. That is what they are for. Have you read many?'

'Some,' she replied. 'I particularly like Miss Jane Austen. I have just finished *Persuasion*.' She handed him the book, trying not to notice the livid scar on the accepting hand.

'It is good to enjoy a particular author. Please feel free to borrow any of my books. I will tell Mrs Vellaby that it is all right.'

'Thank you, sir,' she nodded her head. 'I'll take great care of them.'

'I know you will,' he said, smiling in that shy way he had. 'Good night, Lizzie.'

'Good night, sir,' she gave a small curtsey as she left the room.

Quest thumbed through the pages of the novel, remembering the first time he had read it. He laughed aloud as he put it back into its place on the shelves. He now had Sticks and the maid Lizzie enjoying his books. They were probably better read than he was! He laughed again and sank down into the armchair by the now extinct fire.

EIGHT

Ned was dying. That was certain sure. Every day he was getting weaker and now he could not move at all. His face, his body, the very form of him had wasted to almost nothing. The eyes that looked at his friend had no light left in them. His lips, which had always been pale and colourless, were now turning a ghastly shade of blue. He raised a hand to summon the boy.

'Billy?'

The boy knelt down beside him, putting an ear close to Ned's mouth. The words were slow in coming and barely audible. The taste of death came in a vivid stench from between his lips. Billy, quite used to a stinking world, had to turn his face away.

'Billy,' Ned began...

'Best not to talk,' Billy replied. 'Save your strength. I'm going out to get some food in a bit. You'll be stronger after food.'

Ned shook his head and the effort seemed to tire him even more.

'Sleep now,' Billy continued. 'Won't be gone long.'

He massed the old blanket up under his friend's head and smiled down at the dying boy. 'Back soon!'

It had been three weeks since they had left the rookery. The money he had stolen had lasted much of that time, supplemented by the sale to a fence of two pocket handkerchiefs. They had found a small room in the Borough. Better than the St Giles hole, in that they had it to themselves. But not much better at that. Still cold, still damp. The countryside would have been better, Billy thought. If only Ned had had the strength to get there. He knew that Ned could not last more than a day or two. And then?

Billy's only thought now was to get his friend the Christian burial he knew he craved. But how? He knew he couldn't possibly steal enough to pay for one. Not in time, anyhow. Better to get the boy into the workhouse before he died. That would at least get him a pauper's grave and a few holy words. He would have to carry him to the nearest Union. He hoped Ned would not die before he got him there.

~

'And this is all you have?' Raikes waved a hand over the small pile of documents on his desk, looking up at Anders disdainfully. 'No evidence? A trifle of speculations?'

'It is proving difficult,' Anders replied. 'We are not dealing with some common criminal...'

'The Prime Minister is extremely concerned at the murders of prominent members of society. Not to mention the humiliation of a police constable. Lord Aberdeen is concerned that there might be some political motive for these crimes. He is concerned about the possibility of riot and rebellion.'

'As I'm sure are we all,' said Anders.

Raikes sat back in his chair, intertwining his hands in an attempt to resist tapping the table. He looked up at the detective officer, not particularly liking what he saw. Anders seemed to be a man of integrity, someone far below his own station in life. A plodder. A man with too much patience and compassion. Life was too short to let this policeman have a completely free hand. He half-closed his eyes as he considered the matter. Then opened them to release that devastating stare at Anders.

'You will please send round regular reports of any new developments.'

'May I ask on whose authority you act?' said Anders. 'You see, I don't know who you are, other than that you appear to represent the Home Secretary.'

'Isn't that enough?'

'I'm afraid it isn't,' Anders replied. 'I have brought these documents to you out of pure courtesy. Even my Commissioner, Sir Richard Mayne, doesn't know I'm here. Without his authority I am not sure I should release any documents to other parties.'

Raikes leaned forward, the unblinking eyes fixed firmly upon the policeman. 'I did hope, Inspector, that you might be more cooperative. You will receive a written authorisation from the Prime Minister himself by this evening. He will not be pleased. He has much to occupy his mind. There are these tensions with the Russians. Lord Aberdeen is in conference even now with representatives of the Tsar. He will find this a great distraction.'

'Even so, I must have some authority to share documents. You might spare the Prime Minister and send a note of request round to my Commissioner.'

Raikes sighed. 'Very well. So be it. I will despatch a note to Sir Richard even now.' He rang the little bell on the desk. 'And all the documents if you please, Inspector...'

~

Anders paced up and down Whitehall for a good hour before returning to his office at Scotland Yard, thinking of the man he had just met. He had not enjoyed the company of Mr Raikes. He had not liked the gaze of those green eyes. It had been something like being scrutinised by a particularly vicious lizard. Yes, that was it. Something inhuman. As he told Sergeant Berry, who was kicking the coals of the office fire back into life, having Raikes in their lives was something to be regretted.

Berry frowned. 'Of course, we don't have to *literally* show him everything, do we sir? Better to keep him a pace or two behind us if he's half the menace you think.'

'It is a thought. Just the necessary then. And everything a day or two late. But beware! He has the ears of the Prime Minister, the Home Secretary, and probably the Queen herself. Steady as you go, Berry.

We can discuss at the end of the day exactly what our Mr Raikes sees. And when he sees it.'

'Assuming there is anything for him to see,' Berry replied. 'We don't seem to be awash with solutions.'

'I've been thinking about that. We have so little to go on and all our usual sources are dried up. Let us look again at the victims. Is he picking them at random because of their disreputable lives?'

'It would seem so.'

'In which case,' said Anders, 'it would be very difficult to anticipate his next move. But what if there is a personal element? At least with some of the killings?'

Berry threw a few more coals on the fire and stared thoughtfully into the flames. 'I don't see how there could be.' he said. 'There are no links between the victims. Except for the Bartram brothers.'

Anders sat back into his chair. 'Exactly. Why kill both brothers and travel to Norfolk to slay the first? Neither were charming characters, but surely the death of one would have been painful for the other. And enough to make the point. And a different killing to the others. Gunned down in his own wood.'

'That is true.'

'If we had that killing alone, Berry. If that was our one murder, then we would investigate it as a killing by someone with a personal grudge.'

'We would!'

'Then that is what we must do. We will contact Inspector Gurney in Norwich and I will return there as soon as possible to try and find out why Charles Bartram had to die. Meanwhile you get back out on to those streets. There must at least be gossip to work on. I feel our man must strike again very soon. Let us try and anticipate him.'

~

People stared.

Even though the dead and the dying were common sights on the streets of London, people stared. It was the spectacle of one boy carrying another, one clearly breathing his last, that drew those stares.

There was no weight in Ned. It felt to Billy that the boy's rags were somehow heavier than his body. He tried to be gentle with his friend, steering a way between obstacles, going carefully down gutters and across cobbles as he carried Ned through the darkening streets. The dying boy was unconscious now, his breathing shallow with just an occasional moan from between those pale blue lips. Billy found it hard to look at the death that he held so carefully in his arms. The death that must come to everyone in this way, especially the poor. As he made his way through the dark tunnels between the high walls of buildings, he had, most of all, a deep yearning for open fields and green trees.

They had passed into Southwark now, between taller buildings as the workhouse came into view, gaunt and ugly, great walls of London brick hiding the last of the sunlight. Billy felt a shiver go through his body at the sight of it. He pulled the great chain by the wooden door and heard a ridiculously quiet bell ring inside. After a few minutes the door swung open and a thin grey man looked questioningly at the pair. A pauper himself, earning some extra food by minding the gates.

'Well?'

'My friend...' Billy began. 'He is so very ill.'

The pauper leaned forward, opening one of Ned's eyelids and then resting the back of his hand against the boy's neck. He mumbled to himself and then called out 'Mr Spears!'

'Can you help him please?' Billy asked.

The pauper shook his head.

'Not Gabriel nor all the angels can help him now,' he said. 'He's croaked!'

Billy felt all the strength go from his own body and he nearly dropped Ned where he stood. The pauper reached out and the two of them rested the body down on a long stone bench just inside the doorway.

'He was breathing!' Billy said. 'Just now! And murmuring! I heard him!'

'Not no more. He's a gonner!'

Mr Spears, a weedier man than the pauper, for all that he wore a uniform and seemed to be some sort of official, came up to them out of the black recesses of the workhouse. The pauper took him aside, explaining the situation.

After a moment he turned to Billy.

'He's dead. You'll have to take him away. He's not our responsibility.'

'I can't bury him!' Billy protested.

'Then why should we?'

'He was born in this parish. In this very workhouse. Ned Copper. You look him up. He was born here.' Billy felt tears of anger burning at his eyes.

'There was a boy called Copper,' said the pauper after a moment's thought. 'You tried to get him 'prenticed, Mr Spears, at the horse glue factory. They wouldn't have such a weedling. That's what they said. Went off on streets t'other side of the river. His mother's here still, Martha Copper. Works at the oakum.'

'Damn!' said Spears. 'The guardians'll loathe the expense.'

'He will get a burial?' Billy asked. 'Holy words and all?'

'Not many holy words,' Spears replied. 'But enough for a bag of bones like him. Take him inside, Wilfie, then send out for Doctor Wills. After that you can go up to the oakum and break another mother's heart.'

~

Billy walked away from the workhouse and along by the Thames, picturing in his mind the events surrounding a pauper's funeral. The cheap coffin, a bored parson, a grave with a hundred other corpses in it. Such was the way the poor died. He spat into the water. At least death was an escape from it all.

He sat for an hour on a bollard, watching a ship from the Baltic bringing its load ashore. Then looked as the lightermen worked away, unloading barges bringing cargoes up from the bigger ships moored downstream. Vaguely he searched around for something he might steal or some passer-by he might rob. He felt a great desire to get caught, get lagged, transported perhaps, or even to feel the hempen rope around his neck. A memory came back to him of his own father swinging in the breeze on a country hilltop. Was being topped really so bad?

Perhaps it wasn't, after all.

And now here was a sight that might send him there. On the edge of the dock a shipmaster was yelling at the crew below. A shipmaster who looked as though he had never been to sea, too well-dressed for a sailing master, with his smart clothes and silver-topped cane. He had come down from the shipping office to one side of the warehouse, impatient at the slowness of the unloading of the Baltic vessel. His yells could be heard clear across the Thames and the *lightermen looked cowed by his annoyance. All but one. A lad of perhaps twelve stood just a yard away remonstrating with his master. Billy couldn't quite hear all the words but got the impression that the boy was saying something about how exhausted they were with hunger, and the fact that the ship had not been alongside the dock for very long.*

The answer came swiftly and brutally. The man raised his cane and brought it crashing across the boy's head. The man was saying something. Billy didn't quite catch what it was. For in the moment that the words were being spoken he was rushing the few yards across the dock and swinging the shipmaster round.

The man looked astonished.

'What the bloody....?'

He raised his cane and brought it swiftly down towards Billy's head. But Billy had met the owners of angry canes before. He stepped quickly to one side and brought the side of his hand hard against the shipmaster's head. The man staggered but did not fall. He dropped the cane. In an instant Billy had the weapon in his own hand, delivering a mighty blow on to the shinbone of its owner. The shipmaster screamed in agony and fell to the floor. He looked up with fear as Billy raised the cane high above his face. He saw the deadly look in the boy's face. He felt the nearness of death. Until the day he died that shipmaster was never as close to that fatal moment.

A voice came from the ship.

One of the lightermen, anonymous in the crowd on the deck, ''e's not worth gettin' topped for, son. There's runners comin', so leg it!'

Billy looked along the dock. Two Bow Street runners were coming towards him at a furious pace, one swirling his warning rattle and the other brandishing a club. They were both shouting at him to drop the cane and stand still. Billy threw his weapon in their direction and turned and ran.

The runners were fit young men and only a few yards behind Billy as he sped away from the river and into the winding alleys of Southwark. He knew them well, this jumble of decaying streets and courts. Far better than the runners, for within a few minutes he had left them lost and bewildered in the maze of alleyways. He leaned back against a wall, closing his eyes as he got his breath back.

'A damn near run thing, as the old Duke o' Wellington said after Waterloo.'

The deep voice muttered into his ear, jolting Billy back into the world. He raised his fists defensively and looked into a battered face, just a few inches from his own.

'A damn near run thing!' The man said again. 'Saw it all. You attacking that bully. Know him well. Needed takin' down a peg or two that one. Nearly done it mesself a time or two. But you was lucky to get away with it. You'd best come with me back

87

across the river. There'll be a right hue and cry for you all over Southwark before the day's done.'

'How...how did you find me....?'

A laugh came from somewhere within the bruised round face.

'I've known these alleyways since Jack was a lad. Better'n you, I reckon. Better'n those crushers after you. I knew just which way you'd come. I was here afore you. If you're goin' ter be a real flash villain you need to outsmart folk like me. Need to do better.'

'How are we to get back over the river? They might be watching the bridges for me.'

'Well, we'll have a long walk upstream, how about that? Then meet up with an old pal of mine with a boat. Back in St Giles by the mornin''

'Why should you do this?' Billy asked. 'And how do you know I come from St Giles?'

'No mystery. I've seen you in the tavern there. You're Billy and you're a dip. I've friends who think well of you.'

Billy looked again at the man. He looked familiar and he had recollections of seeing him before. But not just in the taverns of St Giles. Somewhere else. He searched his mind until his memory flew to the lonely countryside to the north of the city. A great crowd assembled around a scratch square of a prize ring.

This very man putting out the lights of another bruiser in a bare-knuckle contest that had lasted two hours with rounds beyond count. He had seen engravings of him in the little books on prize fighting that they sold outside Newgate on hanging days. There hadn't been such a bruiser since the heyday of Tom Oliver as...

Billy turned and looked the man in the face.

'And I know you! I've seen you fight. You're Albert Sticks!' He gasped in disbelief.

'Sticks you might call me,' the bruiser replied. 'Never heard of the Albert. An' I'll box your ears if I hears you say it again.'

NINE

Mrs Bendig, keeper of one of the most prosperous whorehouses in London, was fat and ugly. She was also, as Sergeant Berry knew to his profit, extremely garrulous when prodded enough and when money changed hands. He knew her well, for she had a fine whoring background in his home town of Manchester.

Then the rot had set in.

Her looks had long gone, even before she arrived in London to open her infamous night house. Legend had it that she had cut the throat of her former business partner in the north, decamping with the money he had made running brothels for twenty years. His name had been Bendig. To Sergeant Berry's knowledge there was no evidence that the two had ever legally married. And a dozen prostitutes had sworn that Mrs Bendig was elsewhere on the night that old Bendig was topped, lying in his own bed. The dozen whores had lied convincingly enough to fool the authorities in Manchester.

And there she sat at a table at the long room in the night house off Leicester Square; until dawn some days, conducting her business, making sure the young blades around town had a good time and were paired off with the best of her girls. Making a nightly profit as huge as herself. Older age meant that she only did a few nights a week *in person* as hostess to the debauched of London. At other times she had cultivated a whole new immoral industry elsewhere. One that, for its scale, was even more profitable.

In this other life she lived as Mrs Smythe in a respectable little house just west of Soho Square. It was from here, and under that name, that she trawled the rookeries of London looking for virgins, or at least girls who might pass as virgins, who could be deflowered by the most discerning of her gentlemen clients.

When not busy with this work, she posed as a widowed lady, somewhat distressed financially but still respectable. Her neighbours thought well of her and the parish parson smiled benevolently at her when she occasionally occupied his front pew.

Which she did at times when the gin wore off and she had nightmares of hellfire.

Her fat fingers closed around the coin proffered to her by Sergeant Berry, as they sat in the little shadowed space that she called her withdrawing room. It was mid-morning and the night house was closed as both clients and girls sought some rest.

'Still poisoning the girls are you?' Berry asked.

'Oh, Sergeant Berry! You are a caution!'

'That's what they say, Molly. That you poison the girls that want to go and work somewhere else.'

Her face flushed a deeper red, the great rolls of fat almost hiding her eyes. She reached out and poured more gin out of the bottle the policeman had brought with him. She pushed a glass towards him.

'Your good health!' she said.

'I'm sure it will be, as I brought the bottle. Wouldn't trust one of yours. Might taste of arsenic.'

'You're the living end!' she replied. 'And how long have we known each other? Since you were a young peeler on the beat in Manchester! Funny we should both end up here!'

'Funnier still if you got lagged, Molly. Or sent over the water. Or topped. There's a rumour about you and young girls. Not pleasant rumours neither. Kind of thing that could get you into trouble.'

In an instant all the jollity vanished from Mrs Bendig's fat face.

'What you after?'

'Well,' said Berry, 'Mr Henry Bartram. Knew him did you?'

'Can't recall the name,' she replied, swigging back the gin.

Berry laughed. 'Come on, Molly! He was cut almost on your own doorstep. Just by that little house you have in Soho.'

'He might have been to my establishment a few times,' she said at last.

'And was coming round to see you in Soho, by all accounts,' said Berry. 'Why was he coming to see you, Molly?'

'Can't conceive! Have some more gin?'

Berry shook his head. 'And the constable, Johnson. Assaulted in the Dials the other day. Know anything about that?'

The violent shake of Mrs Bendig's head sent her cheeks wobbling.

'Why should I?'

'Rumour has it that he was giving some of the girls on the street a hard time. Working for you was he?'

'Never met the man!' she growled at Berry.

'You know, Molly, there are people in this city who think you should be put out of business. Closed down. Arraigned to the Bailey.' He held out another coin. 'The truth is, Molly, we're having a bit of a busy time. Haven't got the hours for you. If you don't know who topped Bartram, tell me about the attack on the constable?'

'And end up with a sword through me?'

'Nobody will ever know,' Berry patted one fat beringed hand. 'Come on, Molly? For old times' sake and another few coins?'

Mrs Bendig poured out another gin and poured it speedily into her throat. She leaned forward, her great chin seeming to envelop the top of her bosoms.

'All I can tell you is this,' she said. 'One of the girls Johnson had been leaning on. Sally her name is. Used to work for me. Just before the constable was attacked it was. Mr Watkins, who keeps the door for me. He saw her in a tavern close by where they're building the museum. Queen Street. The Dog and

93

something they used to call it. They've changed the name.'

'Dog and Duck?'

'That's the one,' she tapped the glass nervously on the table. 'Well Sally was there talking to a fat man and a ruffian bludger from the Dials. Name of Bill. He's a footpad, I b'lieve. Often in the taverns in the Dials and St Giles. Lives there mebbe? Mr Watkins thought it odd to see him and Sally there, off their patch. Didn't think anything of it 'til Johnson was attacked. Everyone knew your constable had been leaning on the girl.'

'That's all you know?'

'God's truth, Sergeant. That's all I know,' she said pocketing the coins as he counted them out on to the table.

'You know this fat man?'

She shook her head. 'Mr Watkins's seen him about. Flash gent. Well dressed up. Now please Sergeant Berry, leave me alone!'

~

Jasper Feedle followed Berry as he walked out of Leicester Square and down towards Piccadilly. Even with his crutch he could move faster than most men. He had been following the sergeant for much of the day. Watched him as he talked to a dozen men and women in the Dials. Trailed him as he went into Leicester Square. Saw him bang down the door of

Mrs Bendig's night house. Watched as the fat old woman opened the door, protesting until Berry proffered the bottle of gin. When it became clear that Berry was heading back to Whitehall and Scotland Yard, Feedle turned in the opposite direction towards the City. To Josef Critzman's walking stick shop in Cheapside.

~

It was a busy morning in Norwich as Anders walked along Tombland and through the Erpingham Gate, into the quieter peace of the cathedral close. The sight of the great cathedral with its magnificent spire made him pause. He had only seen it from a distance on his previous visit and was overwhelmed by the spectacle as he drew near. A few rooks circled the topmost heights of the spire, tiny and black against the faint blue sky. Anders shuddered at the thought of actually being up so high as that. Only the dedicated masons who built it or the insane would ever go up so high. The spire looked as though it was scraping the very entrance of Heaven.

'Quite a sight, our spire,' said Inspector Gurney, who had come, unnoticed behind him. His smile grew even broader as he took Ander's hand in greeting. 'Went up it a few years ago...'

'*You went up it?*'

'They were repairing the stonework at the top. My uncle was a mason. He took me up.'

'Why?' gasped Anders.

'Boyhood ambition, I suppose. A strange world up there. Do you know, you can feel the whole spire move in the wind? And it feels so fragile as you touch the top. Like one of those papery wasp nests.'

'You must be insane!'

'Perhaps. But not that insane! Once was enough. Let's stroll around the Close and I'll give you my news.'

'You have news?'

'News! And somebody you must meet.'

They strolled down the Close towards the river, Gurney occasionally touching his hat to passers-by.

'Can you stay in Norwich for a day or two?' he asked.

'As long as maybe if there is a solution to this dilemma,' Anders replied. 'You received my communication relating the assault on the constable?'

'I did indeed. And the warning note from our killer. A man on a crusade, evidently.' He paused and turned towards Anders. 'Do you feel ready for a breath of country air?'

'If it helps...'

'Then tomorrow we will journey to the estate of Lord Colbor.'

'And is his lordship material to this investigation?'

Gurney laughed. 'Not really. His lordship has been dead these past twelve months. The title is extinct. It is his widow, the Countess, we are to see.'

Anders looked quizzically at the Norfolk detective. 'And she is relative because?'

'Because,' said Gurney, waving his hands apart like a conjuror performing a trick, 'she is a widow twice over. She married the Earl of Colbor some eight years before his death. They were both quite elderly at the time. Her first husband died a dozen years ago. He was Charles Bartram, father of two of our victims. And now the Countess herself is dying and wishes to unburden her soul before she meets her maker. No priests for her. She wishes to talk to the police!'

~

'The problem is,' said Isaac Critzman, 'we don't know whether that dreadful old shrew told the policeman anything at all.'

Isaac and his brother sat by the fireside in the back parlour of the walking stick shop, drinking tea and eating muffins. The muffled sounds of the city street, the cries of traders, the neighing of horses, and a thousand muted conversations became a blur of noise as background to their talk.

Jasper Feedle looked up from warming another muffin over the fire.

'Berry was in there a time,' he said. 'With a bottle of gin. That old trout'd sell her soul for a thimbleful.'

Josef nodded. 'We must assume that she was particularly helpful. It is the safest way.'

'But what could she have told him?' Isaac asked. 'What can she know?'

'That is what we must find out,' Josef replied. 'But the best way...?'

'The best way is to go a-visitin',' Jasper spoke through a mouthful of muffin. 'Pay the old witch out. Send Mr William round a-calling.'

'Perhaps,' said Josef. 'We will see what our young friend thinks of all of this. In the meantime, Jasper, keep your ears to the ground and your eyes open. It is not yet winter and I already feel the ice getting thin. These policemen are better than I thought.'

As Jasper walked back towards Seven Dials, the tune of a song came into his mind. An old tune, one that he remembered from years before on the ship that brought him back from Napoleon's wars in Spain. The sailors had often belted out that shanty. He had heard it many times since, always with different words. They sang it sometimes in the taverns of St Giles. He hummed it, quite softly to himself, as he made his way through the pressing crowds of Cheapside:

'Where have you bin all the day,
Billy boy, Billy boy?
Where have you bin all the day
Me Billy boy?
I bin out with Nancy Gray,
She has stole my heart away,
Oh me Nancy,
Tickle me fancy,
Oh me darlin' Billy boy.'

For a moment the words brought back another occasion when he had heard it being sung. In a foul alehouse in Field Lane, so many years ago. A boy had smiled up at him, draining a tankard, as he said: *'but that's my name!'* A boy long dead, as all boys must die. He remembered slipping the boy a tanner, and saying to him: *'It's what's stolen with hearts that's the problem, me lad. It's what's stolen with hearts!'*

TEN

Anders thought the driveway to Colbor Hall was going to go on for ever. They had passed through a huge gatehouse, which itself was far bigger than many a London home. Then plunged into the darkness of woodland, which seemed to fringe the entire estate, itself surrounded by the tall park boundary wall that had accompanied their journey for almost two miles along the highway.

A gamekeeper, old gun tucked away under his arm, looked up at them from the edge of a line of beech trees, touching his cap more at the driver of the growler than the two detectives. A little further along the drive the carriage slowed. Anders leaned out and watched as the driver shooed at least a hundred pheasants out of his path, picking his way carefully through the recalcitrant dozen who refused to budge. Then the driveway was hemmed in on both sides with dozens of rhododendrons, which almost blocked away the light of the autumn day. Anders considered how magnificent they must look at the height of their season.

Then the woods were left behind and a great plain of parkland opened up in front of them, and in the distance a red-bricked house. A dozen men were scything the grass on one side of the drive. From somewhere a peacock cried, the sound reverberating back across the park, into the edge of the woods. It took a further ten minutes to cross the parkland and arrive at the house, passing on the way several smaller cottages and a considerable stable block, with its own gateway and courtyard. Several grooms were cleaning a pair of carriages, paying particular attention to the coats of arms on the doors. Horses whinnied from deep inside the building, getting a frenzied response from the pair that pulled the growler.

And then the house itself, a massive impression of red bricks, with a great gatehouse that seemed to be the oldest part of the building. It was by far the largest country house that Anders had ever seen. How on earth could one family rattle around inside something so big?

Two bewigged and liveried footmen ran out as the carriage swung under the arch of the gateway, coming to a halt in the courtyard beyond, just in front of a gigantic double door. The footmen opened the carriage doors on either side of the growler and Anders and Gurney stepped down on to the cobbles.

For a moment they looked up at the overwhelming red-bricked walls, then at the huge door, unsure where to go. Anders half-expected another liveried flunkey to come out and inquire as to their mission. But the man who came out to greet them was dressed perfectly normally, a typical country gentleman.

He nodded and smiled. 'Gentleman, My name is Ives, Arthur Ives. I am the steward of the estate. Her Ladyship has asked that I come and bring you to her. If you would please follow me.'

Ives led them across the courtyard to a smaller door within the arch of the gatehouse. Immediately beyond was a steep flight of spiral steps leading into the dark heart of the building. Their guide ascended them at a terrific pace. As Anders followed in his wake, gasping for breath, he muttered to Gurney 'I see we are taking the tradesmen's entrance!'

For the first time since he had known him, Anders saw Gurney frown. 'It is the way they do things in Norfolk,' he said.

From the top of the steps they were led through a seemingly endless series of narrow corridors, before they emerged on to a wider balcony above a grand staircase, rising up from the main entrance. 'All the way round the mulberry bush!' Anders spluttered. 'We might have come in that way!'

'Not far now,' said Ives, as they headed into a wide walking gallery that seemed to run along the entire southern end of the house. Massive windows, reaching up from floor to ceiling, gave a view over the park and a tree-lined lake, while the interior wall was crammed with family portraits. At the far end they came to a pair of ornate wooden doors.

Ives paused, his hand on the doorknob.

'A word, perhaps, before I take you into the library to see her Ladyship. A somewhat delicate matter...'

'We quite understand that her Ladyship is unwell,' said Gurney.

Ives looked pained. 'Worse than that. She is near to death. Her mind is...how can I say?...not at its best. There are hours in the day when she doesn't even recognise me or the house or even realise who she is. Then she gets moments of great lucidity. She heard of your visit to her late son's home. She bade me write to you, even dictated the letter.'

'We will be understanding,' said Gurney. 'My late mother went into a similar condition before she died.'

'Then I will take you in,' said Ives. 'But one more point. I wouldn't take for gospel anything she might say. Something...some ancient wrong...is playing with her mind. She won't tell me what it is, but she wishes to relate it to you gentlemen. Whether you accept the credibility of her tale, whether it is just her fancy, well...?'

He opened the door and led them into the library. Books lined most of the walls on three sides. On the fourth were three grand windows of a similar size and design to those in the gallery. A fire burned in a cavernous fireplace, with a life-size portrait above. Leather-jacketed books and inked papers were piled on the several tables placed at random around the centre of the room. It took Anders and Gurney a moment to spot the old lady sitting to one side of the fireplace, such was the shady nature of the room.

'Bring them close to me, Ives.' A strong voice echoed across the library. As they approached, Anders had a sense that for all her present frailty, this had once been a strong and domineering woman. A woman who had never been beautiful, but definitely striking in her way. Even now he could sense that certain magnetism that might have drawn men to her. She was, perhaps, seventy years of age, but her face was lined with many more years, no doubt, Anders thought, with the pain of her illness. She was dressed all in black, the dark veil, pulled away from her face, hiding much of her iron-grey hair.

The two detectives bowed, both said 'Your Ladyship'.

She waved a crabbed old hand towards the armchairs facing her.

'You may sit. And Ives, you may leave us. I will ring when I want you back.' The hand fluttered a gesture of dismissal. So much did the Countess dominate the scene that Anders hardly noticed the estate steward leave the room.

She waited for the door to close and then looked again at the two men. She breathed deeply, the gnarled fingers playing around her lips, as though deep in thought. A minute or two passed before she spoke, pointing up at the portrait over the fireplace.

'My late husband, Lord Colbor,' she said in those strong tones. 'A good man. A religious man. Gone now to meet his God. A better man than ever I deserved. *Much* better than I deserved!' she added with a bitter flourish.

'Your Ladyship...' Anders began.

'Please do not interrupt!' the voice echoed around the library like a whiplash. 'I will not be interrupted...'

Anders nodded and looked across at the pair of fiery blue eyes that seemed to be scouring into his mind.

'So little time,' she continued. 'And that is why you must not interrupt. My late husband was good to me you see. A good man. A holy man.' She laughed a bitter laugh. 'Brought me to religion, a trifle late...' She gave another laugh. 'But I've no time for priests. Only for practicalities. Which of you is the London detective?'

Anders bowed his head.

'So you saw my son Henry's body?'

'I did. And Inspector Gurney was called in after the death of Mr Charles Bartram.'

'Both murdered?'

'We fear so...'

'Fear so? Better to hope it was so!' She drew her fingers across her lips once again and stared into the fire for a moment or two.

'That fire there is not hot enough for my two little bastards. Nor the fires of hell!'

'Your Ladyship!' said Gurney. 'However they lived they did not deserve such a terrible end!'

Anders thought he had never seen anyone look as shocked as his fellow policeman did at that moment. He leaned forward. 'You think they deserved such a death?'

'Ah, yes!' the Countess replied. 'We are leaves on the same bough, Inspector. You see the world as it is, as I do. You are a pragmatist, not a romantic fool. That is good.' She took a deep breath. 'This world, which I am soon to leave, is a better place without the devils I spawned. And I will tell you why. And I will tell you why because I am fearful of God. Both of my husbands gave me a terror of hellfire, in their different ways. I am determined that Satan will not sear my flesh! And that is why I have summoned you here.'

She looked again into the fire for several moments, her hand waving in the air, almost as though it was cranking memories into her brain. And then she spoke in that clear and loud voice, slowly first and then more speedily, seeming to see the past play out in front of her eyes.

'First of all, let me tell you that my sons and my first husband deserved the deaths they got. Their deaths were too quick for them. They should all have had a longer suffering, stretched out and screaming with pain. That would have been a just punishment!'

Out in the grounds a peacock shrieked. The old woman started at the noise, breathed uneasily and continued with her tale.

'The Bartram estate was far too near Norwich. Always troubled with the riff-raff from the town. And the villages around... hardly a week went by without us being troubled with poachers. A whole band of them from Cossey came once and troubled our keepers. I remember the noise as they exchanged shots. My husband was a magistrate. Those he didn't have hanged he had transported. He and his friends on the Bench were not renowned for their mercy.'

A grim smile crossed her face as she said 'And now he has been called before the bar of heaven. I wonder what punishment Almighty God has passed on him?' There was a pause of a full minute before she added: 'It will be hellfire, Inspector.'

She looked up at Anders, a dancing merriment in those piercing blue eyes. She stroked her lips before continuing.

'But it is not of rascal poachers I wish to talk, but of deeper matters. You are from London. You may not realise what a lawless county this has always been. Riot and rebellion! The many seeking justice from the few.'

She looked puzzled for a moment.

'What was the year? Oh, God I am forgetting again... 1830! '32! No, perhaps a year or two after? Oh my mind...my mind! A rebellious year anyway. There was a great deal of trouble. Incendiarists firing the hay. Machine breaking. It seemed that a great haze of smoke filled the sky over the whole of Norfolk. Cattle, my first husband called them, those working men and women of the fields. Cattle to be driven. Cattle to be worked until they dropped. But you know, Inspector, you can drive beasts only so far before they turn.'

'Indeed,' Anders replied.

He remembered well the time of the Swing Riots in his native Wiltshire, when the agricultural workers rose up man to man against poverty and injustice. He recalled the secret meetings under lonely oak trees and in deep dingles. Marching crowds. Smashed threshing machines in fields. Houses and haystacks ablaze. Villagers who were never seen again after they were led to the gallows or transported to Botany Bay.

'I felt...some pity for them,' the Countess went on. 'You can put that to the credit of my soul. But not enough. Not enough to speak out. My then husband. My boys. Dealt with these matters with the utmost viciousness. At first within the law. Then outside it.'

'Outside the law?' said Gurney. 'How outside...?'

She held up her hand to silence him.

'There was a man in Norwich. A good man by all accounts,' she continued. 'William Marshall. He worked for a while as a clerk for Simpson, the lawyer in Tuck's Court. Might have made a lawyer himself. He acted like one when he could. For the poor. Then he had a little bookshop by the cathedral. They closed it down for selling the books of Thomas Paine.'

'I have heard of Marshall,' said Gurney. 'He gave advice to the men charged at the time. He and his three sons disappeared. Just as well for it is said that all four of them were to be arraigned, even the youngest. The rumour was that Marshall may even have been Captain Swing. Nonsense, of course, for no such man really existed.'

'Please do NOT interrupt. I am losing the thread of all of this, I fear. But disappear they did not! At least not in the sense that you mean. They were murdered! Every one of them? I think every one of them. No! That can't be right...?'

She looked puzzled, screwing up her eyes as though fighting to see the pictures in her mind and not the room beyond.

'They came to our estate. My husband agreed to see them. To negotiate terms. He told me that he was willing to talk. I was out riding that day. Now what happened? At the edge of the estate was a great hill amid the coverts. A great hill, with several massive oaks. I was out riding that day...'

For a moment she seemed to have difficulty breathing. She pressed her hand hard into her chest. She breathed more steadily and continued...

'I saw them there. Marshall and his boys. Strung up in the trees. Their legs kicking in the air, soiling themselves as they died.'

She looked up at the detectives.

'But there was worse to come! I said to my husband and my boys: "What have you done?" The three of them just laughed. "This is the justice these scum deserve!" my husband said to me. "Ain't that right, my friends?" My husband and the boys were not alone. His lawyer was there...a young man of ambition. And that odious gamekeeper, Walsham. One or two more. The Banningham boys who drowned in the Broad the next year. But then they did something monstrous and cruel...'

The gnarled hand waved again, almost slashing the air in front of her face.

'They had not hanged the youngest Marshall boy. He was a child...no more than that. I thought they were showing him mercy. I was wrong. They were going to hang him with the others. The lawyer and Walsham had hold of him. But then the boy kicked out. Caught the lawyer on the shin. My God, but there was a man of law who was livid! But as his pain faded away, I saw an evil smile cross his face. He got Walsham to hold out the boy's hand. Then brought his riding crop crashing down on the back of it.

Once! Twice! Thrice! The hand seemed to break across its length and turn red with the boy's blood. A horrible sight. Then I saw another look on the lawyer's face. A look I thank God I have never seen since. A malevolence, but more than that...I dread what might have happened next. I saw a look of fear and revulsion even on the face of my bastard husband, then it vanished with a cruel excitement as he cried out:

"Here is one for the hunt!"

I asked him what he meant, but they all laughed...just laughed! "Run!" my husband said to the boy. "Run! Or you'll swing with your bastard father and your brothers!" And the child ran and ran, clutching his poor broken hand. Ran towards the wood. And then they chased. Chased him like a foxhunt, while the ranter and his other sons swung in the breeze... the Marshalls are buried on that hill to this day...I remember the fear and tragedy on that child's face. Did they catch him? I don't know. They had certainly broken the poor child! Running and crashing through those woods. I heard him...my husband and his...sped down the rides to cut him off...'

She broke off, as though having difficulty breathing. She glared down into the fire. Then her voice was calmer.

'They deserved to die, my husband and my bastard sons. They had dark souls! Dark as pitch! But I'm to be with the angels, for I have told you all that has been haunting me! My soul will be at peace. Go in peace yourselves. Or so I would like to wish you. But I cannot. For I know there is no peace for men like you in this sin-ridden bloody world!'

~

Benjamin Wissilcraft pulled back his horse into the shelter of a copse a hundred yards from the lodge gate of Colbor Hall. He was a heavy thick-set man with thinning dark hair. With the bulk of him and with the great cloak he wore, there seemed little visible of the horse bar its head. It had been a long journey from Norwich on the trail of the two policemen. Holding back from sight of the growler, pausing at bends and corners and riding through fields to avoid the toll bars. For a stranger to Norfolk it might have been impossible. But Wissilcraft had been born in this corner of the county and knew it like the wart on the back of his hand.

He watched through the trees as the growler made its way back up the drive and through the lodge gates. After waiting for the carriage to go out of sight, he turned the horse's head and set off in a slow pursuit. As a spy and government agent he had a great curiosity. He followed and he observed. He reported back to Mr Raikes in Whitehall. And then he made notes of his adventure for a third party.

ELEVEN

It was a hot autumn night in Soho.

Unseasonably hot, Molly Bendig thought, as she turned once more in her vast bed chasing elusive sleep. She reached down and scratched an itch on the side of one ample thigh. She yawned and rolled over in bed.

It had been a profitable day, two virgins sold to valued customers. Well, not quite virgins but little whores from Clerkenwell with innocent faces. They had screamed most delightfully for the benefit of her rich clients. She had rewarded them well and promised to sell them as virgins again in a distant part of town.

And the night house in Leicester Square was doing such good business that she felt no need to be there on more than a couple of evenings in a week. If the police and her enemies and interfering Christians left her alone, then there was no reason why she should not soon retire from this foul old city. Brighton! Yes that was the place to spend the money. How lovely it would be to promenade, flaunting her wealth and jewels and becoming a member of some fashionable set. A rich widow, she would be. Maybe even take a lover again. But not marriage! Oh, no, never again. No runty little male was going to get his grubby hands on her wealth.

Molly Bendig chuckled at the thought of it all, closing her eyes with delight. And it was the movement of the thick folds of skin around her neck as she laughed that were the first indication that something was wrong. Her flesh felt something, long, hard and cold. She opened her eyes and raised her head. Now there was no doubt. Someone stood over her holding a blade across her throat. The laughter died in her mind. Her deepest and darkest fear had materialised. Her enemies had caught up with her at last. She tried to speak, but a finger pressed against her lips.

'Shush,' said a voice. 'Not a word, not a cry and not a scream. Nor a movement, for my blade is very sharp and it would tear into your fat flesh without even trying.'

So this was it, Molly Bendig thought. The terror of death. No future. No Brighton. No lover. No time to spend all the money accumulated during all those years of trials and tribulations. What a terrible, terrible waste!

The finger withdrew from her lips.

'Now you may talk, but very quietly,' said the voice. 'And do remember, my knife is still against your throat.'

'Who are you?'

Molly Bendig looked up, straining her eyes to make out the slight figure illuminated by the moonlight. Her assailant was dressed in a fustian jacket and country breeches, with a red diklo scarf around the throat.

'I am your worst enemy!'

'Oh my God!'

'A trifle late to call on God,'

'Are you here to kill me?' Molly Bendig gasped. 'I have money, lots and lots of money. Whoever sent you, well, I can pay more than them.'

'I might be someone with a personal grudge.'

'I know you not. I'm sure I don't. Wait, you are just a boy! Not a man at all!'

'You think that is so?'

Then the realisation.

'But no, one moment,' Molly Bendig said, looking this nemesis up and down. 'You are not even a boy'. She looked up with a sense of wonder. 'You are a woman in a man's raiment! What kind of devil are you?'

'The very worst kind of devil,' said Rosa. 'One who doesn't care if you live or die. Whether you are still breathing in five minutes is up to you. If you tell me all you know I will spare you. One lie and this bed will be drowned in your blood.'

Molly Bendig looked up, trying to search the face that loomed over hers. 'Are you someone who has worked for me? Is that it?'

'Fortunately not,' Rosa replied. 'I work for others, and you are a Christian saint compared to them. I can spare you the vengeance they have demanded, but only if you tell me the truth. And the truth straight away. One lie, one piece of this history omitted, and I will kill you.'

Mrs Bendig tried to rise on the pillow, but the blade forced her back down again.

'Anything,' she cried out, 'anything you wish to know. But please do me no harm?'

'The policeman, Berry? What did you tell him?'

'Ah, so that's it! You're with that footpad bludger from the Dials. Bill...I know not his other name.'

Rosa smiled down at her. 'Nor will you ever know. And you should thank your devils that it's me here tonight and not him. For if he came...if he came...well you'd die very slowly. Talk of him to the crushers again and you still might. He is a man without any understanding of mercy. And nothing could stop him getting at you.'

Rosa drew the flat of the blade very slowly across Mrs Bendig's throat. Even in the half light of the room she could see how pale the fat woman had gone.

'Talk,' she said.

'My man, Watkins. He saw him...'

'Where?'

'Dog and Duck...at the Dog and Duck. With that whore Sally and the fat man that's always about.'

'Did he hear what they said?'

'No...no. He just saw them. And when I heard that crusher had been attacked...the one that's always at Sally...well, I knew...I just knew.'

Rosa put her face close to Mrs Bendig's, turning her head a little at the stench of drink.

'And that is all?'

''S'welp me, yes. God's truth. Please don't kill me...'

'If *he* finds out you've lied...'

'I 'aven't, I 'aven't...'

'If he finds out you've lied...or if you talk to the crushers again...he'll be here for you. At the moment you least expect it. And you'll never know such pain as you'll get then. You'll be praying for hell long before he's finished with you.'

Rosa slipped the knife into her jacket. 'I could tie you up and gag you, but I won't. You know what will happen if you arouse anyone before morning, don't you? Sleep well and enjoy your nightmares...'

In an instant she was gone, slipping somehow into the dark shadows at the edge of the room. Mrs Bendig neither saw nor heard the door open. She lay rigid in the bed until dawn, shivering with fear and scarcely hearing the tolls as the church bells marked the passing of time.

~

The tavern in Field Lane was so crowded that Billy and Sticks had to force their way through an unwashed mass of humanity to reach a table. It had taken them several hours to cross the river and walk up through the city. There had been one frightening moment when they had had to clutch themselves against the wall holding back the Thames, as a pair of runners walked the pier-head above. Billy had been more concerned about the leaks in the tiny boat that had ferried them across the water, and the fact that the ferryman was quite gone in inebriation.

'Safe enough here,' muttered Sticks as they pushed their way across the dark room. 'Even the runners avoid this hell-hole.'

He dragged a pair of drunks from the benches lining the furthest table and deposited them on the floor. The two fat men groaned but slept on.

'Barney, bring a jug of ale,' Sticks yelled at a scared-looking youth who peered pale-faced and anxious from a back room.

'D'yer drink boy?' he pushed his battered face close to Billy. 'Have yer sold yer soul to the ruin?'

'A little...sometimes...not very much really.'

'That's good,' Sticks replied as he regarded the jug of ale and three tankards that Barney slammed down on the table. 'Drink is the abomination of the world, ain't it Barney?'

'We all 'as to make a livin', Mr Sticks,' the youth replied, 'not bein' blessed with your talents.'

Sticks poured out three tankards of the ale.

'My mother drank herself into the pit. Mostly in taverns like this. Choked on her vomit in Saffron Hill, she did. But the night before she died she made me pledge never to drink.'

'But yer do, don't yer, Mr Sticks?' said Barney.

Sticks regarded the tankard and then sipped a little ale. 'Every day I swears to give it up. This could be the very day I does. Yer know boy, I always had a fancy to be a lettered gent. Read books, lots of books. I can read, they taught me in the workhouse. Can you read boy?'

Billy nodded. 'My father had a bookshop. A long way from here. He could read Latin and Greek as well as English. And a young man in a lawyer's office where he worked before, a Mr Borrow, taught him French and German.'

'A bookshop!' Sticks looked down at the boy with genuine admiration. 'It must be the most wonderful thing on earth to be brought up along a books! And to know languages!'

He regarded the tankard once more.

'You heard of White Headed Ned Baldwin?'

Billy shook his head.

'You should 'ave done! What a fighter he was! Bested Tom Oliver and me, though I got him back in a fight near Chessington.'

'Was he old then, that his hair was white?' Billy asked.

'Just very fair,' Sticks replied. 'Very fair. Oh and a good fighter, though he didn't stay the course for long. Opened a tavern, he did, here in London. Not for long, though, not for long! Drank hisself to death. A real loss to the fancy!'

He looked up as someone approached the table with a thudding noise. Billy turned to see a man in a green jacket, leaning on a crutch, his long dark hair hiding a very brown face.

'And here's the third for our party,' said Sticks. 'Sit ye down, Jasper, sit ye down! Jasper, this is young Billy, or Mr William Marshall to yer good self.'

Jasper put a hand against his chest and gave a low bow.

'I was tellin' the lad as how the Duke of Wellington said Waterloo was a damn near run thing, Jasper,' said Sticks, as the newcomer sat down.

Jasper heaved his one leg over the bench.

'He did indeed. Said it to me on the night after the battle. Riding by me on his horse as I lays on the ground, with me leg shot off! "Ain't they killed yer yet, Feedle?" he asked. "Just me leg!" I says to the Duke. "The rest of me will make old bones." "Them Frenchies have got Lord Uxbridge in the same way," the Duke said, "so the ladies'll be dancing without yer both!" And then he sent me over to his surgeon, rather than leave me a-lying on the field. "A damn near run thing, Feedle!" he said, as he rode off to

Hoogymont. Him and me went way back, through Portugal and Spain, you see lad.'

Billy was filled with admiration. 'He really said that to you?'

'Good days, lad, good days!'

'Pity yer Duke didn't stay out there, instead of politicking' said Sticks. 'Fine mess he's made of the country since he gave up the army.'

'Ah, well, its horses for courses, horses for courses,' Jasper said. He looked round at the drunken men and women lying on the floor and against the walls, shading his ears from the raucous singing coming from an inner room.

'And what do you, me lad?' Jasper asked Billy.

'This and that...'

'He's a dip,' said Sticks, 'and not just cly-faking...guineas and sovereigns and the odd watch. One of the best. Our company has been keeping an eye on him. But the lad has aspirations. Wants to be a flash villain, one of the swell mob. A cracksman perhaps?'

'That would do...' said Billy.

'Ah, yer need to serve an apprenticeship under a master for that,' said Jasper. 'As it happens, I knows a lot about locks. I worked in a locksmith when I come home from the wars. I could teach yer all I knows.'

'Would you?'

'I would,' Jasper replied. 'But can yer clamber, me boy? Climb up walls and into high windows?'

'Used to climb trees...'

'It's a start. Well, what do yer think, Sticks? A little test for the boy?'

'Dunno...is the lad ready for a test?'

'I'm sure I am,' Billy declared.

'There's a drum we know,' said Jasper confidentially, 'not a particular flash drum...a modest premise in Albemarle Street. Yer'd need to climb up on the roof, then down through a narrow winder. It's always open...'

'Is it jewels?' asked Billy, 'or money?'

'Inside the room's a desk and a top drawer with some dockyments. That would be what we want yer to get...the dockyments...'

'Documents?' said Billy. 'Where's the value in that...?'

'Important to us, lad. Important to us. Get in and bring the dockyments to us. Sticks'll show yer the house.'

'I'll do it! But you know, I hate thieving really...'

'So do we all,' said Sticks, 'but it's a cruel world...'

The singing from the next room grew louder. Someone was accompanying the drunken chorus on a penny-whistle. Billy listened for a while, recognising the tune, though not the words. Then some man with a beautiful voice sang them alone, the quality of *his singing silencing the rowdies in the tavern for a few moments:*

'Where have you bin all the day,
Billy boy, Billy boy?
Where have you bin all the day
Me Billy boy?
I bin out with Nancy Gray,
She has stole me heart away,
Oh me Nancy,
Tickle me fancy,
Oh me darlin' Billy boy.'

The boy smiled at Jasper, draining his tankard as he said: 'But that's my name!'.

'So it is!' the old warrior replied. 'And here's a tanner on account of yer future work.' He slipped the sixpence across the table. 'A lovely song, but it's what's stolen with hearts that's the problem, me lad. It's what's stolen with hearts!'

'It's what's stolen with drink that's the problem,' said Sticks. 'Health and wealth and the muscles of yer body.' He poured the remnants of his ale on to the floor. 'And that's the last of the foul doin's that'll pass these lips.'

He threw the tankard across the room causing many heads to duck and curse. He grabbed the boy by the shoulders.

'Billy me boy? I wants yer to go out and get me a book. Any old book. And pay for it too. Take this half sovereign and get the best book you can find. I will be a lettered gent!'

TWELVE

'You make a most admirable boy!'

Quest undressed Rosa, garment by garment.

'You must be thrilled at all of this opportunity to play-act,' Quest continued. 'I often wonder if players of the stage like you remember who they are underneath all the costumes and the parts?'

'More than you, I have a suspicion,' she pouted. 'Take away your costumes and the parts and...well...just who is William Quest? Or Bill the bludger, footpad of this parish...ow! don't tug at the breeches like that... I may have use for them again, and you nearly twisted my leg off...or any of your other characters that threaten the streets.'

'But my parts are of necessity not entertainment.'

'I suspicion they are entertaining to you!'

'You may be right,' he replied, dragging her naked on to the bed. His hands began to explore her body and his lips and tongue sought her mouth.

'You are sure that the woman told you all?'

'All...all,' she moaned. 'I'm sure she was tell...telling the truth. Oh God! All she...she knew. Which was not a...not a...lot. Oh God, let me breathe! Oh...oh...she knew next to nothing. Oh God, you do that so...'

'What a good job it is that your father, the vicar, can't see you now.'

'Come here you bastard!' she replied, pulling him into her. 'Time to stop playing all those parts!'

Quest had known many women, but none quite as ardent and expert as Rosa Stanton. This was one of the rare occasions in his life when he lowered his guard and let himself go. For a while the world that usually occupied his thoughts span away. And then Quest fell into sleep, her arms holding him very tightly.

~

For a while he thought there was no way through the blackthorns that blocked his path. He was cut and bruised from his run through the woods, his shattered hand hot with pain. And, despite all the denseness of the undergrowth, the green and browns and greys and russets that limited his vision to just a few feet, the sight in his eyes were of those who were hanging. Choking and throttling, lips turning blue and eyes bulging, looking helpless, knowing there was no hope, croaking sounds from between their lips.

The boy closed his eyes, then opened them and looked down at the ground. He could hear the crashing of horses and the cries of men behind him. Nearer and nearer. Crying and screaming with delight. Then he saw the animals runway beneath the bushes, the avenue of a badger or fox. He threw himself down and crawled and crawled, his vision blinded by tears and sweat. Instinct and the barbs of the blackthorn guided his path. He felt rather than saw the edge of the small cliff as he reached it, then fell, fell, into the darkness of the water. He cried out just once as the river swept him away.

~

Quest woke with a start, his mind filled with the crush of undergrowth and the tearing of the blackthorn. For a moment he didn't know where he was. Then the room came alive to him. That pleasant bedroom filled with theatrical costumes, lit by the first yawning of dawn. The sound of horses and carriages hurrying up the busy road to Tottenham Court. The girl breathing gently at his side.

He rested his head back on to the pillow, listening to the rapid beat of his heart. He thought of those men crashing after him through the undergrowth on a day lost in time. He considered them one by one. Two dead. Both Bartram brothers. At his hand. No four dead. The Banningham brothers had drowned in Horsey Mere the year after, when their punt overturned as a sudden gale swept in from the sea. Yet there had been more than four men on the hillside. Two? Yes! Two more! The lawyer and the gamekeeper. Three? No not three men, for the third had been a woman. On horseback like the rest. A striking woman who had been shocked at the sight of his father and brothers hanging on the bare hilltop. A woman who had sought mercy for him. That's how he'd remembered it. If she lived she was safe enough. But the others? The others? 'Two more to die!'

'What did you say?' Rosa murmured, stirring by his side.

'Two more to die!'

She opened her eyes and looked at him with real concern.

~

Jacob Raikes strode along by the Thames, tapping the ground with his stick with every step taken. Benjamin Wissilcraft puffed and panted as he strove to keep up with him. He hated walking really. Much better to be on the back of a horse.

'And that's it?' said Raikes. 'They spent an hour with Lady Colbor and you know not what was said?'

'There was no way to know what was said...'

'Never mind that. This you could have communicated to me without leaving Norfolk. Why are you here? You should be there, following Anders around. This knowledge amounts to nothing!'

'Anders and Gurney returned to Norwich. I spent a day trailing them around the city. They indulged in little more than a sightseeing tour.'

'And today? Where are they today?'

Wissilcraft was silent. Raikes walked even faster. His agent struggled to keep up. Then the spymaster stopped suddenly, turning to obstruct the stout man's progress.

'Get...back...there...'

Wissilcraft nodded and turned away. As he paced along the Thames he smiled to himself. 'I'm not as green as I'm grass looking, you smug bastard!' he said aloud.

~

Josef Critzman was toasting muffins over the fire in the room at the back of his shop. His brother yawned in the armchair.

'I think you live on muffins, Josef.'

Josef looked across at him. 'I find food very difficult. Very little tempts me. I like muffins.'

'You used to eat most prodigiously, when we were boys in Poland.'

'Ah, but that was before we starved. I have found it hard to regain that appetite.'

'Not a difficulty I share. Yet we both starved after they killed the beasts and burned the crops in the field. It obviously didn't affect me in the same way. You really should try to eat more! And not be so influenced by the tragedies of the past. Remember how Josiah faded away with grief?'

'I think he ate little in those last few years...'

'Exactly! Look how thin you are! You need a good whole chicken. Or a beefsteak. Proper nourishment! A few muffins a day is not enough to keep anyone healthy or alive. Ah, here's William...'

The door from the shop opened and Quest entered.

'I was saying to my brother that he needs to eat more,' said Isaac. 'I am sure that you agree?'

William leant back against the wall, his arms folded. 'I do think you need to look after yourself, Josef. We have all the money in the world. Why don't you take a tour? You always said that you wanted to see the great cathedrals. What better time? A respite from all of this business. Lots of sleep and good food. The rest of us can manage. Jasper can mind the shop.'

Josef looked up in horror. 'Jasper would have me in the debtor's gaol in a week! He has many talents but commerce is not one.'

'Then I would mind the shop,' said Quest. 'I've done it before. Take a month, old friend. Take two months.'

Josef considered the muffin for a moment before putting it on to his plate.

'Perhaps...' he said. 'Perhaps when our new business is attended to. Yes, when that is done I will go away for a while. I will accept your offer. And a month or two in the shop might be a good rest for you, my boy.'

'What new business?' asked Quest.

'A trifling matter,' said Isaac. 'A gentleman whose continued existence on the earth is an insult to God and man.'

'Do I know of him?'

'Sir Wren Angier MP.'

'The moneylender?'

'The usurer!' said Josef 'A man who has grown prominent in society on the misery of the poor and desperate. A monstrous creature who has driven many to starvation.'

'You want him taken out of the world?'

'A pretty way to put it...but yes.'

Quest sat down and looked into the fire for a few moments.

'I will attend to it,' he said at last, 'but there is a task I must undertake first. The old business in Norfolk.'

'I thought you had done with that,' Josef replied. 'The Bartram brothers are gone. Can you not leave it alone now?'

Quest shook his head. 'I had overlooked the possibility that the gamekeeper Walsham was alive. From the way he drank I'd imagined him in the pit long since. I will go up to Norfolk in the next day or so and deal with that outstanding matter.'

'Let Walsham drink himself to death,' said Isaac. 'Why take the risk?'

'Because it may be the only way to end my nightmares.'

THIRTEEN

Jacob Raikes crossed London Bridge and made his way deep into the Borough. As he walked the streets his eyes were everywhere, scanning each crying costermonger, every gutter beggar and the window of every house. Sometimes he would pause and look into the windows of shops and houses, pondering the reflections in the glass.

He was sure he was not being followed, but it never paid to take chances. That had always been his philosophy. It was why he continued to live.

His palm played with the handle of the ornate sword cane he carried. He had killed eight men and two women with its blade, and enjoyed every single death, loving the look of fear in the eyes of his victims. So satisfying, so much better than despatching someone with a distant pistol shot. If anything a trifle too quick. The look of fear would have been so very much more enjoyable if it had lingered. And these had not, after all, been murders, but executions sanctioned by his Masters.

That thought always added to his satisfaction.

He turned off the High Street into the court of the George Inn, one of London's oldest. Its long galleries would have been familiar to Shakespeare, whose plays were Raikes's one literary indulgence. He had once seen Charles Dickens supping there. Watched him in his dandy clothes being the centre of attention for near an hour. Studied him with contempt, not being able to abide the gross sentimentality of his writings. Raikes had never been able to see what all the fuss was about. The writer had seemed loud and overblown in real life. No doubt the George Inn would feature one day in another of his mawkish volumes.

A coach, painted in a garish combination of yellow and black, was unloading passengers in the inn-yard. Raikes paused for a while to regard the six men who alighted, just to make sure that none of them were known to him. They were not, though he had seen the pickpocketing youth who hovered nearby once before. The wretch had tried, not long before, to pick Raikes's pocket as he had made his way on State business along the Bankside. Raikes had taken him by the throat into an alley and taught him a most unpleasant lesson. He drew back into the shadows as the youth and the passengers drifted away.

Then he entered the inn.

He recognised the man he had come to meet almost at once. A plump individual, whose great ham of a face was broken only by a vividly dyed black moustache. He watched him for a moment, sitting there, drinking some dubious white liquid that he suspected the George Inn never served. He took a good look around the room before approaching.

'This is a dangerous place to meet,' he said to him as he sat on the opposite side of the table. 'We could have had this interview at your house.'

'You are Mr Thomas?' The fat man spoke English with just the trace of an accent.

'I have many names. Thomas will do for now.'

'My house is, I fear, being watched. It might have been even more dangerous to come there. Our countries may soon be at war. Well, that is the feeling in St Petersburg.'

'There is still time to avoid that catastrophe,' said Raikes. 'Time to look at alternatives. We are not yet at war, though Tsar Nicholas has been most unwise. It may well be that war could be averted. Or that my country might be persuaded to play no part in the conflict between Russia and Turkey.'

'I am a simple man,' said the Russian, pouring back the last of the white liquid. 'War would be a sorrow to me. I love your London. I much prefer to live here than in Petersburg or Moscow. It would be a sorrow to me to have to leave.'

'You may not have to leave at all. As I said war is not inevitable. You have influence with your Tsar. I have a great deal of influence with those men who rule Britain. We can, I am sure, come to an accommodation.'

'For a price?'

'For a price!'

~

It was a narrow but tall house of London stock brick, just off the Bear Gardens. An anonymous green door led in from the street, seemingly always guarded by a burly gentleman in fustian. He watched Raikes as he approached, giving a slight nod of acknowledgement. Raikes ignored him, climbed the steps and jangled the bell chain hanging down. The door opened almost instantaneously and a thin man with brown hair, plastered down on his head to hide a balding scalp, greeted him. At first glance he looked young, but the gaslight from the hallway showed that to be an illusion, brought on by a clever veneer.

'Ah, the legal gentleman. It *has* been a long time, Mr Phillips! Do come in.'

He led Raikes into a narrow hallway where a boy gave a low bow and took Raikes's cloak and stick.

'What fine autumn weather we are having, Mr Phillips, though the evenings are drawing in, do you not think?'

He led Raikes along a corridor that seemed to lead a long way back into the building, passing several doors which partly concealed quiet conversations. The man was terribly thin and dressed like an undertaker. He walked softly along the corridor, as though worried that he might awaken something. Then brought Raikes to the end of the corridor where a stout door barred their way. He turned and smiled an ingratiating smile.

'It will be a sovereign,' he said. 'Unless you wish to indulge in something different?'

Raikes shook his head, handing over the coin. The man opened the door.

Beyond was a large room painted entirely in red, with a long padded seat, covered in velvet along one wall. Three fair-haired youths stood as they entered and bowed to him. One held out an arm towards a wooden frame that hung down from the ceiling. A second youth began to unbutton Raikes's jacket, whilst the third walked forward and draped his hand down Raikes's face.

'I will leave you for now,' said the thin gentleman, 'and see you on the way out. I do hope that in future you will visit us more often!' He closed the door as he left.

The three youths encircled Raikes and calmly proceeded to undress him. They led him to the wooden frame and, in a quick movement, grabbed him, shackling his wrists to the topmost wooden bar. Then they removed their own clothes and paraded in front of him, simpering and mouthing quiet obscenities. As one of them knelt like a worshipper in front of Raikes, another reached into a wooden case and removed the birch. The third lay down on the ground, grasping Raikes' feet. As the birch crashed against him, Raikes closed his eyes and entered his paradise.

~

'A fruitless few days,' Gurney smiled at Anders as they negotiated – with some peril – the horse fair in Tombland. A stallion had broken away from its seller and had stirred the other animals into open rebellion. A tatterdemalion gathering of farmers and Gypsies formed a ring and closed in to try and bring order to the chaos. The two detectives ducked under their arms and walked hurriedly in the direction of Gurney's house in Elm Hill.

'Well, not altogether fruitless,' Anders replied. 'We have found that the people of the city held William Marshall in some high regard. To them it remains a puzzlement as to how and why the man and his family should simply disappear, not knowing them dead. And we know that the youngest son, if he was not murdered like the rest, never came back to Norwich.'

Gurney opened the narrow door of his cottage, which led straight into the small, dark raftered room where he mostly lived. He lit the fire and hung a kettle above the infant flames.

'Do you really think that the boy lived?'

'I believe it to be probable,' Anders replied. 'Whether he grew up to be our killer though would be the wildest speculation.'

'Well, we have no way of finding him.'

137

'No, but there are others we must search out and question. Lady Colbor talked of a lawyer. We must seek him out. And I would very much like to return to the Bartram estate and question that gamekeeper, Walsham. Perhaps you might be able to bring him to the gallows?'

'A foul ruffian! We could question him on the morrow. And somehow I would like to ask my superiors if we might find that hill top and recover the bodies of Marshall and his sons. They were probably thrown into one pit. A body missing would confirm Lady Colbor's account.'

~

Quest walked along Monmouth Street and turned into Neal's Yard. He was dressed as the unshaven footpad villain, which was the *persona* he preferred in Seven Dials. The yard was quiet in the early evening, for most of its inhabitants were in the taverns or working the streets. A solitary beggar smiled up at him and waved a hand. Quest bent the old man's fingers around a shilling. 'And get food with it this time!' he growled into the wizened old face, before unlocking the door and making his way up to his room.

He sat for a while in the battered chair and contemplated the spiders that journeyed across the ceiling. Did they consider? he asked himself. Did they have any concept of wider life? Did they appreciate what humans were and how dangerous they could be, how with one strike they might crush a spider out of existence?

'What a foul and cruel bloody world this is!' he said aloud, in their general direction. And it was true, he reflected. Any one of us, spider or man, could be sent tumbling into the dark without a moment's notice. He had sent men into their own eternity, with as little forewarning. Seen the puzzled look in their eyes on the occasions when they had a second to consider their own deaths. Quest wondered how it would be for him? Would there be a moment to kiss this life goodbye? Days and weeks, perhaps, in the condemned cell at Newgate waiting for the quick march to the drop? Or the quick stabbing punch of a blade? Or the thundering blow of shot?

He doubted, somehow, that it would be in old age with his head against a soft and peaceful pillow. That was not the death for the kind of life he had lived. He thought for a brief spell of Mrs Vellaby and that maid at his country house and envied them their quiet existence.

There had been those happy years of childhood when he had no conception of mortality. Days in green woodlands or watching the quiet flow of the water as he sat on the banks of a river. When he had stood in wonder as great crowds of starlings formed changing patterns in the great open skies over Norfolk. Those times when he would look up from his book at the great giddying spire of the cathedral, wondering if he could ever have the courage to climb to its pinnacle.

He had had no fear of death when he was young.

He had no real fear of it now, though he felt the need for some preparation before it overtook him. His difficulty had always been the fear of life, that terror that he pushed away so often and blotted out with the experiences of existence. As he considered these matters he had a sudden yearning for the peaceful walk he loved so much at Hope Down and the quiet rest against the wall of the little churchyard.

And then there was Norfolk?

Did he really want to go back there, even to account for Walsham? Was there a point to all this vengeance? Possibly not. The world would still spin whether or not a few individuals breathed upon it. Time would level everyone in the end, the innocent as well as the guilty.

Quest sighed as he stood up and considered how he would make the journey. He took from the corner of the room a stout dark walking stick, the kind a countryman might use to batter the overgrowth on a footpath or fend off a dangerous animal. A twist of the handle revealed a short but deadly blade, a vicious instrument that had had much use. He drew his finger over the sharp point and remembered those who had died, though their faces were now indistinct in his memory.

Putting the stick to one side, he opened the great chest against the wall and rummaged through the old clothes within. He scattered them around the room, considering and then rejecting. That one for a city merchant, then the costume of a gentleman out to visit his club, that other the down-at-heel respectability of clothes fit for a man out to visit a gambling hell, another the wrecked garments of a street beggar. At last he found what he was looking for, holding it against him and regarding himself in the cracked and stained mirror. He gave a wistful smile at the sight before him. He really should have gone to the stage like Rosa.

What a pair of thespians they would have made!

~

Jacob Raikes stood stiffly as he looked out of the window at the bustling horse traffic in Whitehall. The pain of the beating still throbbed, exquisitely across his back. Not that it should be something to be indulged in too often, for it could still incapacitate his body for hours. At first it had been a week or more. A week or more of lying face-down on a couch, sipping water and relishing all the memories of the experience. Then only days of rest were needed. Now hours of pacing around and not resting at all. He still enjoyed the activity, but felt a need for other indulgences. By morning it would be as though the beating had never happened.

As the sky darkened, the street beyond the window seemed to vanish and he saw only his own face reflected in the gaslight. A face that had not changed much in all those years. He could still see there the features of the boy he had once been, in those endless days in the dark halls and corridors of Eton. How they had sneered at him, those children of peers who had made him fag for them and thrashed him on a regular basis. Those annoying little bastards who would never have to do a day's labour in their lives, while he slaved at this uncongenial toil. His own father had struggled his way into the grave to send him to the College. He had come home from time to time and assured his father that he loved being there. His father had told Jacob that his long-dead mother would be proud of him. Jacob Raikes wished both parents and his indulgent wider family in hell.

Now his schoolfellows were well up in the world, so many idle on their great estates, others as idle in Parliament, when they deigned to turn up. A few, more dedicated to public service, in government, in the Cabinet even, stifling yawns as popular opinion forced them into legislating for reforms that they must have hated.

And Raikes knew them. He knew them all so well. Knew of their nasty little schoolboy habits. Their deceits and hidden criminalities. And they knew Raikes as well. Regarded him as he sat in quiet

142

corners in Westminster, eyes closed as though he might be contemplating the past. They all dreaded that those piercing eyes might open to regard any one of them in particular. For Raikes knew what they knew. Knew of their pasts. Remembered the way they had treated him. Recalled their ferocious and disgusting behaviour in those long dark nights in College. Those activities that had now become a way of life for so many, albeit in feared secret.

Raikes had come to Westminster only recently, after an entirely different career. He had gone as far as he might in that previous direction and made too little money. So he had returned to London and sought out those old schoolfellows, including his predecessor as Queen Victoria's spymaster. After just one conversation with Raikes that poor individual had taken a pistol and blown out his brains. A few other conversations had put Jacob Raikes in his place. And it would do. It would do for now. But not for ever. Oh no! There had to be a better way. He wanted to be like those other parasites from Eton. He wanted money, estates, power over the poor. And not to work at all. Not to do anything but indulge in a nether world of pain and pleasure.

And Raikes didn't care at all how that was achieved.

He took a little silver snuff box from his pocket, engraved with an illustration of Greek gods cavorting in a woodland glade, and had a pinch. The powder was so strong that it forced his eyes to water and then shut tight. He shook for a moment with the sensation, then opened his watering eyes and looked at the documents on a table which took up so much of the room. He still could not sit, so he bent over to examine them again.

There was an Ordnance sheet of Norfolk, Wissilcraft's written reports, intelligences from the police, and pages of his own notes. Raikes felt an annoyance that people were not keeping him well informed. It seemed that the Queen's spymaster had to do all his own work for there were damned few spies and no spy service as such to command. How ridiculous the whole thing was. How it could have been so much better handled, if he had had his way and sufficient funds.

Raikes pulled the chair away from the table and sat down with a suddenness that sent a sharp and pleasant rip of pain through his body. He took out the little box and took another pinch of snuff. Holding his head back he looked up at the panelled ceiling and let out a stream of profanities.

FOURTEEN

Josiah Quest found a solace in walking in the green fields near to his country house. The peace of nature and the books in his library were his only comfort now. He felt older than his years and he felt ill. There was not much time left to settle his affairs, he knew that.

As he sat down on a stile, he thought of his friends in London, even now carrying out what he considered to be the last great project of his life. He needed time to see it accomplished. Just a few years to carry out all that was planned. To put matters to right. To fulfil an obligation to an old friend. His heart beat faster at the thought of it. Beat a trifle too fast. He breathed deeply and wished the weariness would go away.

He had not been this way along the country path for a long time. Not since the death of his son, that dear gentle boy, William. Was there a Heaven? Somewhere they could all meet again, the boy, and the boy's mother, his dear wife Adelaide? He wasn't sure anymore, though he had always been a religious man. Perhaps there was only oblivion. The last thought in the brain being the last thought for eternity. Any yet, if there was a Paradise he yearned for it to be like these green fields, bird-thronged hedgerows and the quiet shade under the green mantle of the trees. He closed his eyes and dwelt for a while on the past.

As he opened them again he became aware of the robin just a yard away, perched on the wooden fence, regarding him without any fear. He made a few tutting noises and held out his hand. The bird hopped and perched on his palm. For a minute or two the man and the bird looked at each other as though they were the only two creatures in the universe. Ever since he was a boy the robins along this hedgerow had been as friendly. He had hoped to see one again. He reached into his pocket with the other hand and brought out the small paper bag of crumbs he carried in anticipation of this moment. How young William had loved these birds, making the trip to the hedgerow every day when he was at the country house. He must tell...well, if the project in London came out as he hoped. He scattered the crumbs and put the robin down on the fence. Suddenly, he felt a little bit stronger.

~

The man who alighted at midday from the train at Victoria Station in Norwich looked no different from a dozen other farmers who had shared all or some of the journey from London. He was wearing full length trousers, a shirt without collar and a moleskin waistcoat, with a bright red coloured kerchief around his neck. A battered jacket that had seen better days and an oilskin cap completed the outfit. A knapsack was flung very casually over one shoulder and in his right hand he held a thick walking stick.

Quest had marvelled at the speed of the train from London to Norfolk. Just a few hours. He recalled the five days it had taken him to walk the other way. But then he had been very young - and hungry for much of the journey.

It was strange to be back in Norwich. For a while, as he walked through the city, the streets made no sense. He had remembered them differently, narrower in places, heading in different directions. He had thought that he might see lots of people he knew but, apart from an old man in Rampant Horse Street who gave him a second glance, no one paid him any heed and nobody looked familiar.

Then why should they? he asked himself. The citizens of Norwich that he had known were transfixed in ancient sunlight, not the light of today. People who were elderly then, friends and acquaintances of his father were probably dead and lost in time. The younger folk that he might have known would be older now, looking different with an unfamiliar way of life. The younger people would not have been born. The world had moved on since the days when he would run along Tombland to his father's bookshop or make rafts to explore the swilling waters of the Yare. But, as he made his way to the livery stables, a kind of familiarity came back to him. And the great spire of the cathedral and the rising ground of Mousehold Heath still dominated the buildings all around.

As he rode the hired horse westwards, he was glad to leave the city behind, relieved that he had not encountered anyone he knew. Having crossed higher ground he descended into a broad river valley, passing the little church of St Mary at Earlham, where his grandparents were buried. The horse wavered, almost as though it was aware that Quest was contemplating going in to see their stone. But he patted the animal and rode on along the lane, faster now at a good canter and out into a wilder countryside of meadows, wooded coverts and lonely stretches of heath. It had been a long while since he had ridden a horse. He had almost forgotten how exhilarating it could be.

~

'This is very lonely countryside,' Anders said to Gurney as the carriage pulled up the long road from Norwich to the Bartram estate. 'Very much like the place where I spent my boyhood.'

'Did you enjoy your youth?'

'It wasn't always the easiest time,' Anders replied. 'My father was a small farmer on a tenanted farm. He had poor health and we could barely cope on a hundred acres. We never made any money. It was one reason I joined the Salisbury City Police and then the Wiltshire Constabulary.'

'Ah, so you were a rural policeman originally?'

'Five years a constable in both, before I came up to London. I think on reflection I preferred policing the countryside to the town.'

'There is a great deal of villainy in both,' said Gurney. 'This is a particularly lawless county, though rather calmer than when I was a constable in Aylsham. We need more constables on the ground and a better organised detective force. And, like you, we have boundaries to cross. The county constabulary, the borough police, the city police. I seem to float everywhere and am never too sure who I am serving.'

'I understand your confusion. Our Commissioner Mayne is a stickler for boundaries. If we could keep the politicians away from the task of policing then life would be a great deal simpler. I sometimes yearn for a return to the country lanes of Wiltshire.'

'We could certainly do with a detective of your calibre in Norfolk. Should you acquire a taste for our county it could certainly be arranged. My chief was asking after you the other day. He is well aware of your excellent record in London.'

'Well, it's a thought,' said Anders. 'Who knows what might happen in time. But back to present matters. Does Walsham know we are coming?'

'I sent out a note yesterday by the carrier, insisting that he remain at his cottage for the afternoon. He is a foul individual, you know. It would be to the better good of the countryside if we could put the hangman's noose around his neck. On some cold dawn outside Norwich Castle.'

'I heard you hang at dawn.'

'The belief is it keeps the crowds down,' Gurney replied. 'Not that I've ever noticed. These public executions are a positive disgrace. They simply encourage crime. Norwich on a hanging day is a festival for pickpockets, thimble-riggers and heaven knows who else.'

There was a silence for a moment or two as both men sat back and regarded the countryside they were passing through. Then Gurney put his head out of the window.

'Someone in a hurry,' he said.

The words were scarcely out before a horseman rode past them at great speed. Anders caught a glimpse of a shabbily dressed farmer on his mount, some sort of bag and a great stick slung across the saddle.

'Perhaps he has word that his house is on fire!' he said.

'Well, he can certainly sit a horse. He'd have made a fine highwayman if he had a better sense of dress.'

~

Walsham had been in a foul mood since groaning into life with the coming of the late dawn. He screwed up his eyes against the light before he reached across the table and grasped the bottle from the night before. He sank back the dregs before slamming the bottle down, the crash making his head feel like bursting. He was in no mood for food, so broke off a plug of tobacco to chew. The gamekeeper had tried to stand, but his legs were too weak.

No work today!

And why the bloody hell should he? The family were still away and Bartram's bloody widow and her snivelling brats could rot in hell as far as he was concerned. The estate had long gone to pot, for old man Bartram had not wanted to pay out for under-keepers. These past few months every poacher in the district had invaded the pheasant coverts. The man traps and spring-guns were no longer set. And he had no intention of risking his neck by taking long solitary walks into the surrounding woods where thieving bloody peasants with a grudge might lurk.

He regarded the filthy room of his cottage, with its broken furniture and shabby bits of cloth hanging over the windows. It needed a woman's touch, that was the thought that came vaguely into his mind. He had had a wife once. A grubby little whore who had moved in to share the drink and the roof above. Where had she gone? In his stupor he could hardly remember. Norwich was it? No? Dereham, that was it, Dereham, where she had found a carter to move in with and filch. Whore! Better dead than have that ugly old shrew in his bed.

There had been other women, but he had kept them at a distance. Or rather they had kept him at bay. Some had complained about his stink. Well, so what? A countryman had to deal with the stenching reality of the countryside, eh? And why shouldn't he spent his wages on drink? It was the only comfort he had had.

Not that he didn't still lust after women. There had been that peasant girl only the last month. The one he had pinned down against the hedgerow and took against her will, putting a grubby hand over her mouth to blot out her moans and pleadings. Little whore! Bet she would have been willing with anyone but me! And she wouldn't talk, not her. He could still get her parents evicted. Walsham smirked and spat out the tobacco. When he felt better he might take her again.

And then he looked up at the man standing there. A man with a full bottle in his hand. As he watched, the stranger put the bottle down upon the table.

'Remember me?'

The voice was refined. A gentleman. Yes, you could always tell, however they were dressed. Something about them, all clean and cosseted. Bastards!

'Drink up the bottle,' said the voice. 'Pour it all back. I've brought it along especially for you. As a reminder of past days. You do remember me?'

Walsham wiped his eyes with the back of a hand and looked up at this mysterious benefactor. There was something familiar. Someone he knew, recognised....Yes! That was it! Though older...older than when he was...'

He looked up at the man and gave a smile as he recalled that last time they were together. For a moment his addled brain had a vision of a field and trees. Of other people surrounding him, of...but why bother remembering...'

He regarded the bottle for a few moments before pouring the contents down his throat.

Life had suddenly got very much better.

~

'God, it stinks in here,' said Gurney as they thrust open the door of the gamekeeper's cottage. 'Stinks of a filthy man and his drink. Walsham!' He yelled the man's name.

'Clearly not here,' said Anders. 'Probably lying drunk somewhere,' he added, looking at the empty bottle on the table. 'The drink might yet carry him off before the hangman.'

'Not if I have my way,' Gurney replied. 'If what he helped to do to Marshall and his boys is true, well...I'd have him drawn and quartered as well.

Walsham!' He shouted again, though once more in vain.

'There is, of course, the possibility that he has heard that we have seen Lady Colbor and taken to his heels. We may have the pursuit of a fugitive on our hands.'

Gurney nodded. 'It is possible, though I had thought that he might be too drunk and indolent for escape. However, before we set off a great hue and cry we should search the estate. Come back here again later, for I see there is still some gin un-drunk.'

Anders stood in the doorway to get away from the stench and looked out into the surrounding countryside.

'I would very much like to walk to the high point of this estate, to see the place where these hangings are supposed to have taken place. Is it far?'

'I think not,' said Gurney. 'Less than a mile. I noticed the high ground on our last visit. I suspect that the broad path up through the covert goes there. Let us go then, but for God's sake watch out for spring guns and man traps!'

~

All Walsham wanted to do was sleep, but the stranger had insisted they keep moving. As they journeyed upwards through the wood, the man kept muttering to him to hold on, hold on. It took Walsham some time to realise that he was on the back of a horse, his hands tied together by a cord which encircled the animal's head. Reaching the open countryside on the heights of the estate he fell asleep.

And then he was awake, somehow sitting up on the horse, with his hands tied behind his back. Even that brief interlude of unconsciousness had roused his mind and his memory a little. Looking down he saw the stranger holding the horse's bridle. He knew the man for certain now. He was sure of him and he suspected just why he had come back to that place.

'Why'm I here?'

The man held out an arm expansively.

'Can't you see where you are?' he said. 'You must have memories of this place? Thoughts of days agone must have crossed your mind every time you wandered through these fields. Surely, Walsham, you recall that day. No? I think you're lying! Just look up, go on, look up at the branch above your head...'

Walsham moved his head with difficulty, for there seemed to be some obstruction at his throat. But gradually, and with discomfort to his drunken brain, he held back his head, his weary eyes taking in the blue of the autumn sky before catching the edge of the tree's browning canopy...and then the thick branch a dozen feet above him. And there was the rope, hanging taut and vertical, coming down from the branch and burning with friction against the back of his head. And he knew, he knew what was to happen and felt sick with fear.

'But you were...you were...'

'Life isn't fair is it?' said the man, no longer a stranger. 'Some are meant to die and some survive. You are meant to die so that I *can* survive. Not fair at all!'

And with a flick of his wrist he pulled the bridle forward and the horse danced away, whinnying, as though desperate to relieve itself of the load.

Walsham felt the first pressure of the rope like a great blow against the back of his neck, as the knot cut in to the tender flesh. Then the pressure spread all around, feeling as though it might sear away his head. He looked down and saw his legs shaking and then kicking, as if desperate to dance through the air. He tried to move his tied arms but nothing would happen. For a moment he was aware of an uncomfortable sensation and knew that he had soiled himself. His legs kicked harder and further, harder and further, as though trying to expel the foul matter that seemed to be congregating in the top of his boots. As he looked up the colour of the field appeared to change before his eyes. The green and brown tints of the autumn day were swept away. He saw the land before him now only as a deep purple and then a violet and then a black. He tried to unscramble his thoughts as he felt the deep pain tearing apart his head.

And then there was nothing.

~

It was the greatest shock of William Quest's adult life.

He had tethered the horse just off a ride, deep in the shooting coverts of the Bartram estate, a little glade he remembered from boyhood. He had climbed the slope through the trees. Somewhere in these woods would be Walsham. He had to be. Either that or drunk in the village alehouse. He had not been in the cottage or anywhere in the immediate vicinity. Quest could not hear a sound of anyone in the woods. The fields beyond then. Those fields that Quest was so reluctant to revisit, those hilltop pastures of such bitter memory.

He walked carefully up among the trees, but even so his movements alarmed several pheasants. A pair of pigeons jinked overhead as they noticed him crossing a ride. For a moment he paused to check that the blade came easily out of the great wooden walking stick. He knew that he must be prepared for a sudden attack by the heavier and ferocious gamekeeper.

As he neared the grassy plateau at the top of the trees he moved even more carefully. It was on this fringe of the coverts that Walsham had been wont to set man traps and spring guns. But Quest was too near now to be deterred by any such threatening engines of destruction. He paused to listen. Voices. Yes, well one voice, distant and indeterminable, words that he could not make out but spoken in a clear and authoritative air. He was minded of the tone of a judge passing a sentence at the Bailey. It was a haunting voice and somehow familiar. A memory echoed for a split second through his brain before being lost, as the stimulations of the scene around crashed and overwhelmed it in his mind.

And then, at the edge of the trees, he could see across the open ground.

For a moment Quest thought that he had gone quite mad. Or that he fallen unconscious and lapsed into that oh so familiar nightmare. There was a man astride a horse, a rope leading from his throat to the bough of a tree. Another figure stood close by, a man in dark clothing, waving an arm and talking up at the condemned individual. Then, even as Quest watched, the dark figure jerked his arm, pulling at the horse's bridle. The hanging man fell but slightly and then danced a sinister jig through the air as the hempen rope choked the life out of him. Even as he died and went still - a period of time that to Quest seemed to be hours - the man in black mounted the horse and rode away across the field. Just as Quest remembered him riding so many years ago, with a rakish confidence in his abilities as a horseman. Though without the yells and laughter of that previous occasion. He watched as the rider disappeared into the trees on the far corner of the meadow.

For a while Quest dared not look back at the hanged man.

He stared down at the ground and then along the line of his dagger-stick. Things that seemed rooted in reality. He drew the blade and scarred it across the palm of his hand, bringing a thin line of blood to view, and then a vivid pain that shot up through his arm. But still he did not wake from his nightmare. For as he looked up the man was still hanging there, the corpse swaying slightly in the breeze.

Quest knew who it was.

The gamekeeper had changed little in the intervening years. The long locks of hair greyer and the body, once stout and muscular, turned more to fat. Hanging there. *And from the same tree!*

And then the gamekeeper's body seemed to vanish and other bodies, hanged bodies, appeared. All swaying in the breeze that swept across the wide Norfolk sky. For a moment his father's face seemed to be in front of his own, his tongue swung out of the edge of his mouth and the skin a deep purple. His father's voice seemed to cry out to him, trying to form the sounds of his name. Then the eyes turning upwards to the sky as he died again and again.

Then Quest fled down through the trees, as he had so many years before, running with the same desperation as then, crashing through the trees of the undergrowth, sending the pheasants flurrying through the branches. The fallen leaves of the autumn crowded into the sky from around his swift feet. When he reached the horse, he buried his head for a moment into the long mane. Then he mounted and rode and rode and rode, faster and faster, out into the fields and heathlands, and then back out on to the turnpike road where he sped for a mile before considering the horse and pausing to look back across the countryside.

~

'My God!'

Anders saw Gurney's mouth form the words but no sounds came.

They had reached the top of the ride, at a corner of the woods, when they heard a hint of distant voices. And as they emerged into the open they saw Walsham swinging from the tree and a man in black watching, mounted on a horse, just a few yards away. Even as they paused the man spurred the horse away.

'My God!' Gurney said aloud.

Then they ran across the field to where the pathetic corpse of the gamekeeper swung so freely.

'We must get him down,' said Gurney.

'We must,' Anders replied, 'but there is no doubt that he is dead.'

'And that man...that horseman...'

'Our killer...probably. I'm afraid Walsham must hang for a while longer. Get back to the house and get one of the servants to send for reinforcements. I'll head across the field to see if our horseman might be tracked. And Gurney...I want labourers here. I want this field dug up. If Marshall and his sons are buried here then I want them found. I want to know whether there are four bodies here or only three.'

FIFTEEN

'That book, boy. The one you got for me. I read it the other day. It's full of criminal doings,' said Sticks, as he and Billy walked through Piccadilly on the way to the house in Albemarle Street. 'Are you sure it's a right and proper book?'

'It's by Daniel Defoe,' Billy replied. 'One of our greatest authors...a favourite of my father. The book is really all about morality. I don't think it's meant to be a primer on crime...though you could read it that way.'

'But this Moll Flanders. She's a thief! A dip at the least. She robs a child on the kynchin lay and is tempted to top the little girl as well. And she becomes a tail, sellin' herself on and off the streets.'

'I think Defoe was suggesting that people go to crime because poverty and desperation drives them that way.'

Sticks halted and gave a big sigh. 'Well, that's true enough, anyroad. And do you agree with that, Billy, that all crime is down to folk being poor?'

Billy thought for a moment before replying.

'Not altogether,' he said at last. 'There's many a poor man and woman that doesn't go to crime, though their honesty often puts them in an early grave. No, I steal because I don't want to die. And what alternative is there?'

'Well,' said Sticks, rubbing his chin. 'There's the prize ring. I used to make more in a bout than most can earn in a five-year.'

Billy laughed. 'But you're good at the fancy! You have the build and the fearlessness of a bruiser. Not many could do that. Not many would wish to...'

Sticks nodded. 'True enough! You're a thin little thing, though I could train you and fatten you up. Handy to know how to punch back.'

'One day perhaps.'

'An' there's somethin' else. If crime's there because of folk bein' poor, well, how do you explain all those rich bastards who rob and cheat and deceive? They've got enough already and still want more...'

Billy was quiet for a moment as they walked on. 'I knew a family like that once,' he said at last. 'Their name was Bartram. The law never protected the poor from them.'

'An' another thing. It says in the Bible "Thou shalt not steal". Yet everyone I know does...in all their odd ways. Are we all sinners? All bound for the fires of hell?'

'I think we are all human,' Billy replied. 'And I believe that, if there is a God, he will be particularly forgiving of those who were forced to steal from need. It is those who have enough yet still steal that might have a harder time explaining themselves. Need is one thing...greed quite another.'

Then they were silent as they walked the length of Albemarle Street, with its tall and well-proportioned buildings; many were business premises, though there was a sprinkling of private houses in between. One building in the long row was clearly some kind of gentlemen's club for as they watched several carriages dropped off men in expensive clothes, who stopped to chat with their fellows on the steps. They had not long passed one building, which Billy was interested to see belonged to Mr Murray, publisher of books, than Sticks nudged him in the ribs and nodded his head.

'That's the one. That's the tight little crib we wants you to crack.'

Billy looked up at a building of yellow brick, four storeys high, but quite narrow compared to many in Albemarle Street, its windows darkened. They crossed to view the premises from the other side of the road, which revealed three tiny windows built out from the roof tiles, probably the resting places of servants.

'Best to walk on,' said Sticks. 'Don't want to be seen takin' an interest.'

They turned the corner before they halted.

'Whose house is it, Sticks?'

'People of business. People with dockyments. That's all we need to know. There's an alley at the back leads to some low buildings behind the house next door. You needs to get up there and on to the

roofs. Then over to the front. The little windows of those servant rooms are never locked. Then the room you want is on the next floor down, right on the left of the house. Some kind of office.'

'Are the servants living in?'

'Prob'ly no one livin' in. No lights on. But you'll have to be a-careful how you attend to that window. Mustn't be seen from the street. Here, take this.'

Sticks slid a short lead-weighted wooden life preserver out from his jacket. Billy pushed it deep into his pocket.

'Try not to use it. No need for violence unless you're cornered.'

'Very well,' Billy replied. 'Now show me the way into this alley.'

~

'You are very good, Wissilcraft. You really are.'

Raikes sat forward in his chair, head held slightly on one side with eyes now wide open. Wissilcraft knew that posture well, and dreaded it. It was the way Raikes sat when he was in his most dangerous moods. Wissilcraft did not know how to reply. It was hard to tell from the spymaster's tone whether he was being honest or ironic. He gave a nod of his head.

'So the gamekeeper, er...Walsham? He is dead, mysteriously hanged...the day before yesterday?'

'Probably by the killer we have been trailing. Just moments before Anders and Gurney arrived on the scene.'

'And what are these detectives doing now?'

'Digging the field, sir.'

Raikes sat back in his chair and closed his eyes.

'Digging the field?'

'For bodies.'

'Bodies? Whose bodies?'

'I am not clear whose bodies, sir. But old bodies, that is buried quite a while ago. I got that from a labourer who has been engaged on the work.'

Raikes was silent for a moment.

'I need to know whose bodies Anders thinks they are? You will return to Norfolk and find out.'

'But sir, I had hoped to recommence my duties in London. I am too well known in Norfolk. It is the place of my birth. If I continue to be seen in the district then questions may be asked. Better to send up a different Queen's agent.'

Raikes' eyes flashed open.

'Back there, Wissilcraft. First thing tomorrow.' He could not disguise something like anger in his voice. 'You are one of my very best men. If you are unwilling to carry out your duties...well...I would be sad to lose you.'

'I am sure it would never come to that, sir.'

'Then go! And send me a communication each day as to what is happening. If Anders finds out anything of substance I wish to know immediately.'

He waved a hand towards the door. Wissilcraft gave a slight bow and left the room.

Raikes sat for a few moments with his eyes closed. Then he reached forwards and rang the little bell on the desk. Almost instantly Barker opened the door.

'Sir.'

'Barker, when did we last obtain a report from Inspector Anders?'

'Not for several days, sir.' The little man looked terrified as though this absence of reporting was his fault.

'Then pursue him, man! Go down to Scotland Yard. Find out what is happening. And you will now do that at the end of each day and bring your findings to me. Inefficient people tend to end up in the poor house, Barker.'

The little man nodded and shuffled away, closing the door behind him. After he had gone Raikes reached into the drawer of his desk and brought out a beautifully-polished mahogany box. He opened the lid and took out a pair of almost new percussion-cap duelling pistols and a powder flask engraved with his initials. He took one of the pistols and primed it ready for action, before putting the other pistol and the flask back into the box. He slid the loaded pistol into a pocket on the inside of his jacket and stood to put on his cloak and tall hat. Jacob Raikes had business on the streets of London.

~

A short alley led towards the rear of the houses in Albemarle Street. Sticks, checking it was clear, waved Billy towards the low range of outhouses that backed on to the properties.

'Up there, lad,' he said, nodding up to what seemed to be a great dark cliff blocking out the light. 'And take care. If you don't thinks as how you can do it, come down. S'along way to fall!'

Billy nodded and heaved himself on to the roof of the first of the little buildings. Crossing to the main wall he found a thick leaden drainpipe leading up towards the sky. It reminded him of the trees of his youth, though he yearned for something like their rough bark rather than this damp and slippery metal. But the pipe did stand several inches away from the brick, allowing him to wrap his arms through the gap. He could see almost nothing in the darkness but began to haul himself up.

With each movement he slid back a few inches for the pipe was dangerously wet with the rain water of the previous day. The gutter above must be partially blocked, causing some of the drained water to bypass the interior of the pipe and waterfall down the outside. Some way up he paused for breath and looked back into the black pit beneath. His heart was racing and he knew a real fear. He felt a great temptation to slide back down the pipe to the safety of the ground. But his pride wouldn't let him.

He climbed on and on, his breath coming in quick light gasps.

Just when he though his strength might give out, he bashed his head on an obstruction and knew that it must be the gutter. And that presented a further problem. It was at least two feet wide, made of lead like the drainpipe. A formidable obstacle that would prevent even the most daring climber from pulling himself up on to the tiles of the roof. He paused for a moment to get back his breath, then felt along the edge of the gutter to discover just how sound it was. For if any of the lead came away during his next manoeuvre he would be send tumbling into the pit of darkness so far below.

It seemed firm enough, though his forearm, scrabbling along the top, could barely reach the edge of the tiles. But there were only two choices. He could risk putting all his weight on the gutter or retreat back down the drainpipe.

He took three deep breaths and then grasped the gutter with one arm and then the other, his legs still wrapped against the pipe. Nothing gave way. He breathed again. He let go with his legs. For a moment he hung dangling in the air, trying to gain more purchase on the gutter. Then he gradually hauled up what seemed like the great weight of his *body on to the gutter. His heart skipped a beat as the lead creaked and groaned. His two hands scrabbled into the gap between the guttering and the wall and with one desperate heave he pulled himself full-length into the hollow in the lead.*

It held, though there was still an uncomfortable creaking sound from somewhere beyond his feet. Looking across at the sloping roof Billy noticed a ledge, perhaps a foot across, between the top of the wall and the start of the tiles. He half-rolled across the gap and on to it. He breathed a sigh of relief that he was off the metal.

He lay there for a few minutes, regaining breath and strength, and looking up at a soggy London sky. He began to wander whether a life of cracking cribs was quite what he expected. But, immediate danger past, he began to recover his appetite for adventure. Pulling himself together he stood and began to crawl his way up the steep line of tiles to the apex of the roof. The tiles were almost as smooth as the drainpipe and soaked with the rain that had fallen earlier in the day. But speed and four limbs hastened him to the top.

He looked down the roof on the other side. Albemarle Street, far below, seemed to be quiet enough. There were a few pedestrians on the far pavement but nobody was looking up. Billy examined the next part of this mad expedition. The tiles on this side seemed to be even steeper, but there were three small sections of flat roofs above the windows of the servant garrets, just a few feet below. He swung his legs over and, sitting down on the tiles, eased his way down to the one on the far right. Reaching it, he crouched on the top and then reached over to the window.

Sticks was right. It was unlocked and easily opened sideways. In a few seconds he was inside.

One of his great fears was that the room might be occupied by a sleeping housemaid or footman. But, as his eyes grew used to the darkness, he could see that it was deserted. The narrow room had an unmade bed along one wall, with an ancient chest of drawers and a washstand opposite. It didn't look as though it had been used for a considerable time.

Billy crept over to the door and listened. As quiet as the...now there was an unpleasant thought. He rubbed a hand across his chest and felt the life preserver deep in his pocket. Dare he use it? He hoped not. The lead weight might easily top someone and then he might get his neck stretched. One thing was for sure. If he was challenged he would never be able to make a quick escape back over the roof and down the drainpipe.

Slowly, oh so slowly, he eased the door open. It was dark beyond and it took a good couple of minutes before he could see anything at all. Even then he sensed more than saw the uncarpeted narrow corridor linking the garret rooms, a steep flight of steps going downwards at one end.

He made his way out, gently pulling the door closed behind him. The first step creaked. Damn! If one creaked then they all might. The sound seemed to fill the air. Billy pulled back to consider the problem. A solution. He put a hand on the banisters on each side and lowered himself down a little at a time. He thought he counted twelve steps in the dark beneath him. There were no more creaks.

The corridor below was carpeted and silent beneath his feet. It was much wider, evidently part of the living area of the owners of the property. At one time, he surmised, all of the five doors off the corridor would have been bedrooms. Perhaps they still were, though the building he had looked at from the outside had seemed to be offices. But who was to say that nobody lived in? And perhaps there was a watchman.

Billy made his way along the corridor, taking care not to bump into a side table and a pair of chairs that stood against one wall. What had Sticks said? The furthest room on the left of the house. He made his way to the corresponding door.

No light shone under the doorway. He listened. There were no sounds within. Very slowly, very gently, he turned the doorknob, easing the door back, first taking a peek and then entering. He closed it behind him. Gaslight from Albemarle Street half-lit the room, showing him a writing desk and a few chairs. Nothing more in the way of furnishings. It felt to Billy that no one had been in that room for a considerable time. As his eyes became accustomed to the dim glare he noticed a second door which obviously connected to an adjoining room. He tried the doorknob. It was locked.

The documents must be in the desk, then. If Sticks had indicated the correct room then they could be nowhere else. Billy eased forward the writing lid. There was nothing there, all the tiny shelves were empty. He closed it. Then the drawers. Four of them. He began at the bottom as Jasper had taught him. Empty and empty and empty. He tugged at the top drawer. Locked or jammed? Locked! He reached inside his jacket and took out the wallet containing several picklocks – "Bettys" Feedle had called them, though Billy couldn't imagine why. He tried the first picklock in the wallet against the keyhole. Too big, though it was really difficult to check in the half-light from the street. He wished he had brought a bulls-eye lantern with him, though he could not imagine how he would have carried it on his climb. Jasper had never instructed him in the art of the screwsman in such darkness. He tried a second picklock. Then a third.

Click!

The lock had turned. Gently. Very gently. He eased the drawer forward. It was not unknown,

Jasper had said, for careful people to install a bell inside drawers containing valuables or sensitive property. But there was no sound as Billy opened the drawer. And there they were. The documents. Certainly a package sealed with red wax. Billy took it and pushed it inside his jacket.

The cold round piece of metal against the back of his neck and the words came together.

'Move and I'll blow your brains out!'

~

The fat Russian with the dyed-black moustache looked across the table at Raikes, a smile seeming to split his great ham of a face.

'I am impressed, Mr Thomas,' he said, 'really I am. And you can get more like this?'

He patted the pile of documents on the table.

'If you can get more gold to pay for them.'

The Russian laughed. 'The one thing the Tsar is not short of is gold. My masters are most appreciative of the contribution you have made so far to our cause. These are worrying times. Soon our countries might be at war.'

'Very probably. You should have let the Ottomans slumber.'

'And you should not have sent your navy to the Dardanelles. But never mind. No fatal blows have been struck so far, well, not between Britain and Russia.' He laughed, though Raikes noticed little humour in his eyes. 'But we are old allies. Fighting together for God and Christ. It makes sense that we are both on the same side, does it not?'

Raikes nodded. 'It makes sense to me that everyone is on the side I choose, certainly. But I only work for gold.'

The Russian smiled, his thick hand patting the table.

'Then you shall have your gold. Bags of gold for documents like these. Wealth beyond your imagination...if you can use any influence you may have to hold back Her Majesty from going to war with the Tsar.'

~

It was cold as Raikes left the tavern in Whitechapel. Cold as though autumn was about to surrender to the first blows of winter. Cold as though the blast was coming in from Russia itself. And perhaps it was.

The streets were crowded, despite the lateness of the hour. Sufferers of society's ills lay strewn across the pavement, shivering and moaning in the cold. Some women were trying to sell themselves for tuppence. A few dangerous characters caught Raikes' eye, but looked away as soon as they glimpsed that menacing glare. Raikes had hidden the bag of gold deep within his coat. The pistol was handier, in a pocket, ready to be used.

And he thought it might have to be used for as he walked he had the feeling that he was being watched.

Not by one of the street villains but by someone with an interest in him. This instinct of knowing that he was being singled out from the crowd had come with the long practice of his profession as spymaster. He felt it now. And he was seldom wrong.

He had to know for sure.

As he turned into Houndsditch, busier even than the streets of Whitechapel, he suddenly swung into an alley, a shortcut into the city. It was an alley with a foul character. A cutting between high buildings that had a reputation for being particularly unsafe by day and night. Yet, in its way, it was one of the safest thoroughfares in London. Its legend of danger kept nearly everyone away, honest man and rogue.

Raikes sped along its narrow length and turned at the first corner. Somewhere behind him he heard what sounded like just half a footstep, a tread going gently down. So indistinct that it was barely there. But there it was.

He took out the pistol and levelled it along the way he had journeyed.

'Come!' he shouted. 'Show yourself!'

His words echoed up and down the alley. But all he got back was the sound of the wind sweeping along Houndsditch and the dripping of water down the sides of the high buildings and into the alley. Raikes waited for a moment then, still gripping the pistol in his hand, walked on.

~

As the sound of Raikes's footsteps faded away, a large man leaned against the wall to one side of the entrance to the alley. A few passers-by eyed his bulk and wondered where he could have got so much food. The man smiled to himself. Raikes was good, well-deserving his reputation. Out of all those vast crowds he had realised that he was being followed. On the other hand perhaps it was just jumpiness. Men – prosperous men, not dressed in rags - who journeyed into this neighbourhood had a very good chance of being followed. No, Benjamin Wissilcraft considered, Raikes was better than that. He had known that someone was dogging his footsteps because of who he was.

But it had taken Raikes a time to realise that he was being pursued. He had given no indication of that knowledge on the long journey from Whitehall and into the East End. His meeting with the Russian in the tap-room of the Grave Maurice had proceeded in such a careless way that the spymaster must have felt safe enough. Careless, Wissilcraft thought. Very careless. Only now was Raikes taking care. Over-confidence, Wissilcraft thought, led so often to human blunders.

The breeze sweeping along Houndsditch had grown even colder. Wissilcraft raised an arm and a closed carriage came and picked him up. He was grateful, for he hated walking. After wrapping a blanket around his great body, he burrowed inside and brought out a flask of brandy.

He could get to like London.

He really could.

SIXTEEN

'Slowly...slowly...to your feet boy,' said the voice. 'And don't turn round until I tell you to. Slowly...and keep your arms away from your pockets. Nothing sudden...gently...or I'll spatter your brains against the wall. Right...now. Turn round. Cautious, boy. You wouldn't be the first I've shot...'

Light appeared suddenly as the cover was removed from a bulls-eye lantern. For a moment Billy was dazzled by the glare. Then he made out the scene. The man stood now in the centre of the room, aiming the pistol at Billy's head. He had a round face and he was losing his hair. What had once been a muscular body was turning to fat. Billy looked across at the second man, the one holding the bulls-eye lantern. He was thin, as wasted as a beggar on the street. There was a sad expression on his face. He looked much like those pictures of saints and martyrs that Billy had seen in one of his father's books. Despite the circumstances, the boy felt a strange sympathy for him. For the thin man seemed to be bearing all the agonies of an unjust world.

'Please put those documents on top of the desk,' the thin man said. 'And tell us just why you were attempting to steal them?' Billy noted the strong foreign accent.

He reached inside his jacket and took out the package. He placed them on the top of the bureau.

The thin man walked over to the wall and brought up the gaslight.

'Just to see you better,' he said. 'Well, what a young villain you are!'

'Villainy is villainy, brother, whatever the age of the villain,' said the man with the pistol. 'And villainy has consequences. Who sent you here boy?'

Billy remained silent and looked down at the floor.

'I think you will tell us. The consequences of silence will be particularly unpleasant.'

'Go to hell!'

'Listen boy,' said the thin man, seeming to struggle with his English. 'We have no wish to harm you. You are clearly the...the...tool of older villains. Please just give their names and we let you go.'

Billy looked him in the face and shook his head.

The fatter brother sighed.

'Ah, well. Then we must compel you to talk.'

'But how brother?' asked the thin man. 'Should we send to Bow Street for the Runners?'

'I think not. They would not be particularly helpful and might ask questions that we do not want to answer.'

The thin man looked appealingly at Billy. 'You will really not tell us? It is in your interests.' He waved an arm at his brother. 'He is not patient, you see.'

'If you do not tell us who sent you then I will make you. Brother, the fire in our office downstairs, it is lit?'

'Roaring...'

'Then we could roast the information out of him...'

'Please tell us now,' the thin man seemed really anguished. 'Just a name, just one name. They will never know from us that you spoke.'

Billy shook his head.

'Or I could shoot him dead, brother. No - better to maim him. Let him end his young days as a cripple in the workhouse. A shot through the knee perhaps?'

He walked nearer and lowered the pistol, aiming it directly at Billy's right leg. Despite the cold Billy felt sweat pouring down his body and the thumping of his heart seemed to bellow into his head.

'I will give you...one...last...chance,' said the fat man, holding the pistol just three feet from Billy's kneecap.

'What...are...their...names?'

'Never!' Billy shut his eyes. 'Go to hell!'

The room seemed to explode around Billy as the pistol fired, its flash forcing his eyes open. He fell forward on to the bare wooden floorboards and the world seemed to crash in on him.

~

Lady Colbor sat in the window seat and looked out across the parkland of the estate, her gnarled hands grasping the tiny walking cane without which she could no longer move. Her breathing had become very shallow in the past few days, as though her lungs were losing their capacity to take in air. Soon there would be no breaths at all.

It had not been a pleasant day.

Ives, her estate steward, had organised the traditional pheasant shoot for the neighbouring gentry. The first time that she had been absent as hostess since her marriage to the Earl. She had watched them, out there on the gravel of the carriage turnaround, dressed to kill, all of them, waving their guns around, drinking her brandy.

She had watched their return later in the afternoon, mud-spattered from the coverts, two hundred dead birds, at least, piled upon the keeper's cart. And nobody, not one of them, had deigned to come up to see her. And they could have done. They had all come crawling when the Earl was alive, virtually kow-towing to the host and hostess. Now they wanted nothing of her...nothing.

She grasped the stick tighter, her knuckles white. They were really all bastards. Everyone she had ever known was a selfish bastard, all except the Earl. He had been, in his way, the gentlest of souls. They really should have had more time together. Met when they were younger, when she might have borne him children. Someone to care for her now. But these people who came shooting. Out for themselves. All of them. She stamped the stick on the ground.

She couldn't see the point in living to be humiliated any longer. She wished the breaths would stop. She wished she could always remember the past with the clarity of today. Some of the past at least. Not just the worst of the past.

She noticed the man by the distant window. Saw him out of the corner of her eye. Ives? No, not Ives. A stranger. Someone had come, she thought, some member of the shooting party *had* lingered. She turned to look at him, but could not quite place him in her memory. And he was dressed like a peasant, well a farmer anyway. His clothes stained with mud and the other marks of swift travel. She bowed her head a little as he walked nearer. Then looked up, her mouth open and her eyes challenging.

'You are?'

'It doesn't matter,' Quest said. 'Just someone from the distant past.'

'And how did you get in here?'

'That doesn't matter either. I am here.'

'You are an intruder! Have you come to kill me?' she asked.

'You ask that question almost hopefully?'

The old lady leaned forward on her stick and nodded her head. 'Well, look at me. I might measure my life in weeks, days perhaps. There is no joy in this decaying state. If you beat me to death you would do so with my gratitude.'

'I mean you no harm,' said Quest. 'I just want you to name a name...'

'A name?'

'A name from the past. From a day in the past when you saw your first husband hang...murder...William Marshall and his sons. You recall that day?'

A cold shiver shook Lady Colbor's wasted body as another bad memory occupied her mind. She looked up at the intruder and spent several moments examining his appearance.

'Of course,' she said at last. 'You are the one they chased. I can see the boy yet in your face. You are Marshall's son. So you *have* come to kill me.'

Quest shook his head. 'No, I mean you no harm. It was not your doing. I remember...I remember so vividly the look of horror on your face.'

'But you *have* come for revenge?'

'Not against you...'

Her voice rang out, shrill and clear. 'Then who? Who is left alive? My husband...my Bartram husband...is dead. My sons have been slain by...by you? *Yes, by you...*'

'It was necessary,' Quest said.

The countess laughed and gasped for breath before speaking. 'Oh, don't think that I blame you. I salute you! They were ungrateful cubs, the pair of them, from the very moment they were whelped. The world I am leaving will be better for their absence. I wish I had had the courage to drown them in the well when they were born, like any other unwanted curs.'

'You speak harshly of your children?'

'Little brats begot on drunken nights!'

'The Banningham brothers were drowned the next year.'

'That is right, that is right! There is the gamekeeper, Walsham. He was there.'

'He is dead too,' said Quest. 'I saw him hanging from a tree only this morning.'

'So you killed him?'

'No, somebody else.'

'A poacher perhaps?'

'I think not. His murderer had all the appearance of a gentleman. A man I have seen before. The other man who was there that day. I knew him the moment I saw him on horseback.'

'Ah, the lawyer then, though what that monstrous man had to do with law is beyond me. He was there that day. Even now I can see the pleasure in his eyes.' She paused. 'And you want to know who he is?' She laughed and, once again, took some moments to recover her breath. She nodded at the silver tray on the table. 'Then pour us both some brandy and I will tell you.'

Quest did as he was bidden. He sipped from his glass, but the old lady threw most of hers down in one quick swallow.

'We had a shoot today. I was not invited. I missed out on a drink.' She held up her glass with its tiny remnant of Armagnac. 'I salute you, Mr Marshall. Now come close, before this brandy takes away my memory. And I will tell you the lawyer's name and where I last heard of him....'

After she had spoken she looked out the window once more. Darkness had fallen and she could see only her own reflection in the glass. The intruder had gone, though she had scarcely noticed him slip away. She looked at herself in the window. Soon there would be no reflection of her anywhere at all.

~

'Just a heap of bones in the ground,' said Anders, looking down into the pit that the labourers had dug. The two detectives were just a dozen yards from the tree where they had found Walsham hanging. 'Funny isn't it?' he looked across at Gurney. 'All of our hopes and our dreams. All those stupid worries and the nightmares we all have. And they only dissolve to a heap of bones in the earth.'

Gurney nodded. 'I know what you mean. The way everything in creation seems to rot away. Is there anything more than these bones? "Can these dry bones live?" Where is that in the Bible?'

'Ezekiel,' said Anders. 'The parson at Liddington often used the text in his sermons, when I was forced to go to church as a boy. I could never puzzle out the possibility of whether they could or not. I used to have dreams of the bones in the churchyard burrowing back through the earth and dancing into life.'

'You do not believe then that they ever will?'

'I fear not. I suspect that death is the end, though I would wish to be proved wrong. But until we know it is all the more reason why we should reverence life.'

The two men were silent for a moment. A chill wind blew in from the east, stirring the branches of the trees and sending a confetti shower of russet leaves down on to the three skeletons. The bones had clearly been buried in a great hurry, their limbs intertwined and the skulls almost touching each other.

'Walsham's work, I suspect,' said Anders. 'I cannot imagine any of the other murderers dirtying their hands. He was probably told to bury them deeper than we found them. How apt that he should swing almost over their poor remains.'

'Three of them,' Gurney remarked. 'The father and two of the sons. So the youngest Marshall boy escaped?'

'I think it likely. There is of course the possibility that they caught him during that foul chase and buried him elsewhere. Lady Colbor was unsure of the outcome.' He looked across the field to the fringes of the wood, trying to picture the events of that day. 'But no, I do not believe that we will find

187

the dry bones of young William Marshall anywhere near here. We must assume that he is out there avenging the deaths of his father and brothers.'

'Then how are we to find him?'

Anders shook his head. 'I cannot imagine how we will find him. But one matter is clear. His vengeance is not restricted to those who were present on that day. He has widened his revenge on to much of society.'

'It might not be Marshall at all.'

Anders smiled across at the younger man.

'I will tell you why I think it is Marshall. The cord left by the bodies. The miniature hangman's noose found by both of the Bartram brothers and his other victims.'

'Aye, but not by Walsham's hanging corpse. We searched. There was no such token.'

Anders frowned. 'And that is a great puzzle to me. We saw the assassin. He could have had no idea that we were watching him. Yet no noose. Why? I cannot contemplate why he would not leave a noose?'

'Forgot? Perhaps in the anger of the moment?'

'I don't think so,' said Anders. 'It is not how he operates. Yet there has to be some reason.'

'There is another possibility,' said Gurney. 'That Walsham's killer was not the same man.'

Anders rubbed his forehead. 'And that is the worry that has been haunting my nightmares. But here is where Walsham was killed. Hanged just like the

Marshall father and sons. That cannot be a coincidence. It cannot be, Gurney! It cannot be!'

~

The smell of the powder filled the room, the sound of the shot echoing away into the corridor.

Billy felt no pain. He turned over and glanced down at his leg. There were marks of powder from the closeness of the pistol, but no mark of the pistol ball, no wound, no blood...

He looked at the two brothers. The fat one was cradling the pistol, the older thinner brother nervously rubbing his hands together. They both looked down at him. There seemed to be an expression of pleasure on their faces. The older brother pulled the chain on the gas lamp, flooding light into the room.

'It was not a misfire,' he said. 'The pistol was never loaded.' He looked even more agitated than before. He turned towards his brother. 'It was a cruel trick to play, Isaac. I said it was before. The boy did not deserve such a trick.'

'He did not,' the fat brother replied. 'But we had to be sure...had to be sure.' He looked down at Billy. 'You are a brave man, Master Marshall. You could have spoken out. Spared yourself the ordeal. But you were willing to be maimed or killed rather than betray your friends.'

'How do you know who I am?'

189

'We know most things,' said Isaac. 'We have been trailing you since you came to London. We know that you are the son of our dearest friend William Marshall. The man who helped us so much when we had to flee our home in Poland. We are the Critzman brothers. I am Isaac and this is Josef. But for your father neither of us would live.'

'You knew my father?'

'Very well. We knew him and we knew you when you were young. We know that your father and your brothers have gone. We suspicion that they were done away with. Is that correct?'

'Murdered.'

Billy told them how.

Isaac Critzman sat down, turning pale as he listened to the boy's words. Josef leaned back against the wall, tears pouring down his face.

'That was abominable,' Josef said at last. 'In England, such a crime. Such things are familiar in our land, but here?'

'And now you seek vengeance?' asked Isaac.

'I want to see the Bartram family in hell!'

'And you will,' said Isaac, 'you will. And others like them, perhaps? You will forgive us. There is much to explain. We were in communication with your father. And then the messages stop. We are puzzled. We make inquiries in Norfolk. What we hear from our comrades there makes us fear the very worst.'

'You thought well of my father?'

'He was the bravest of the brave. A man determined that the world should be better for the many and not just the few. If the rioters had listened to him, if they had let him organise, then this might be a fairer land. But they were impatient.'

'It is understandable,' Josef added. 'This is a country of great injustice, but much could be done. The few who hold down the people are indeed a very few. Your father...we his friends...have dedicated our lives to bring about social justice in the fastest ways possible. Some might call us revolutionaries...'

'There is much that is good in England,' said Isaac. 'We are outsiders from a broken land. But even we can see how little needs to be done to alter the balance in favour of social justice. Until we die we try to tip that balance.'

'And we would like the help of the young Mr William Marshall,' said Josef. 'We have watched your life in Seven Dials. Saw your interests. We observe as you pick pockets. You are good at what you do. But we think your talent might be put to better purposes. The real criminals are the ones that exploit the poor for their own ends and profits.'

'You could be a criminal of very great talent,' said Isaac. 'Make a good living as...what is that phrase, brother?'

'One of the swell mob.'

'A flash villain,' Isaac laughed. 'Yes, indeed!'

'Or you could use those same talents to forward your father's work,' said Josef. 'Use them on behalf of the poor and desperate. Fight back against all this cruelty and injustice.'

'But how?' Billy asked. 'I steal because there is no other way of putting food in my mouth. There might be a thrill in it, when I look back, but I have to survive.'

'And survive you will,' said Isaac, 'and with a kind of life you cannot possibly even imagine. Tell me boy? If you were rich would you abandon all thoughts of the poor and what you have seen? Would your dreams of vengeance be cast aside?'

'Never!'

'Rich you may well be, by the standards of Seven Dials. It is no crime to be rich, as long as it is not achieved in an unjust way. And as long as you use that advantage to the benefit of those who are not. My brother and I are men of business ourselves. We wish to see everyone rich and nobody poor.'

'And the lion will lay down with the lamb?' said Billy. 'I doubt such a world is possible.'

'Well the best that might be achieved then...' said Josef. 'Would that be too much to ask?'

Billy considered. 'Tell me more about my father and I will consider what you say.'

'Very well,' Josef replied. 'Come downstairs to that fire that roars and we will toast some muffins. Some friends await you there. Sticks and Feedle.

Incorrigible rogues! To bring a young man to such menaces!'

SEVENTEEN

Lord Palmerston was not in a happy mood.

Parliamentary business as Home Secretary had stretched the day out beyond all human endurance. He had been on his way home when the message sent him back to his private office. He sat back in the chair by the fireside and looked up at Wissilcraft.

'You are sure of this?'

'Without a doubt,' Wissilcraft replied. 'It would appear to confirm your lordship's suspicions. Raikes is holding deep conversations with Russians who are close to the Tsar.'

A worried look crossed Palmerston's austere features. 'My worry is that we are wrong. I am aware that I asked you to get close to Raikes, to become his man, his very best spy. The past year has been a triumph in that direction. The man thinks of you as his finest agent. You are trusted.' He paused and took a sip of water. 'He has never guessed that your first loyalty is to me?'

'I think not.'

'This work in Norfolk. Hunting the killer of a certain gentleman. Raikes is pleased with your progress?'

'He thinks well of me, but is annoyed at my slowness in reporting back and discovering the identity of the assassin.'

'And Raikes has never suspected that you are much in London? That your time in Norfolk is limited to swift excursions?'

'I think not.'

'You have followed Raikes with great diligence...'

'As best I could,' Wissilcraft replied. 'There have been times when his insistence that I be in Norfolk has hampered our work.'

'But we cannot overlook the fact that he is Her Majesty's Spymaster. If we were to confront him then would he not say that these meetings with Russians were a part of that duty? Even to the extent of him taking money from them? We may think him traitor but he be yet patriot?'

'Of that I cannot be sure. But is it not the usual practice for such compromising meetings to be reported to you as Home Secretary?'

The Home Secretary nodded. 'That is so. And you have reports of other difficulties concerning Raikes? Distasteful matters of a private kind? I have read your reports.'

'I feel that such practices leave a man vulnerable to pressure.'

Palmerston gave a wry smile. 'You may be right, though there would scarce be a politician at Westminster who would not be equally vulnerable. It is the nature of man to be at times...unwise.'

'Then I await your instructions, my Lord. I am, at present, supposed to be in Norfolk. I will return there tomorrow morning. I suspect that there will be little more to report on the occurrences there. It would be helpful if I could receive instruction to be in London on some pretence. It would give me a greater opportunity to follow him.'

Palmerston sighed. 'I will see what I can do. But go carefully. Recall that Master Raikes is very well connected. He may not be liked but he has been a most effective spymaster. And he holds information on some of the greatest men in the land.'

Including yourself, old mongoose, thought Wissilcraft. He nodded in agreement and smiled at Palmerston.

'Trail him. Bring him to heel, but discreetly, Wissilcraft. And I am to be consulted before any deed is done which might cause embarrassment to the government. You understand?'

Benjamin Wissilcraft gave a low bow and left the room.

~

'A collection?' asked Anders.

'A collection,' Gurney replied. 'Once the news reached this town that the bodies of William Marshall and his sons had been found it was decided that a collection would be made in order to facilitate their proper burial.'

The two men were strolling along the edge of Mousehold Heath, looking across the rooftops and church towers of Norwich. They were filling in some time before Anders caught the late train back to London.

'Marshall was that well regarded?' he asked.

'He fought for the people of Norfolk. Anyone who needed help, irrespective of class. Yes, he was very well regarded. The collection has already raised enough for a proper tomb in the churchyard of St Mary at Earlham. Even those Gypsies you see camped on the edge of the heath gave several guineas.'

'Do you know who started the collection? Or was it spontaneous from several quarters?'

'If anyone led the way it would be Mr Bell. He publishes a newspaper in the town. A somewhat radical gentleman, rather like Marshall used to be. Though held in great affection. Even by the Tories in the town.'

Anders smiled, 'You seem to live in a most tolerant community!'

'It was not always so,' Gurney replied. 'And this can still be a most rebellious and lawless town and county. But the events of a few years ago, the riots and burnings. They frightened people. There is no doubt that the pot is still boiling. At the moment people still wish to keep the lid on the pot.'

'And this Bell? He knew Marshall?'

'Very well indeed. They were companions in arms during the riots. At that time Bell was a tailor and not a profitable one. A clever man, and well read. In communication with many a radical member of Parliament. Bell was put on trial at the Assize but the jury refused to convict. The judge was said to be so frustrated that he went back to his lodgings and promptly had a stroke. He had been looking forward to stretching Bell's neck.'

Anders smiled, 'That sounds like a lot of judges I encounter. So how did Bell acquire the newspaper?'

'A bit of a mystery there. He had always had printed some seditious broadsheets. It went with his rebellious trade. But once all of the troubles were over he suddenly had the money to acquire premises. A printing press arrived. Within a week the first edition of the *Norfolk Reporter* was published. It sold few copies those first months. But then word went round and it became a triumph.'

'And the tone of this sheet? It is still rebellious?'

'Very much so,' said Gurney. 'Bell has been threatened with seditious libel on many an occasion. But no one wishes to take the lid off that pot by pursuing matters through the court. To answer your question about the money. Rumour has it that certain radical gentlemen in London fund the sheet.'

They walked in silence for several minutes, off the heath and down towards the river. A strong wind in the night had robbed the trees of many of their leaves providing a thick carpet of brown and gold to quieten their steps.

Anders turned to Gurney.

'Before I take my train...I think I would very much wish to interview this Mr Bell.'

'We can go there now. He is seldom away from his printing machine.'

Anders nodded. 'Good. And this collection? You have contributed?'

Gurney smiled and turned red. 'Ten shillings.'

Anders dug into his pocket. 'Then I will match that to give those dry bones a goodly burial. Should I give my donation directly to Mr Bell?'

Gurney turned even redder.

'I did,' he said.

~

'Where is Quest?'

The Critzman brothers looked up from a ledger as Rosa flung open the door of Josef's walking stick shop in Cheapside, sending the bell into a wild jangling.

'My dear young lady, do sit,' said Josef. 'You seem to be in a state of agitation...'

'Where is Quest?' she demanded. 'Have you seen him at all?'

Isaac stood and guided Rosa into a chair.

'We had rather assumed that William was with you,' he said. 'Is he not?'

'No he is not! And I haven't seen him for days. Not since he journeyed to Norwich. He was supposed to come to see me on his return. I have been to his house. Sticks knows nothing of his whereabouts. Not that he was very helpful. I could scarce tear him away from the final instalment of *Bleak House*. *Bleak House*! So from there I went around all of Quest's lurks. Not a sign! Then round all the taverns inquiring into all of the other characters that Quest plays on the stage that is London. He is not to be discovered!'

'He may have been delayed in Norfolk,' said Isaac.

'Then he should have damned well let us know!' Rosa stood so swiftly that the chair fell over. 'For all we can be aware he might have been lagged on that foolhardy errand. Or killed in a fight with the gamekeeper. I told him to leave it alone, but he cannot. It is his obsession. Madness!'

Isaac picked up the chair and sat Rosa down in it once again.

'Please do calm yourself,' he said. 'I will have inquiries made in Norfolk. We have a good network of friends there. And I will get Jasper to search London again in case he has returned in the meantime. My dear Rosa, return to your lodgings. He may turn up there and worry if he finds you missing...'

'Missing! Aye, that would be his way. To complain if he finds *me* missing! If you see him before I do tell him...oh, tell him...Aargh!'

~

Bell was drunk.

Drunk and sorrowful.

Drunk and in a reminiscent mood.

Anders liked them like that. Just drunk enough to be talkative. Just drunk enough to be indiscreet. He hoped that the newspaper proprietor and printer might be very indiscreet. Mind, the man was fat and could probably hold a lot of drink. Bell was, perhaps, sixty years old, almost as broad as he was tall, with a ragged beard, untidy hair and printers ink splattered over his clothing.

'Good of you...' the printer said. 'To give money in this way. Your health!' he raised the tankard. 'And you could not have known dear Marshall and his boys?'

Anders shook his head.

'A good man,' Bell continued. 'A fine man. A champion of the poor. No, not just the poor. All in distress. And well connected. Well thought on across the land. They say those Bartram swines killed him. Well, I can see why they would. They tried to kill a great many...'

'Did you know William Marshall for a long time?' asked Anders.

'Aye, a very long time. Through trouble and sorrow we fought...' he almost sang the words. 'Nor shall we be defeated...'

'Marshall had three sons? The youngest may have survived.'

'Young Billy? A brave lad, though he struggled as an infant. His poor mother died when he was but two. A shock to all!'

'We think he is alive,' Gurney remarked. 'Would you know of his whereabouts?'

Bell poured more drink down his throat and sank back into the printer's chair.

'Unlikely,' he said. 'Where would he be? Mind, I have not been in communication with any of our friends outside Norwich for many years. Others may know of him elsewhere...'

'Others?' said Anders.

'I think it likely that young Billy Marshall is dead. If he were alive why would he not have returned to Norwich?'

'Who are these others?' Anders persisted.

'His father had friends in London. In political circles. They might possibly help you in your quest.'

Bell closed his eyes against the sunlight that streamed in through the window. His head nodded forward and he gave a grunt that was somewhere between a sigh and a snore.

'What others?' Anders asked in a gentle voice.

'Marshall had many champions. Not just in the days of Swing but before and after. He corresponded with fierce old Cobbett and they struck up a great friendship. Did you know that? And radical members of Parliament such as Chapman and Quest and Roebuck. Ah, if only people had listened. If only people had stuck together.'

Bell fell asleep as the two detectives left his office.

'I'm not sure that that was helpful at all,' said Gurney as they walked to the railway station. 'Old names from the past. William Cobbett is dead! No help there.'

'We have very little else,' Anders replied. 'Roebuck sits in the Commons. I can talk to him. I know nothing of Chapman and Quest. I will make inquiries in London. When is the funeral to be?'

'Two weeks tomorrow.'

'Then I will return to Norwich for that. It is just possible that young Billy Marshall might make an appearance. Just possible.'

~

Sergeant Berry looked up through the gloom and tried to see anything of the sky. The autumn night was drawing in. He shivered as a blow of cold and stinking wind blew into the alley from Monmouth Street. Another wasted day in Seven Dials. Just as the day before had yielded nothing in the way of information in the perilous quarters of the St Giles rookery.

It was too late to be about in such a place. The stench seemed to grow worse as the day progressed. Somewhere in the distance he could hear raised voices as two women scrapped over something important to them. He pulled over to the wall as a donkey pulled a small cart past him, led by a dowdy man who seemed to be walking in his sleep thanks to the long hours of toil. For a moment he recalled similar scenes in his native Manchester. What a mess life was! Was it any wonder there was so much crime in these rookeries? Hard crime often. More often soft crime, the kind of petty offences that anyone living there had to commit just to continue a miserable existence. A number of times that day he had watched as crimes were committed. Watched pockets being picked, saw items being lifted through the doorways of the shops around Covent Garden. And he had done...

Nothing!

What was there to be done?

Was there any point in lagging a man or woman or child just because they were hungry? And yet, if a policeman didn't what would ensue? Would it all get much worse? More violent?

It always amazed Berry that these poor pathetic people didn't sweep into the City and Westminster and all those restful Avenues and peaceful Squares to seek their revenge against the privileged. As they might have done in days of old. But no. They were too beaten down, too demoralised, just too hungry to march. The fight had been knocked out of them. Berry's own father had starved to death in a

Manchester slum. Berry knew just how these people felt. And yet there were times when he had to battle their predations.

And just then was one of those times.

There were three of them. And each one of them was holding out a knife. The leader was a tall man with an eye patch. He waved the knife with an upward gesture.

'Money.'

His lips formed the word, but so quietly that Berry scarce heard a sound.

'Money.'

Louder now as the man closed in, holding his knife ready to sweep across Berry's face.

'Money...'

He had scarcely finished the word before Berry swung out his billy-stick and smashed it across the man's wrist, sending the dagger flying through the air. Eye Patch yelled with the pain, bending over towards the wall, swearing and blustering.

'A crusher,' Eye Patch gasped out. 'Get 'im. Finish 'im.'

Berry held the stick out before him as the other two men closed in. He swung it at the nearest but misjudged the distance. The man stepped briskly to one side, grasping Berry's forearm as he closed, forcing the detective back against the alley wall.

'Top 'im,' Eye Patch yelled again, closing in to help to force the policeman against the wall. 'Go on. Go on. Cut 'im. Now!'

Berry watched dazed as the third villain closed in, pulling his knife back ready to thrust upwards into his chest. For a moment the alley seemed to swirl around him. He could still hear the distant voices of the women arguing somewhere back on the street. He saw the knife coming at him.

He couldn't move.

And then the third man seemed to fly sideways through the air, only to crash on to the hard and filthy cobbles. As the second assailant turned to see why there was a delay, a life preserver cracked against the side of his head, sending him spinning on to the ground. On the edge of his vision, Berry saw Eye Patch raise a protecting arm in front of his face. It did him little good as the life preserver speared into his stomach.

Within three seconds of expecting death, Berry looked at all three attackers as they lay groaning on the alley cobbles. He shook his head. It all seemed like the flash of a nightmare.

He was aware of a man putting the billy-stick back into his hand and leading him out of the alley and back into Broker Row.

'It was not wise to walk that alley,' said his rescuer. 'It is never safe. The men you have just met hang around it like carrion crows hunting for a feast. A police detective should know better.'

'It was fortunate for me that you were passing.'

'Fortunate indeed. I was on my way to take a railway train. Otherwise I might not have come this way.'

It was hard to see anything in the dark. The man was well-dressed, like a country squire. He was tall but Berry could not make out his features. He still carried the lead-weighted life preserver in one hand and a heavy country stick in the other. He led Berry into a more crowded and safer part of the street. As they reached its light the sergeant stumbled, but the man reached out and caught him. The right hand, the one that held the life preserver, was horribly scarred across its back. The man noticed Berry looking down at it.

'An old wound,' he said.

'You've been in the wars before!' Berry replied.

'A little too often!' the man said in a quiet voice.

'I should know your name?' said Berry.

The man laughed.

'Just call me the policeman's rattle,' he said, gently easing the detective into the midst of hurrying people. Berry took a deep breath and looked all around.

His saviour was nowhere to be seen.

~

Lady Colbor looked up at the sky. Looked at a cloud of curious pink that seemed to be blowing gradually towards the house. The parkland reflected the colour, but then the ground became a deeper crimson as it absorbed the light from the heavens. And then, as the cloud drew nearer, each solitary tree which broke up the plain of the grass became a most vivid red.

'And when that cloud is overhead I shall die,' the old woman said to herself. She thought the cloud and the reddening landscape quite the most beautiful thing she had ever seen. As she sat within the open window she looked down at her hands. Watched as the pale skin turned as red as the nature outside. For a moment she caught her reflection in the glass of the drawn open window. She looked up at the sky once more. And then she tried to take a breath. It did not come.

EIGHTEEN

'Why does he sit like that for so long at a time?' asked Lizzie Paynter, looking out of the window of the library at Hope Down. A distant figure could be seen on the edge of the downland, his back against an oak tree, seeming to be gazing down at the house. The maid leaned on the sweeping brush and frowned. 'He seems to be so sad since he arrived.'

Mrs Vellaby, the housekeeper, stood by the fireplace, looking up at the portrait of Josiah Quest. Remembering again his quiet voice and gentle smile. She shook her head.

'He has had these moments of melancholy since he was younger,' she replied. 'He used to sit at the same spot for hours on end even then. Or take long walks across the downland. I remember seeing him once, as I was coming back from town on the carrier's cart. He was sat just so against the wall of the little churchyard at Stoke. Looking as though the world had ended for him.'

'And was he like that as a small child?'

Mrs Vellaby was silent for a moment, as though she was thinking how to answer. At last she said, 'I didn't know him when he was very little. He was almost a young man when he first came to Hope. I remember so well when...'

The girl looked round at the old woman. There seemed to be a reflective sadness in the look that was returned. Mrs Vellaby shook a duster into the fireplace. 'This isn't getting the work done!'

'I do wish we could cheer him,' Lizzie persisted.

Mrs Vellaby frowned.

'Well perhaps we can. When he was a boy and I used to see him sitting there, I would take him a jug of my lemonade. It often brought him out of himself. He would swig a glass back and tell me I was a saint. A saint!' She laughed. 'Perhaps you could do that for him now. There's a fresh jug in the kitchen. Take it up to him with a glass. And tell him that if he doesn't eat his dinner tonight he'll have me to answer to. Well, go on, girl! Off from under my feet! I'll finish in here.'

~

Hope Down.

Named after the family that had lived there in the seventeenth century. A hundred years before it was acquired and rebuilt by newcomers to wealth called Quest. He remembered jesting with old Josiah, raising a smile during the old man's last days of illness. 'Why *Down*? Should we all keep our hopes *Up*?'

William Quest had always admired the downland that gave the house the second part of its name, loved how the wide bare chalk ridges tumbled into valleys lined with hangers of beech trees. He had always felt so at home in the beautiful house, standing so sprightly in its modest park. He was always glad that it was not too big. He had never wanted a house that he could rattle around in too much. As he leant back against the tree and regarded the property his mind went back to the little house in Norwich. Then to the rookery slums where he had existed when he arrived in London. He felt those pangs of guilt that he always did when he compared his home to those of the desperate and struggling masses in the city.

He was glad that Hope Down had no tenants. He could not have borne the idea of playing squire to better people. The nearby village of Stoke was an "open" village, with no manorial lord to lay down the rules. Quest was glad of that too. He liked the people there, was pleased that they had to show no deference to anyone. The cottagers owned their own homes, for Josiah Quest had given them to the people when he came into his inheritance. The old manor of Hope Down was no more. It was a community. William Quest often worked in the fields during harvest time. Provided alibis when cottagers were accused of poaching on neighbouring estates. Shared in the Christmas celebrations. Let the few fields of Hope Down so that they might be worked and grazed as a kind of communal farm. And the cottagers recognised that he had come from nothing to be amongst them. William Quest was liked. And he liked them back.

He knew that one day, once all the other tasks were done – and if he were allowed to survive – he would come here and hardly leave again. For it was at Hope Down that he was mostly able to banish his demons. His few days here had refreshed him, given him a time out of the world. But now it was right that he should go back.

~

The hired carriage made its way up the gravelled drive to the house at Hope Down. Billy looked eagerly through the window at the grand property before him.

'And this is the home of a revolutionary?' he gasped. 'A man of the people?'

'Very much a man of the people,' Isaac Critzman replied. 'I can see your difficulties my young friend. But in a way Mr Josiah Quest has travelled a greater journey than yourself. It is easy for us, for you, people like us with modest backgrounds anyway, to be rebellious at the evils of society. Mr Quest need not have been rebellious at all. His father was a wealthy manufacturer. He left his son a considerable fortune, far beyond the riches you see here. Mr Quest could have lived in idleness and splendour for ever.'

'Many do,' added Josef. 'Yet the world would be a better place if they did not.'

'Mr Quest chose not to indulge himself in riches,' said Isaac. 'He has given much away, even more so

since the death of his only son. Even before that he sat as a radical member of Parliament. Fought for reform. Took the part of the people during the recent troubles. He was nearly imprisoned for his views.'

'But why?' asked Billy.

'Because he believes in the values of Christianity,' said Josef. 'Oh I know many of the wealthy say they do, but Mr Quest genuinely believes that the first task of a man is to do good for others.'

Isaac looked down at the floor of the carriage before speaking again. But as they came up to the house he looked across at the youth.

'My brother and I came to England destitute,' he said. 'Exiled from our homeland. Our family murdered. We had nothing. But Mr Quest had read some of Josef's pamphlets about Poland and sent for us. Invested in our undertakings. Shown us the greatest friendship, even though we were not of his religion. We would sacrifice our lives for Mr Quest. He would do the same for us.'

~

Quest watched as the girl came around the side of the house, bearing a jug and a glass. He knew what was coming. He smiled at the memory of all the times his black moods had been vanquished by Mrs Vellaby's lemonade.

The girl smiled, shyly, as she came nearer up the slope, walking with great care so as not to spill any of the liquid from the jug. Quest, who was not good at dealing with the folk who worked for him, avoided catching her eye.

But he smiled.

'Mrs Vellaby is a saint,' he said. 'And you are a saint to carry it all that way. The least I can do is offer you a drink of it?'

Lizzie flushed. 'Oh no. I couldn't. Besides there is only one glass.'

'Then we will share it,' Quest said as he poured out a drink for her. 'Go on. I insist...'

She took a sip out of the glass, quite nervously and then passed it back to him.

'Which book are you reading at the moment?' he asked.

'The second volume of *Lavengro* by George Borrow,' she replied. 'A most interesting man, though a trifle opinionated.'

Quest laughed. 'Yes, I suppose he is. My... Someone I knew a long time ago worked with him in a lawyer's office. He was opinionated even then. An interesting writer, though. You must discuss him with Sticks when he arrives at Hope Down. I know for a fact that he read *Lavengro* but a short while ago.'

'Is Mr Sticks coming down?'

'Several London friends will be arriving later today,' said Quest. 'It didn't take them long to track me down,' he added quietly, almost to himself.

'I'm sure you'll be pleased to see them.'

Quest sighed. 'Yes, I will, though it will mean my return to London in a day or two.'

'And you would rather stay here at...?' she stopped. 'I beg your pardon, sir. You must think me impertinent!'

He laughed. 'No, not at all. One of the best things about Hope Down is that I don't have to be a gentleman of the town. There is no impertinence in an honest question, Lizzie.'

'Even so...'

'Even so. And are you happy here?'

'I am, sir. Everyone is very kind. The house has a lovely atmosphere.'

'It always had, well, anyway, since I was younger...younger...'

~

'Your father was my dearest friend,' said the old man. 'As good as a brother to me.'

Josiah Quest and Billy sat on opposite sides of the fireplace in the library at Hope Down. A great fire burned in the grate and a stiff breeze rattled the windows.

'I do remember you sir,' Billy replied. 'I really do. You came up to Norwich just before...'

The old man looked terribly sad.

'What happened to your father and to your brothers, John and Alfred. It was appalling. At first I thought they were just missing, perhaps hiding from the authorities. But what you have told me. The foulest of deeds. And what they did to you...'

A tear ran down Josiah Quest's face. He was quiet for several moments.

'And you are now a young criminal? That is what they have driven you to?'

'I have to survive,' Billy replied. 'But it is more than that. I wish to avenge the murder of my family. It would not be difficult now, but better if I were to be equipped with a gun. And it is hard to get at them, on their country estate with their keepers and their servants to protect them. What I wish to do to them can wait. Until I can be sure that I will succeed.'

Josiah looked thoughtful.

'There was a time when I would have dissuaded you from this course of action,' he said at last. 'I have always tried to maintain my Christianity. You mind the words in the Bible? "I will repay, vengeance is mine, saith the Lord?"'

'I mind them well enough,' said Billy. 'But who is to say I am not meant to be God's instrument?'

'There is an arrogance in that, but I can sympathise with it. Others may describe your last comment as blasphemous. But I do not. You see, I too have lost someone so very precious to me. There was a time when I thought myself a man of peace, a man totally opposed to violence. But how can we stand by while these agents of the Devil prosper and the vulnerable suffer?'

The wind outside the window grew harsher as though all the elements of nature were concurring with the old man's words. Billy shivered, despite the heat of the fire.

'I had a son,' Josiah began. 'Oh, such a good lad, not unlike yourself in looks. You shared a name. He was William Quest, and I oft called him Billy when he was up to mischief. He died. And he died long before his time. And in many ways his death was my fault, a fact that haunts me to this day...'

'But how could it be your fault?'

'I have always fought for the radical cause,' Josiah replied. 'Took my part against the evils and injustices of the world we live in. When I was a younger man most actively. First out in the world, speaking at demonstrations against privilege and selfishness. Then, at last, I was elected to the Parliament. A radical member, though I dislike the word. I thought of myself as representing the values of common decency. We achieved some things, but not enough, not swiftly enough...'

The old man got to his feet and walked over to the window. He pulled the sash further down to quieten the rattling sound caused by the wind. For a moment he looked up at the rain that was sweeping across the downlands rising high above the house.

'My young William,' he said, turning to face Billy, 'favoured the church as a career. He was not much older than you at the time of his death. But even then he had spent several years helping the poor. Taking nourishment to them in their homes. Interceding on their behalf with the most villainous of landlords and masters. We still ran our manufacturing business in those days. It was what made my father his fortune. But my young William and I changed the way it was run. We made it fair for everyone involved. Oh, we were mocked, laughed at, told we would fail.' He slammed a fist on the window ledge. 'But we did not fail!'

He sat down again by the fire.

He smiled across at Billy for a moment, but then a great sadness crossed his face.

'During the troubles of the 'thirties, when the people revolted. It was a quiet Sunday morning. There were crowds in a town not far from here, returning from a meeting. I had spoken that day. So had others. The people were on their way home. It was all over. They were on their way home...but the magistrates had called out the yeomanry and instructed them to clear the streets. There was no need for that!'

Josiah seemed far away, as though he was back there.

'The people were going home, there was no need to use the yeomanry. They were mounted on horseback, blocking the street. My young William went across to them. Told them who he was. Asked them to stand aside to let the crowds through. They agreed. They said to him "go back and tell them to come along, we will not impede their progress." William walked back towards the crowd. But even before he was halfway back the yeomanry charged! They charged! Rode him down before he could even pass on their assurances. And then rode into the crowd, beating people down with their horses, cutting them with their sabres...'

The old man stopped as though he was having difficulty taking a breath. Billy stood and leaned against the fireplace, seeing in his own mind the horror of the event. It was a while before Josiah spoke again. And then...

'My young William had never been strong, you see. His mother died of a consumption. I fear that her weakness was in his blood. But even so he lingered for a week, despite the most appalling injuries. He never became conscious again. He died in a room in the local inn. The landlord was a friend of mine. William was too weak to move far, though I would like to have taken him home. He died and I believed that I had lost everything.'

Billy didn't know what to say. He knew grief himself and sometimes it was best to stay silent. The old man was silent again, but at last broke into a smile.

'And so you see,' he said, 'that is why I have brought you here. I have no family left. None at all. Your father was a brother to me. When we were young and foolish we fought with Wellington in Spain. A pointless war! But your father saved my life on two occasions. We didn't realise then the greater battles that needed to be fought at home.' He laughed. 'It was there that we met that rascal Feedle. Caught him looting! Should have been hanged really. That was Wellington's rule on looters. But we turned a blind eye.'

'Was Sticks in the war?' Billy asked.

'No, not Sticks, though he would have made a mighty warrior! He was too busy prize fighting, though he worked in the dockyard at the time. But he too saved my life. Fought off three footpads that accosted me on the Dover Road. He has worked with me ever since.'

'Worked?'

'Our fight for liberty goes on. We were there supporting "Captain Swing". And we took our part in the Chartist protests. We achieved very little, so that is why we decided to take more direct action. We are fighting that battle now. And with your father gone, well, we need you, Billy.'

'Me?'

'We knew you had left Norfolk, though we didn't know why. You were trailed to London. We have our spies everywhere. But they were not as efficient as we thought. They lost track of you on the streets of London. It took us quite a while to find you again.'

'I was trying not to be found.'

'And you succeeded magnificently! Your ability to blend in with the background could be of immeasurable help to our cause.'

His eyes met Billy's.

'Have the others told you about Monkshood?'

'Monkshood? It's a plant by the wayside. A poisonous plant.'

Josiah smiled and shook his head. 'No, not that Monkshood, though the other takes its name from the plant. Still, no matter. You will be told of that later.'

Billy felt confused. 'I still do not understand why you had me brought here? What can I do to help?'

'You share your father's views?'

'I do.'

'Then you can join us! We need someone young to carry on the fight.'

'But how?'

'With my son dead, I had intended to bequeath all I own to your father. Now that he is no more I intend to bequeath it all to you.'

'What?'

'I want to invite you to be my heir?'

'But all of this? I'm a thief from the Dials! I'm not a country gentleman!'

'And neither am I in any real sense of the word. This property, the monies I have left, the status. They are but a cover for our work. Your father would have understood. In order to remove the worst excesses of the society that rules and makes miserable so many lives...well...you need to burrow away from the inside to bring the whole rotting edifice crashing down. Your anonymity, your disguise, your way of getting in close comes from blending in with that background.'

The afternoon light was fading away, the room lit now only by the firelight.

'And there is another matter,' said Billy. 'The Bartram family and their friends are members of the society that you wish to bring down. Once they find out I am still alive, and it would soon be obvious if I do what you suggest, they would have me hanging from a tree as well. Either quietly by murder or through some trumped-up charge at the Bailey. And if not that then they would expose me and make impossible the campaigns you have in mind.'

Josiah nodded. 'We have considered that. My associates and myself. Our solution is simple. You stop being William Marshall. You take the name of my poor dead son. In order to continue with my work you become William Quest.'

~

Quest leaned forward in the library chair and threw another log on the fire, remembering the conversation of so many years before. The sunlight of the morning had faded away and dark autumnal clouds threatened rain. He looked up at the portrait of Josiah. Sometimes it felt as though the old man was still alive and walking around the house. He smiled up at the picture, remembering those last few years that they had spent together. There had been enjoyable times with the two of them and not just in the preparation of campaigns. William Quest felt fortunate. He had had two fathers and missed them both.

He heard the sounds of a carriage on the drive.

So here they were, those adored but pesky friends from London. Sticks certainly. Possibly Rosa. Certainly one or both of the Critzman brothers. Quest sighed. These days of rest were over. It was time to leave Hope Down and return to the city. Return to killing and vengeance.

There was a tap at the door and Mrs Vellaby entered.

'Is that Sticks, Mrs Vellaby?' he asked. 'And who else?'

She looked concerned.

'What is it, Mrs Vellaby?'

'A gentleman,' she said. 'From London.'

Before she could elaborate the stranger swept into the room. He was tall, with a thick mane of grey hair and greying moustache and side whiskers. He held a small hat in front of him.

'Mr Quest?'

'I am he,' Quest replied standing to greet the visitor.

'My apologies for arriving unannounced. I came down on the spur of the moment.'

'And on what business, sir?'

'My name is Inspector Anders. I am with the detective division of Scotland Yard. I very much wish to speak with you.'

NINETEEN

He was being followed.

There was no doubt about that.

The man was good, Raikes thought. One of the best for there were no obvious signs of him. But he was there, all right. Somewhere in the crowd, thought Raikes, who had been followed many times before in his profession. He had developed an instinct for being trailed. Hunted animals often do. It was pure instinct that warned him now.

He had tried all the standard tricks of his trade. Stopping suddenly. Seeming to be aware that he had taken the wrong direction and then swinging back along his own path. Watching reflections in the windows of the shops. Halting for longer periods while he fastened up his coat or searched his pockets. Pausing to take directions from a constable. Entering a tavern by one door and leaving by another. Plunging into a shop and examining its wares for many minutes.

Nothing.

And yet he knew the man was there.

He pulled into the shelter of a deep corner of wall half way along Threadneedle Street. He watched as black-coated gentlemen in great hats entered and left the Bank of England. And after a few moments the street seemed to quieten. The crowds departed with that sudden and apparent vanishing magic that often absorbs masses of people on the streets of London. Just a few now, strollers for the most part. A handful of junior clerks. A merchant in a carriage. But still no one who seemed to take an interest in him. Raikes looked up at the many windows of the great buildings. Nobody seemed to be looking out. He waited there for several minutes and no obvious candidate came into view.

He took out his hunter watch and flipped back the cover. Five o'clock. It was already starting to get dark as the autumn nights drew in. Darkness would provide a wonderful cover for his opponent. It was a risk Raikes was not prepared to take. He would abandon his meeting. He turned and walked back to Westminster.

~

Raikes was good, Wissilcraft conceded. A hard man to follow. Twice he had nearly caught him out in his long walk from Westminster to the City. Close by St Martin in the Fields the spymaster had turned, very suddenly. Only a stone pillar of the church had been enough to hide Wissilcraft's great bulk. Then, close by Somerset House, Raikes had come to a sudden halt and leaned against a wall for a number of minutes. Had Wissilcraft not hung back he would have been spotted.

Then there had been the greater problem of speed. Raikes was strong and fit. He could walk at a considerable velocity. Wissilcraft, as a much fatter man, had some difficulty in keeping up. That was why he had been so cautious in his trailing. Better to lose Raikes than be discovered. There was no feasible reason why Wissilcraft should be in London at all. Explanations, bogus excuses, simply had to be avoided.

And it all been for nothing. Raikes had been as spooked as a horse. He had abandoned his mission. Wissilcraft turned a corner in Threadneedle Street and watched as Raikes returned the way he had come. It happened like that sometimes. People being followed had a feeling that they were being trailed.

Wissilcraft followed at a great distance as Raikes returned to his rooms in Albany. A waste of time and energy. But still...

'Never mind,' Wissilcraft said aloud. 'I'll have you yet my lad!'

~

Sir Wren Angier was bored.

Not that there wasn't a lot to do. There was often too much. Sometimes he had to concentrate on business matters for several hours a week. But what to do now? He could journey over to a sitting in the Commons, but he could really see no need. There was not to be an election that year and, besides, his parliamentary seat was safe enough – it had been in his family for years, along with the baronetcy that gave him title.

His business affairs were in good order. Coming from a wealthy banking family there was always plenty of money. So much so that he lent a fair bit of it out to people who were in the way of small business, the tinier manufacturing enterprises, shopkeepers and even individuals struggling to stave off poverty. Helping to keep open the arteries of a trading nation. Most paid him back. Some who did not had to survive in the debtor's gaol until their families could come to some accommodation with him.

Not that imprisoning those who owed him money was Angier's first choice. No. It increased the difficulty of getting money back. As a first option he would always offer to increase the original loan at a much greater rate of interest, secured where possible on any property the defaulter might own. If this generosity was thrown back in his face he would send round his man Wicks and some decent fellows to give the debtor a hiding. Only if everything failed would he resort to the law.

His associates in Parliament thought him generous in his treatment of the poorer members of society. They always gave him a cheery greeting on the few occasions in the year when he might attend a debate. They feasted him, invited him back to their mansions for cards or to meet their daughters – for Wren Angier, not yet forty, and handsome in a slim, fair-haired way, was judged to be a catch. Not that the man himself was anxious to be rushed into marriage. He had such a pleasant time whoring in Mrs Bendig's night house, or tupping the wenches on his country estate.

A man really could not ask for more.

And yet...and yet...

When these pleasures were not occurring he was subject to great fits of *ennui*. As though there should be much more in his life. Not that he wasn't pleased with his achievements. He certainly was. He had accumulated much wealth beyond his inheritance and the country house and vast estate that came with it. He had as well a splendid property in Highgate, though he seldom spent a night there. It was too lonely and inconvenient. For social purposes he stayed most days in his set in Albany. There were bachelor friends there, men that he had been with at Eton and Cambridge. Not that he had much in common with them, but they could pass a merry hour. Be used to advantage. Keep him abreast of useful gossip.

Then there was the family bank, far away in the city. Wren Angier seldom travelled so far from Westminster. He had people there to do his bidding, that unctuous crowd who had so adored his father, another Sir Wren Angier. Those who had mourned the passing of the Old Man. Let them get on with it! It was not difficult to be a banker, after all. The lowliest clerk was competent enough. Angier read the accounts once a sennight, a boring duty. He was rarely dissatisfied with the profits. That was surely enough!

The money-lending business was run from a smaller office in Soho from which Angier's man Wicks operated. It was a convenient location. Wren Angier could call by making a small diversion on his regular nightly journeys to Leicester Square.

And he could do that now. It would pass an hour. Then on to Mrs Bendig's? Why not? That might be just the instantly disposable company he craved. Angier put on the jacket, cloak and tall hat he used for such excursions. He picked out an ebony walking cane with a silver rondel handle. Yes, that was the one to take in case there was any danger on the streets. He twisted the rondel to make quite sure the long blade came freely out from the stick. It did. And then he set out. It would all pass some time.

~

'So what is Monkshood?'

Billy and the Critzman brothers were on the way back to London. The carriage had rattled along the turnpike road at considerable speed for some miles from Hope Down. Now it had halted at a toll bar while the driver paid the toll fee to the keeper.

Isaac and Josef looked at each other in a thoughtful manner. Isaac smiled at the youth.

'Mr Quest has told that we may use our discretion in explaining certain matters to you. You know of the Monkshood plant?'

'I do,' Billy replied. 'I have oft seen them growing in Norfolk.'

'The Monkshood is a shy plant. Not so very common, I think. It has an attraction for the botanist. Aconitum Napellus. A shy plant but a deadly one. One of the more poisonous plants in the world. It is said that retreating armies would use it to poison wells to hinder pursuit. In Asia its juices were used to smear arrows to make death more certain. And there it sits in the countryside, quiet and deadly. And our Monkshood is something to akin to that. Just as quiet and deadly.'

'Monkshood became our symbol of covert rebellion,' Josef continued. 'After the risings of the past few years. Those who had struggled openly for justice were forced underground. Waiting for the next time. Just as secretive as the plant...and just as deadly.'

'So you are part of the Monkshood?' asked Billy.

'We are,' Joseph replied.

'And there are, of course, hundreds of others, scattered around the land,' said Isaac. 'Waiting and waiting, secretive and deadly. Seeming cowed and respectable. Obedient and honest men and women. But all the time fighting behind the scenes, fighting for justice in so many ways. Some openly, taking part in acts of revenge. Most quietly, passing on information, trailing our enemies to see where they go. They are there all the time. Mostly working people, the labourers on the land whose eyes are everywhere even as they poach or gather the harvest. The little tradesmen in a town, tailors and cobblers. The printers and small country lawyers. Ostlers and coachmen. Toll Bar keepers such as that man out there,' he waved a hand at the window of the carriage. 'And then there are thieves and sailors and brothel-keepers. There are many of all of these in the Monkshood. Most are lowly in the eyes of society. But there are gentlemen too. Brave individuals like Mr Josiah Quest. Country squires with a conscience. Even men in Parliament.'

'Waiting for the day when we can rise openly together,' Joseph added. 'It was members of the Monkshood who trailed you from Norfolk to London.'

Isaac laughed. 'And that is where you demonstrated your own talents. Not all the skilled members of the Monkshood could keep a watch on you in London. We lost you for three years. Three years! Three years when we might have given you aid and comfort. It was an appalling situation. We searched and searched, sometimes hearing rumours of a young boy thief who might be you. But every time we came close we lost you again.'

'And then we had better fortune,' said Joseph. 'You picked the pocket of a bookseller in Piccadilly. A good friend of ours. A member of the Monkshood. You thought he had not noticed. He did and followed you into the rookery. From that moment you were watched. Day and night. We were determined that you would not be lost again. Sticks was following you for some time before that incident at the docks.'

'And we had to be sure of you,' said Isaac. 'Certain that you had not become corrupted by the misery all around you. That you were still at heart the son of William Marshall. For we have a need of you. Someone to fight on behalf of the people. To become the secret leader of the Monkshood. To work covertly until we can rise again.'

'I am nothing special!' said Billy.

'You are the son of William Marshall. The heir to Captain Swing,' said Isaac. 'Who better?'

'You think I should do what Mr Quest desires?' asked Billy, after a moment.

'We do!' Joseph replied. 'It puts you in the best position to fight for justice. You have matters of vengeance yourself? They can be dealt with more expeditiously if you accept Mr Quest's offer.'

'But before we deal with that,' said Isaac, 'Mr Quest has set you a task. An undertaking that our friends in London will have to help you with.'

'And that is?'

'To transform you into a skilled criminal. To give you every talent that you will need to be the leader of the Monkshood.'

~

Wren Angier looked across the desk at Wicks.

'There seem to have been several defaulters this week?' he said, putting the account book down on the table. He looked up at his debt-collector, a bulky individual with cropped red hair and an even redder face.

Wicks grinned. 'Not as bad as it seems. Six in all. We've rolled over three debts. They will probably be good for the money at the end of it though they might struggle afterwards. One we've had to confine to the debtor's gaol, though I have a suspicion that the family will scramble around to get him freed.' The grin grew wider. 'We had to give the other two a warning in the old fashioned way.'

'I trust you did not go too far? Remember my instructions – a hiding. No more.'

Wicks gave a low bow, grinning across the room at his two henchmen. 'As if we would, sir. Just the usual mark of our calling. No more, nor less. Both gents'll have the money in the week.'

Angier nodded. 'Good. That is good. I shall call again in seven days to see how matters progress. My clerk will discuss with you the list of new customers in the meantime. These hard times seem very good for business. People always seem to want money...'

'The price they pay for living in a mercantile society, sir,' said Wicks.

TWENTY

A strange man, thought Anders, looking across the room at William Quest.

Something deep about him, a look more thoughtful than you usually get with these country landowners. Something profound and troubled. Approachable, in a way that few of the Class ever are. Personable, not handsome, but fair enough looking in a knocked about sort of way.

And the room itself.

A library, but not one of the great libraries that you see in many a country house. More homely than that. A place where a man might enjoy working. Books obviously read and held as objects of affection by their owner. And he a man of thought, a kindly look in the eyes. He looked up at the portrait on the wall. An old man with a genial expression.

Quest, he noted, held his head a trifle to one side, an expression of curiosity on his face, as he waited for the detective to speak. He looks a little concerned, thought Anders. But then many do when confronted by an officer of Scotland Yard.

Anders was used to grasping scenarios at an instant, summing up very quickly the people he met. Getting to grips with the moral state of those he interviewed. He could see that he might quite like this Mr William Quest.

'You must forgive me. I have been most remiss,' Quest said. 'You have journeyed a long way. May I offer you some refreshment?'

Anders shook his head.

'That is kind, but I dined at the posting inn in the village only a little while ago. An admirable host and a fine table.'

'Indeed! Then a glass of sherry, perhaps? Do take a seat...' Quest said waving a hand, before pouring the drinks.

'Ah, you are left handed?' Anders noticed. 'As I am myself.'

Quest presented the glass to the policeman with that hand, the right buried in a pocket.

'In point of fact,' he replied, 'I grew up knowing how to use both hands with equal efficiency. Useful at the moment, for I wounded my right on a blackthorn a day or two ago. I find the warmth of my pocket eases the pain.'

Anders sat in a chair to one side of the fireplace and rubbed his hands together. 'Your fire is appreciated on such a chill day.'

'I love the scent of burning logs,' said Quest, as he sat opposite the detective. 'It reminds me of youthful days in this library when my father was still alive.'

Anders looked up at the portrait of the old man.

'This gentleman...a portrait of Mr Josiah Quest?'

Quest nodded. 'Indeed. Painted only a few years before he died. This was his favourite room in the house. It pleases me that he still looks down upon it.'

'I can see that,' said Anders. 'He died a while ago?'

'Ten years.'

'Until I arrived in the village I was unclear whether or not Mr Josiah Quest still lived. Most of his contemporaries in Parliament are now gone. Those that survive were unclear as to whether or not he remained with us and not keen to talk of him.'

Quest smiled. 'My father valued his privacy. He was not in the best of health when he left London and the concerns of the world weighed heavily upon him. More sherry?' He reached across and refilled the detective's glass.

'Was it of my father you wished to inquire?' he asked.

'I had hoped that Mr Quest might still live. There are matters concerning his past that I wished to discuss. But the landlord at the inn told me that he was no more.'

Quest sipped his sherry and then said, 'If I may be of assistance?'

'Perhaps you might. Do you know of a family called Bartram? From Norfolk?'

'I am aware of them,' Quest replied. 'I have never had a social introduction to any gentry from that county. But I did read in *The Times* that two members of the family had met unfortunate ends. Would that be the matter you are investigating?'

'In part,' said Anders. 'Have you ever heard of a man called William Marshall?'

Anders noted the younger man's look of seriousness. Quest finished his sherry and looked back at him.

'Mr William Marshall was a very old friend and political acquaintance of my father. He disappeared with his three sons many years ago. It was a matter of great sadness for...' He looked up at the portrait. 'No trace of them was ever found.'

Anders was silent for a moment. And then: 'I regret to have to inform you that William Marshall and his sons were murdered.'

'Murdered...' said Quest very quietly.

'We have all the evidence that we need that they were killed by the Bartram brothers and various others many years ago. On the Bartram estate in Norfolk.'

'You say you have evidence?'

'The testimony of the Countess of Colbor, the mother of the Bartrams.'

Quest put down his glass on the little card table that was clearly never used for its original purpose.

'I understand, again from *The Times*, that Lady Colbor died a little while ago?'

'She gave her evidence to myself a while ago. Most valuable evidence. It has led us to discover where the bodies of William Marshall and his sons were to be found.'

Quest sank forward in his chair, a hand raised to his mouth. A moment or two passed before he spoke.

'You have found their bodies?'

'We have recovered their poor remains, buried in the field where they were murdered. There is to be a funeral on Friday week, paid for by public subscription. In the churchyard at Earlham, just outside the city of Norwich.'

'The poor, poor...I would gladly have paid for their proper burial for the sake of...my father. It was good of you to come personally, to inform me...'

Anders gave him a few moments before he spoke again. A log crackled and fell to the fore of the fireplace. Quest seemed oblivious to the danger so he reached down and, picking up the poker, pushed it back into the safety of the grate.

'It is not altogether the reason that I am here,' he said. 'Mr Marshall had three sons. We found but the bodies of two of them in the grave, alongside the remains of their father. The youngest boy, the younger William Marshall, was not in the grave.'

'Not in the grave...' Quest said in a distracted fashion.

'No, not there, not with the others. The Norfolk police have made many inquiries. He is not to be found.'

'Then he is buried elsewhere?'

'It is a possibility,' said Anders. 'He has certainly not be seen in Norfolk since the murder of his family. I wondered if it is just possible that young William Marshall sought sanctuary with his father's friends and comrades?'

'And that is why you have come here?'

'Precisely so. Not just here. I have sought several of the surviving acquaintances of the older Marshall. You are the last on my list.'

Quest looked down at the fire for a moment and then directly at Anders.

'Has the boy been seen anywhere since the murder of his family?'

'Apparently not,' replied Anders.

'Then is it not likely that he too was slain?'

The detective frowned. 'I suppose it is the most reasonable explanation. The Bartram estate is vast. We could not possibly search all of it.'

'Then the matter would seem to have to lie.'

Anders suddenly sat forward in his chair.

'I notice you have not inquired into the manner of the Marshalls' deaths?'

'Is it relevant?' Quest replied, without a pause. 'Is it not enough that the poor souls were foully murdered? The method seems to be irrelevant to the tragedy itself. I had assumed they were shot or beaten.'

'They were hanged.'

'Hanged?'

Anders noticed the look of shock on the other man's face.

'I believe the Americans have an expression. Lynched. Unlawfully hanged by a mob. It would seem that that is what happened to William Marshall and his two sons.'

'An act of barbarism!'

'Quite so,' Anders agreed. 'Are you often in London, Mr Quest?'

'I divide my time between there and here. Too much time there and not enough here.'

Anders smiled, looking around the room. 'Yes, I can see why you favour such a lovely home. And the countryside is a delight.'

'You are a countryman?'

'From Liddington in Wiltshire. The downland there is not unlike these hills about.'

'It is good country for tramping,' said Quest. 'And the air is much cleaner than the city.'

'Mr Henry Bartram was killed on a dark night in the city – tramping about.'

'So I understand from *The Times*. London can be a dangerous place at night. But was not his brother found dead on his country estate? As I recall the newspaper implied it was an accident.'

'It was no accident,' Anders said. 'He was murdered.'

'We live in dreadful times!'

'Indeed, we do. And that is why I have come to see you. I believe it possible that the Bartram brothers were murdered precisely because of their involvement in the deaths of William Marshall and his sons.'

Quest considered for a moment before he replied.

'But is it likely?' he asked. 'You say that the Norfolk murders took place many years ago. These deaths were recent. If some associate of William Marshall commissioned such a revenge then why wait? Would it not be more likely that the Bartram brothers would be struck down as soon as possible after the original killings?'

'That is indeed a puzzlement,' said Anders. 'And I have no answer to it, though William Marshall's associates may not have found out that they were dead until recently. But by each body was discovered a piece of cord tied like a hangman's noose. Given past events that would seem to be relevant.'

'It would seem so,' Quest agreed. 'But I do not know how I may help?'

'You have no memory of anyone coming here in your father's time? You do not recall your late father being in any way in communication with someone who might be the youngest son of William Marshall?'

Quest looked thoughtful before replying.

'I still think it most likely that young William Marshall died.' He said. 'I cannot suggest an explanation for these tokens left by the bodies of the Bartram brothers. It may be coincidence.'

'I do not deal in coincidences,' said Anders. 'Not as a rule. And there have been other killings...'

'Relevant to your enquiries?'

'In one case very relevant. We know, from the testimony of Lady Colbor, that the Bartrams' gamekeeper, a man called Walsham, took an active part in the slaying of William Marshall and his sons.'

'And you have him in custody?'

'Unfortunately not. He was killed only the other day. Found hanging from the same tree as the Marshalls.'

'A suicide?'

'I think not,' said Anders. 'A local detective and I caught a glimpse of his killer speeding away.'

Quest refilled the glasses with sherry.

'And you found one of these cords, one of these hangman's nooses nearby?' he asked.

'We did not.'

'Then surely the deaths may not be connected?'

'Another puzzlement, I confess. But I find it hard to accept that there is no connection between the killings of the masters and their man. I find it near impossible to accept that it is pure chance that Walsham was hanged from the same tree as William Marshall and his sons.'

'It is not unknown for gamekeepers to make enemies,' Quest commented. 'There was an affray not far from here a year or so ago, a keeper peppered by shot from a poacher's gun.'

'Maybe...but I suspect that the deaths of three participants in the Marshall killings, all within a few months of each other, is not coincidence.'

Quest reached forward and put some more logs on the fire. The dry wood crackled as it was surrounded by the flames. A window rattled in harmony with the conflagration as a chilly wind from the downs beat against the glass.

'You remarked earlier,' Quest said, 'that there were others present with the Bartrams and their keeper. On the occasion of the killing of William Marshall. Are you close to arresting them?'

Anders sighed. 'Not that simple, I'm afraid. The other participants in the killing were two brothers called Banningham. They drowned in a Norfolk water about a year later. The only other person we are seeking who was there is the Bartram family lawyer. Lady Colbor omitted to name him, though a detective of the Norfolk Constabulary is searching through the family papers seeking his identification. Should we find him alive we will put him on trial, though it will be near impossible to prove that he was ever at the scene.'

'I wish I could be of greater assistance,' said Quest. 'The whole business is such a sad tragedy.'

'Perhaps I might take your address in London, Mr Quest? It would be useful for me to talk to you again should I have any further thoughts.'

~

As the carriage pulled away from the house, Anders made notes in his little book of the conversation with Mr William Quest. Not an easy task for the roads were not surfaced too well and the horses seemed to stop and start, possibly alarmed at the crack of the wind through the trees. The task completed he lay back in the seat and closed his eyes to review the meeting. A pleasant man, Mr Quest. So much friendlier than most of the gentry he encountered. Treated him as an equal, which few of the Class ever did. Glancing at the notebook he went back through the conversation line by line, realising that he had been very open with Mr Quest, revealing matters that he would not ordinarily have done in a police interview. It had been like comparing notes with another officer of the law. A strange lapse! Anders felt as if he had known Mr William Quest for years rather than an hour. He rather hoped that he might taste of his sherry once again.

TWENTY-ONE

'You cannot be there,' said Isaac. 'It is quite impossible that you should go to the funeral.'

Quest, Sticks, Rosa and the two Critzman brothers sat in the library. The others had arrived barely an hour after the policeman had left. There was a chill in the atmosphere that had nothing to do with the cold autumn day.

Quest stood by the window looking out at the blustery weather.

'It is the funeral of my father and my brothers,' he turned to face them. 'I intend to be there!'

'You'll be putting your neck in the noose,' Rosa said, sitting back in the fireside chair and finishing the last of the sherry. 'You have already had a Scotland Yard detective here asking questions. How close to the wind do you intend to sail?'

'Exactly so!' said Quest. 'He has been here. We have met. He has no idea that I am William Marshall by birth. He is convinced that I am who I say I am. Where is the danger? Certainly not from Anders.'

Josef sat at the table, placing cards in a game of patience, with a look of worry more than usually grave. He looked up.

'With the greatest of respect, William. It is not the detective that is the problem. It is your face. This will be a very public funeral. You say it has been subscribed for by well-wishers, many of whom would have known your father. Many of whom would remember you.'

'I was a boy when last I lived in Norwich,' Quest protested. 'I wandered the streets just days ago. I was not recognised.'

'Yes, but this will be the funeral of William Marshall. His memory will be on people's minds. You have a resemblance to your father. And you have not changed that much in appearance since your youth. You *will* be recognised.'

Quest was silent for a moment. He pictured the scene Josef had described, seeing in his mind the churchyard at Earlham. Wondering how it might be done, attendance at this funeral. He looked up at Sticks who was standing in the corner of the room. The prize fighter had said nothing.

'And what of you, Sticks? Are you going to reproach me with the prospect of heads in nooses?'

Sticks shook his head for several seconds before speaking.

'Can't say as how I would. I been reading the Bible a good deal of late. And what it says in there is about honouring thy father and thy mother. And I only knows that if it were my father I *would* be there, danger or no.' He frowned. 'He was hanged for killing a man in a brawl when he was digging the canal Leicester way. Then they put him up on the gibbet in Saffron Lane. It was seven months afore I was able to cut him down. Then I had to bury him on a bit of no man's land at the wayside. Buried him with my bare hands I did, what bits of him the crows had spared.'

'You think I should go?'

'I'd think the less of you if you didn't.'

Rosa slammed down her glass.

'You are a pair of impossible dreamers!' she said. 'This is no game!' She looked at Quest. 'They hanged your father and brothers. If you go to this ceremony there is a good chance they will seize and hang you.'

'And we do have business in London,' Isaac cut in. 'The matter of Wren Angier.'

'We have ten days,' Quest said. 'I can easily deal with the moneylender in that time. I will return to London on the morrow. And I will account for Angier, since you seem to consider that matter more important than anything I care about...'

'That is not fair, William,' said Josef. 'Our only concern is your safety...'

'I have taken risks before. A great many risks and on your behalf. Going back to Norwich is just such a risk, but it is one I fully intend to take.'

Josef sighed and put another card down on the table.

'Well,' he said, 'if you are set on this course let us make it at best a calculated risk rather than plain suicide. Let us work together to consider how it might be accomplished. Without putting any of our necks in a noose.'

~

'And have you enjoyed your travels?'

Josiah Quest and William strolled very slowly across the lawn at Hope Down, making their way to the doors leading into the library.

'I found Europe entrancing,' said William, 'particularly Germany. I spent a happy few months in Heidelberg. Swimming in the Neckar and fighting Mensur duels.'

'I am pleased that you came away without a facial scar. They were perhaps gentle with you?'

'Perhaps they were. They said I was scarred enough,' William replied, rubbing the vivid marks on his right hand.'

'Does that trouble you much?' Josiah asked.

'Not so much now. An occasional twinge on a cold day. All of those pickpocketing adventures in London exercised it well. But for those exercises, well, who knows?'

'And your languages?'

'I manage French very well. German a trifle better.'

'They may be of use one day.'

They walked into the library and Josiah sat in his favourite chair by the fire. His face was pale and William noticed how quick and shallow was his breathing.

'William...' Josiah began. 'Do you think I have done right by you?'

'Don't ever doubt it. I have had a wonderful life, both here and in my education.'

'I would have liked to have sent you to my old college in Oxford.'

'Edinburgh suited me very well. Few inquiries were made into my background. Oxford might have been more difficult. And I might well have known many of the folk we now have to deal with.'

'Ah!' Josiah smiled, a tad wearily, William thought. 'You are still set on that course?'

'Do you not wish me to be?'

'I do...I do. For the sake of the poor I do. But I wonder if it is fair to you?'

'Fair?'

'You could have a happy life without any of it. Here at Hope Down and in London. You have accomplishments and money. You could live the life of a country gentleman and put away all thoughts of the past - and the future we intended.'

William leant against the mantelpiece and was silent for a moment or two.

'I could indeed,' he said at last. 'But it would be a terrible betrayal. I have seen much on my travels, in this country and in Europe. Much cruelty. Much injustice. Much absolute unfairness. I cannot stand by and watch these things happen anymore. It is true I could be a country gentleman, but if that is all I became I would be simply a part of all that is wrong with the world.'

Josiah looked up at him.

'It is the answer I hoped for, though I accept it with many misgivings. Please reach behind you and take up that walking stick.'

He waved a hand at a slim cane of dark brown wood that leaned against a chair.

'It is beautiful,' said William. 'I do not recall seeing it before.'

'Josef made it only a week or two ago. One of the first results of his new commercial enterprise in Cheapside. I had it made for you. I know you have a fondness for walking canes.'

William ran a finger along the smooth wood and then balanced the cane across his palm.

'Josef is a true craftsman,' he said.

Josiah nodded in agreement.

'Now twist the top of the handle,' he instructed.

William gave the handle of the cane a gentle turn and it came loose. He eased it away from the rest of the stick and a long, thin and deadly blade came away.

'A very fine sword stick,' William said. 'Tough but flexible. One could do a deal of harm with it.'

'It is my gift to you,' said Josiah. 'Though there will be others, that is the first. Get used to it. May it be your companion on many travels and adventures.'

'I will use it wisely...'

'Do that! Use it wisely. It is easy to take a life. Impossible to restore a man once he is gone.'

'Indeed!'

'Never take the blade out without honour, never put it back until justice has been done.'

'I shall remember your words,' said Quest.

~

'I may go back to the stage,' Rosa said, turning over in bed. 'Mr Jolys has sent me a note to say that he is reviving *The Beggar's Opera*, possibly at the Lyceum.'

Quest lay back and stared at the ceiling.

'You will make a most admirable Captain Macheath,' he said after a moment's thought. 'With your experience of dressing up as men and being a footpad.'

She thumped him on the arm.

'I am to play Polly Peachum, of course. My greatest triumph of past days.'

'Are you not a trifle old for that role?'

She thumped him harder.

'You give me several years, Quest. And you look much older than all the total of those years.'

He turned to look at her.

'And you,' he riposted. 'You are beautifully raddled!'

She turned her face to the ceiling as though she had not heard.

'At the Lyceum I shall find an audience that really appreciates me. Flowers upon the stage and courting johnnies at the door. I may well end up a duchess. Several of my friends have.'

'You may well,' Quest replied. 'I haven't met a duke yet with good eyesight.'

She scowled.

'It is a good job that I can never love you, Quest.'

'Then, pray, what are we doing in bed?'

'Passing the time. Simply passing the time...'

'And if your endeavours on the stage are a success...would we still pass the time?'

She gave a wan smile.

'I don't know. I really don't. It would be difficult with all the eyes of London upon me.'

'I suppose so.'

'That does not mean there is any hurry in all of this,' she added. 'Mr Jolys will not stage his production until after Christmas. There will be a great deal of time to accomplish any outstanding matters.'

'Sir Wren Angier?' said Quest.

'Not just him,' she said. 'That other matter as well. About which I have some ideas.'

She sat up and rested against the headboard.

'Another triumph on the stage of life?' he asked.

'Exactly!' she replied. 'I have a performance planned that will be beyond parallel.'

Raikes seemed uneasy, Anders thought, when he arrived to deliver his report. The Spymaster leaned forwards and backwards in his chair, occasionally stood up and paced to the window and back. Once or twice he leaned against the wall in the corner of the room, a hand tapping the wall. *You'd think the man's got St. Vitus's Dance*, Anders's old aunt would have said had she seen him. She had been a great believer in the idea that people should sit still in conversation with others. She had liked her house and the people in it kept tidy.

After Anders had finished his report, the Spymaster sat down in the chair, those menacing eyes glaring up at the detective, who had been made to stand throughout.

He began, 'I believe I did state that I wanted a report on a daily basis...'

'Not always possible,' Anders replied. 'I have been away a good bit of the time. In Norfolk and at Hope Down. This is not an investigation that can be carried out just in London.'

'And you are firm in your belief that the Bartram brothers were murdered by this same individual?'

'Undoubtedly.'

'The killing of the gamekeeper, Walsham?'

'By all accounts it should be at the hands of the same assassin.'

'*By all accounts?* You have doubts?'

'I do,' said Anders. 'I think there is a...faint possibility that the keeper was killed by someone else. Someone who wanted to silence him.'

'And you say you saw this other man?'

'I saw a man on a horse. In the distance. A man dressed in black. He galloped away before we could get near.'

'But is it not more than likely that it is the killer of the Bartrams? You say there was no corded noose? I would suggest he was aware of your presence and made good his escape before he could drop such a token?'

Anders nodded.

'There is that possibility,' he said. 'It's just an instinct that tells me different.'

'I think, certainly for the moment, that we should assume that we have but one murderer.'

'I agree,' said Anders, 'but I don't think we should entirely rule out other possibilities.'

'And you believe to a certainty that the killer is the son of the renegade, William Marshall?'

'I do.'

Raikes looked down at one of the few notes he had scribbled as Anders gave his report.

'And this William Quest? You believe him to be telling the truth? That he has no idea where the younger Marshall may be found? I say this because his father, Josiah Quest, was a radical and a traitor to his class. A man who should have been impeached, and would have been had I held my high office in those days.'

'Quest seems to be quite content with the life of a country gentleman.'

'Nevertheless, perhaps he should be watched for a while to make absolutely sure that Marshall makes no contact with him.'

Anders frowned.

'I am not sure that Scotland Yard has enough people available for such an enterprise. The detective division is rather small and always busy.'

'Never mind,' said Raikes. 'I will see to that...'

'Quest might be at the funeral of the Marshall family, if that is a help?'

'And it is quite possible that he will meet this William Marshall there. We must bear that in mind.' He opened his little silver snuff box, decorated with Greek gods and took a pinch. He breathed in deeply and then turned those penetrating eyes once more upon Anders.

'Do you believe Lady Colbor's account of the killing of Marshall and his sons?' he asked.

'I do.' Anders answered.

Raikes breathed in deeply once more, his face turning a trifle red, as the effects of the powerful snuff spread into his lungs

'I understand that she had become half-witted in old age?' he asked as he recovered his breath.

'She had moments of great clarity. I have no doubt of her version of events.'

'I see,' said Raikes. 'Well, the Bartram brothers are dead! No loss to the world. But what of the others who were present. You tell me that two are drowned? Yes! And then there is the family lawyer. What do you know of him?'

'The worst of all of them, according to Lady Colbor's account. A monster who beat down his riding crop on the hand of the Marshall boy before the lad escaped.'

'But who is he?'

'Either Lady Colbor could not remember or she would not say,' said Anders. 'But he will not be difficult to track down?'

'How so?'

'It is the lot of the great estates that they generate a great many papers and documents, legal and otherwise. Inspector Gurney of the Norfolk detective force is sifting through all of the documents relating to the Bartram estate. If this man really was the lawyer for the family then it will not take very long before we can identify him.'

Raikes gave a slight nod of his head.

'Then that would seem to be settled,' he said. 'You may go now. Send me a written report on any development that occurs. And send in my clerk as you leave.'

He took another pinch of snuff as Anders left the room. A moment later a nervous Barker tapped on the door and entered.

'Barker, where is Wissilcraft?'

The little clerk looked pained.

'No idea, sir.' He muttered in a nervous voice. 'He came to the office yesterday and implied he was on the track of a man pertinent to his enquiries. Would you care for me to seek him out, sir?'

Raikes held up the little snuff box, looking for a moment at the dancing Greek gods. Barker watched anxiously, trying to anticipate what nightmare might come next. He was relieved when all that Raikes said was: 'No. It doesn't matter now!'

~

Anders was troubled as he walked across Whitehall in the pouring rain.

There was something playing in his mind, a memory lost that needed to be recovered. He could not think what it was. Something he had thought at the time. One of those brief points that come up in a conversation that you mean to note, but which is put out of your mind by the next words spoken. It had almost dashed into the forefront of his brain whilst he was listening to Raikes. Then the fugitive memory had run off again. Something William Quest had said. But what in hell was it?

259

~

Four men sat around the table in the room at the rear of Josef Critzman's walking stick shop in Cheapside, drinking tea and eating muffins.

'And what do you know about where that odious man Wicks will strike again, Jasper?' asked Isaac. 'Will we have time to deal with him and Angier before our excursion to Norfolk?'

Jasper Feedle leaned forward and noisily slurped some tea before replying.

'Oh, plenty of time. He's to call on a house in Soho to teach someone a lesson. An old widder woman and her cripple son. In three nights time he'll be there for the money. She's bin warned to have it ready. She can't oblige. It's likely, from 'is threats, that he'll take desperate measures.'

'The widow and her son? They are in danger?' asked Josef.

'Indeed!' Jasper replied, 'I've known Wicks and 'is scum followers for many a year. They've maimed and killed afore now, though I doubt Angier realises it. On their last visit, the widow, Mrs Jenks, wouldn't open the door. She throws a bowl of water over 'em from an upstairs window. A surprise that Wicks didn't settle the matter there and then. He'll come for the money. I suspicion that he'll settle 'em both, whether he gets it or no.'

'In that case we must put someone inside her house, in case all else fails...' said Josef.

Sticks smiled. 'And that'll be me,' he said. 'And how I'll cherish the prospect of dealing out these villains. You'll join me, Jasper?'

'I will,' said the old screever. 'A rare pleasure it'll be.'

'And William outside?' said Isaac. 'But not alone! There will be Wicks and two others? Yes, two others, that is usually the way of it. I will take a good stout stick and be there in support of William. Not that he is likely to need me.'

'Then that is settled' Josef said. 'And after Wicks has been dealt with we can send William round to account for Mr Wren Angier.'

'Agreed,' said Isaac, 'I will meet William and discuss it further with him. Which brings us to the other outstanding matter. The adventure in Norfolk. You have heard my brother's plan, worked out in consultation with Miss Rosa? What do you all think?'

~

Few passers-by spared a glance at the lawyer's clerk - for the few that did assumed that that was what he was – who walked hesitatingly down through the Temple Gardens. He was a young man of moderate height, with ginger hair and an equally red face, partially hidden by a pair of spectacles. He was dressed in a suit of clothes long past the best and carried a bundle of documents of what looked like a legal nature underneath one arm.

The ginger-haired clerk had spent the whole morning wandering through the Inns of Court, talking to other clerks, and lawyers in worn-down wigs. Holding long conversations on a legal matter, only slipping in a question here and an inquiry there, as though the information he sought was not terribly important. The disconsolate expression on his reddened face suggested that he had received little in the way of helpful answers.

Afterwards the clerk walked down the banks of the Thames for a couple of miles, halting and then starting again, backtracking up alleys and streets, until he reached a tavern of doubtful reputation that seemed to cling desperately to the river bank, many of its rooms and balconies jutting out in perilous fashion over the water. In a small back room, with a sloping wooden floor, its underside brushed by the high tidal current, he met a one-legged old man in the battered green jacket of the Rifles.

'I believe I am being followed, Jasper,' said the ginger-headed clerk. 'And someone good at the task too.'

'Yer tried to catch 'im out?'

'A number of times,' Quest replied. 'I see nothing of him but I know that he is there. He has trailed me all the way from the Inner Temple to here. I doubt he's in the tavern. He's too good for that. But he is not far away.'

'There's that detective?' Jasper suggested. 'He's good at such work.'

Quest considered for a moment.

'It could be him,' he said at last. 'But my instincts tell me not.'

'The man yer seekin'?'

'I think that if it were the man I am seeking I would be dead. I gave him every opportunity to take a shot at me or plunge a dagger into my back. My follower is curious and not malignant.'

'These travels round the courts and cupboards of the law. Did yer find the lawyer yer seek?'

Quest looked out of the tiny window and regarded the swirling waters of the Thames. The river seemed to widen very dramatically at this point as it swept down towards its estuary. It had become rougher and choppier than the waters that flounced through the heart of the city. Like a wild animal desperate to rush away from captivity. He watched for a moment as a sailing barge struggled downstream against the tide, seeking the downward tow of the mighty river to aid it against the wall of water coming up from the sea. Waves battered both its bow and stern as though two aggressive and competitive forces were arguing over a possible spoil. The river's edge spattered against the wooden floor of the tavern room.

'He is not there,' Quest said at last. 'He no longer follows the law, though he is in London still. And there was something more. On one or two faces I saw fear. Concern at the mention of his name. Some of the men I talked with were friendly and helpful at first. But when I told them who I sought they were silent. They would be drawn no further.'

'Perhaps they thought it weren't the business of a lawyer's clerk?'

'My argument was that I had documents pertaining to an estate in the country. That there was a disputed ownership thanks to a badly-drawn will. A matter with which he had dealt at some time in the past. And that I was a clerk to a country lawyer in Shropshire, sent up to town to seek his opinion on the matter.'

'Meat and drink to the legality I'd 'ave thought!' said Jasper.

'So, indeed would I,' said Quest. 'And I have a suspicion that had I made enquiry as to the whereabouts of any other lawyer they would have been beyond helpful. But *this* man...this man I seek...he is somebody extraordinary, someone that even the lawyers of London fear.'

'And since making this inquisition yer feel yer've bin followed?'

'Sure of it, Jasper. Not at first, but late in the day. As though my inquiries had triggered a warning to someone. I was sure of it when I left the Inner Temple. Certain as I walked down through the Temple Gardens. And all the way here...'

'Well, we must be sure beyond doubt,' said the screever. 'When yer leaves 'ere take an open road to the city, just a stoop and a jag now and then to show 'im yer're wary. An' I'll follow 'im what follows yer. We'll try and flush 'im like a rat from a sewer!'

~

It had been a quiet funeral, the day they buried Josiah Quest in the cemetery at Kensal Green. A peaceful spring day under a pale blue sky. The green bank leading up to the bench on which the old man had been wont to sit was yellow with daffodils. William Quest stood between the Critzman brothers as he threw a handful of earth down upon the coffin. Jasper Feedle and Sticks stood on the opposite side of the grave, both tearful as the earth hit the wood.

'We shall not see his like again,' said Josef. 'He would have liked that old Blackthorn.' He nodded at the spreading tree a few yards away.

'He would!' said Sticks. 'He loved nature – a true gent in every sense of the word.'

'Rest in peace, old comrade!' said Jasper. 'I hopes yer find a better world...'

'A better world than this,' said Isaac. 'That is for certain sure...'

They all saw William Quest's lips mouth some words but none of them could be quite sure what he said. After a few more moments he turned to face the next grave, with its inscription on the stone slab commemorating another William Quest. The dead youth's successor knelt down, resting his hand on the cold stone. He read the words once more.

The grave of William Quest.

A William Quest who had found peace.

What was there more in life than that?

TWENTY-TWO

'Our friend's good,' said Jasper. 'Far the best tail I've ever seen. Better'n me! Prob'ly better'n yerself. Not even yer own shadow could follow as well. He was on yer the moment yer left the tavern.'

'Tell me what you saw?' said Quest.

'Well, that's the genius of the feller,' said Jasper. 'Yer don't see 'im. Yer senses 'im. Like when yer knows a rat's in yer room. Just scratchin'. Just hustled movements. But yer don't know for sure 'til yer wakes in the night and there he is on yer belly.'

'But did you see him?'

Jasper shook his head.

'A man in the distance,' he said

'Then how can you be sure?' Quest demanded.

'I'm sure! The way yer was sure yerself. These are crowded streets, hard to pick one man out of the many. In quiet alleys yer can hear the steps of 'is feet – but only just. When yer walked by the great walls of the Tower there was a bit of a shadow too many. Then in Eastcheap I gets a glimpse of someone in the distance, a man with a purpose, unlike all the other drunks an' idlers. An' when yer swung over London Bridge, I was sure that nobody followed yer. But then yer comes back again just as he knows yer would. An' he picks yer up again. Like he can read yer mind. For that's how he does it!'

Quest looked around the crowded tap-room of the Dog and Duck. The only faces he saw were familiar to him, apart from a collection of drunken builders working on the new museum. But they all seemed to know each other.

'He could be waiting for us outside,' said Quest.

Jasper nodded.

'That he could,' he said, 'and on me mother's grave I swears he will be. What we goin' to do? It ain't safe to be in London with a man as good as that on our tails?'

Quest caught the eye of the landlord and raised his eyes upwards. The host gave a slight nod.

'As you know I have a lurk upstairs,' Quest said. 'I keep some of my clothes there for emergencies like this. Time to lose the lawyer's clerk! I have something that approximates to what those builders are wearing. They are getting very drunk and he may not notice if I leave with them. As for you, Jasper, well, you have a good sleep by the fire and leave in the morning. He may not have the patience to stay outside all night.'

'An' that's a triumph of hope over expectations,' Jasper replied.

~

Palmerston looked up at Wissilcraft, a look of distaste on his face.

'This is a pretty thing!' he said, 'A pretty thing indeed!'

'I am in no doubt,' Wissilcraft answered. 'I have been making inquiries into several individuals who have had contact with Raikes in the past months. You would know of the Russian, Serov?'

'Who wouldn't? He is everywhere in society. He dined with the Prime Minister only an evening or two ago. A great fat man!' He looked up at Wissilcraft's bulk, gave a slight cough and hurried on. 'Well, anyway, he dyes his moustache. He is the personal assistant of their Ambassador. Something of a poet and scholar, I believe. Fancies himself as another Pushkin. He's translated Lermontov into English. Everywhere he preaches literature. Most of which I've never read, thank God!'

'And everywhere, away from his friends in higher circles, he preaches sedition!'

'Then we must request that he leaves the country!' Palmerston thundered.

'Not just yet, I think. That would alert Raikes to the fact that we suspect him. Better that we deal with our own traitor first. My own informants suggest that Raikes is proposing to escape England.'

'Then let us place him under arrest,' said Palmerston. 'A custody, a trial, an execution for treason. What could be neater?'

'It may come to that...' Wissilcraft began.

'What else?'

'Jacob Raikes is Her Majesty's Spymaster. And he hasn't spent the past few years just spying on our enemies. By all accounts he has a wonderful catalogue of indiscretions against many a well-placed Englishmen. Even, I might add, amongst the highest in the land.'

'Bad?'

'Governments and dynasties have been brought down with less. I know this for I am aware of many of these indiscretions myself.'

Palmerston slumped forward and held his head in his hands. After a moment he sat back in his chair and looked up at Wissilcraft, his face ashen.

'Then what are we to do?' he asked.

'Better, I think, that Raikes never comes to trial.'

'I see,' said Palmerston. 'You would do it yourself?'

'I think not,' said Wissilcraft. 'But I have a man in mind. Someone who could make the death of Raikes look...neater in the public eye. I will need some authority from you. Power to act. Power to employ. Power to...perhaps...pardon?'

'Who is this assassin?'

'I am not sure, though I have a strong suspicion. A man I have been watching. I will know, I think, within hours. Whether the man will agree to work for me, well!'

'Then compel him!' Palmerston slammed his fist down on the table. 'Whatever it takes.' He added, 'Obviously within reason.'

'Then I have your authority to act?'

'I have discussed this matter at length with the Prime Minister. Lord Aberdeen is of the opinion that you be given full authority. We are determined that you should be Her Majesty's next spymaster. In fact, in everything but the word you already are.'

'That is very gracious,' Wissilcraft gave a slight bow.

'But depending,' Palmerston continued, 'on how successfully you deliver Raikes's head on a platter!'

~

'You had an adventure then, Berry?'

It was near midnight and the gaslight burned late in Anders's office at Scotland Yard.

'Been a bit in the wars, sir.'

Anders looked across the table at his sergeant.

'In truth you were damn lucky. I know that eye-patched villain well, though I've never managed to bring him to heel. There's a Newgate Knot waiting for his throat the moment we lay him down.'

Berry frowned. 'I suppose I should have gone back for him while he was still lying in that alley?'

'You were shaken up and outnumbered, so how could you? And the chances are they would have fled by the time you found the beat constable. Anyway, we can leave Eye Patch and his felons for another day. I have a greater interest in the good Samaritan who came to your assistance. This "Policeman's Rattle"?'

Berry nodded, breathing deeply for a moment.

'No doubt in my mind, sir, but that he saved my life. If he hadn't come along that instant moment they'd have topped me for sure.'

'The Policeman's Rattle? You are sure that's what he said?'

'Absolutely,' Berry replied. 'At first I thought it a joke, for I was rattled myself. But then I remembered what happened to the odious Constable Johnson. And the way the stranger dealt with those three men, well...'

'It could be our man, no doubt about that. What do you remember of him?'

Berry thought for a moment.

'Not much,' he said. 'I was dazed from their blows, my eyes watering. All I can say for sure is that he spoke like a toff and was dressed like one.'

'And his weapons?'

'A life preserver and a thick wooden walking stick. And my he knew how to use them. He could as easily dealt with six of 'em.'

'And you noticed nothing more?'

'We were scarce out on the street before he was gone. Like a wisp of fog blown away by a river breeze.'

'Nothing more?'

'Only the scars I told you of. On the back of his right hand. A cruel injury at some time, though it didn't hinder him in the struggle.'

'Well, that is something he can't hide,' Anders said, 'unless he wears gloves.'

'We still can't be sure it's our man!'

'I'll put a year's wages on it! Do you recall what Lady Colbor said? How the Bartrams' lawyer broke the Marshall boy's hand with a riding crop? What could leave more scars than that?'

Berry poked the coals on the fire back into life as he considered the matter. A cold rain had started outside, its sleety drops falling slowly down the window panes, lit by the gas lights out in Whitehall.

'But we still have a mountain the size of Kinder Scout to go before we can lay him by the heels,' he said.

'I still believe he'll be at William Marshall's funeral,' said Anders.

'He'll be taking quite a chance, sir!' Berry replied. 'Half the people there'll recognise him.'

Anders smiled.

'We must make sure that we do. And...'

He was interrupted by a constable who dashed in without knocking.

'Yes?' Anders growled.

'Beg pardon, sir. Commissioner says you've to go to Daws Alley in Soho. There's been three killings in the street there. Two of 'em with a sword stick, the third's got 'is head bashed in!'

~

On a winter evening, several months after Josiah Quest's funeral, three men sat around the library table at Hope Down. Outside the first snows of the winter swept across downs that were fast disappearing from view as night fell. They had moved the table nearer to the great log fire, so harsh was the cold that permeated the room from outside.

'This will be a hard winter,' said Josef Critzman. 'For the wind comes from the east. From Russia, where they have the deepest winters of all. I remember well how those winds filled with snow buried the fields in Poland, driving the wild creatures deep into the forests. I have fought my way across the Russian steppes in just such weather. No man or woman should be out in such snows.'

His brother nodded in agreement.

'I journeyed to Moscow once. The earth was froze hard as iron. So hard that it hurt to walk upon it. And then came the snows, sweeping across those Russian plains with little to impede their progress. Deep and with a coldness beyond imagination.'

'Mrs Vellaby says she can feel a bad winter coming in her bones,' said William Quest. 'She says this will be a hard one, though there seems to have been a number of such winters since I first came to Hope Down. We must get in more logs.'

'She told me yesterday of how the Thames froze in 'fourteen. When she was young. And how a great fair was held on the ice,' said Josef. 'In Poland it was not unusual for the rivers to freeze, though the snows of my youth were so deep you could never see the courses where the rivers ran. Only the tops of the trees along the banks coming out of a great blanket of white.'

'God help the poor!' said Isaac. 'How many will freeze to death this winter?'

Josef shook his head.

'Too many! That is why we must begin our charitable works,' he said, reaching out to some documents on the table. 'Here are the papers initiating officially our "Metropolitan Society For The Alleviation Of Pauperism". As you will see it is nominally funded by the businesses Isaac and I have founded since we came to England. Though much of Josiah's legacy will go to its work. We shall, of course, request public donations.'

'And the rest,' said Isaac, 'will arrive in its coffers unofficially from the depredations on the rich undertaken by the Fellowship of the Monkshood.'

'All of this thieving, these burglaries, highway robberies, pressured requests for donations. Do we rob everyone who has money?' asked Quest.

Isaac smiled, 'Monkshood has a policy of only robbing those who can bear it. And only those who persecute the poor at that.'

'Positively Robin Hood,' said Quest.

'Something of an inspiration!' said Isaac.

Quest poured them all another glass of sherry.

'While others freeze we are here in the warm,' he said. 'It seems unfair.'

Josef shook his head.

'It would be a pointless gesture, though I admire your suggestion of solidarity. You have other work to do, William. And it is time to begin.'

'Then who am I to deal with first?'

Isaac laughed, 'Not just yet. Perhaps not for a year or more.'

'A year!'

'First you must return to London, at least for some of the time. Back to the rookeries. To St. Giles and Whitechapel and Seven Dials. There to resurrect the boy Billy who left them all those years ago. You must find lurks to hide in, all over London. Gain a reputation as both a flash villain and a harder footpad. Live once more amongst the people you seek to help. Refine those criminal skills you have learned under those disreputable tutors Feedle and Sticks.'

'And you must meet and work with other members of the Monkshood,' Josef added. 'There are others who must instruct you yet. Other talents to acquire. Friends that you must know of. These matters cannot be rushed.' He dug in his pocket. 'Now take this...'

He put a pendant on the table, a small oval disc bearing an engraving of the monkshood plant.

'Keep that around your neck,' said Isaac, 'for it is the symbol of the Fellowship. If you need assistance bring it out where it might be seen, for it is possible that it might be recognised and summon someone to your aid. Watch for others wearing such a pendant. They may need your help.'

Quest fingered the disc for a moment.

'When should I return to London?' he asked.

'Enjoy a Christmas at Hope Down,' said Isaac. 'We know how much it means to you to be here. We'll come and make merriment with you! And bring Feedle and Sticks with us to feed on Mrs Vellaby's good cooking. And then, after that...well, to work!'

TWENTY-THREE

Raikes looked across the table at the Russian. They sat in a private box in a tavern on a street corner hard by Clerkenwell Green.

The fat man fingered his ludicrous dyed moustache and beamed back at him.

'A dilemma indeed,' he said, 'but I am not sure what you want me to do about it?'

'I think the time is approaching when I should leave England for good,' said Raikes. 'I have taken a great many risks for Russia...'

Serov laughed. 'You mean you have taken a great many risks for Russian gold, surely?'

'Even so. The results of my labours have benefitted the Tsar in very many ways, particularly in your present disputes with the Turks. It is possible that our two countries will be at war within months. You will benefit even more from my information once that happens.'

Serov nodded.

'That is possible,' he agreed, 'but before we can accommodate your desire to leave England we will need a little more than the trifles you have provided.'

'Trifles! I have taken a great many risks...'

The Russian silenced him by holding the palm of his hand close to Raikes' face. He smiled at the Spymaster.

'Do not misunderstand me, my friend,' he said. 'Our gratitude knows no bounds. And I feel sure that we may further reward our friendship towards you. What exactly did you have in mind?'

'Twenty thousand sovereigns. '

Serov laughed.

'You intrigue me...'

'And a safe passage by boat out of England. Not from London Port, but from an isolated stretch of coastline. Within the week.'

'To where?'

'Anywhere,' Raikes replied. 'Anywhere away from England. St Petersburg might do, though I would prefer a landing elsewhere in the Baltic. Or mayhap somewhere in Denmark or Prussia.'

Serov sat back in his chair, closing his eyes as if pondering the request. He was silent for a full minute.

'You ask a very great deal,' he said at last. 'The journey by ship is not difficult. We have vessels trading with ports on your east coast all the time. It would be possible for one to take you aboard...'

'Yes, but not in any port. I would require them to pick me up in a small boat from a beach or cove. I fear that the ports are being watched.'

'That would be...not difficult,' said Serov. 'But as for the other matter. Twenty thousand sovereigns! I doubt we have anything like that much money in England!'

'But you could acquire it?'

'We could. But why should we?'

'In exchange for the information I can obtain for you...'

Serov leaned forward on the table.

'And that would be?' he smiled.

'Information in parts.'

'In parts?'

'Some information after I board your vessel,' said Raikes. 'And the rest when I arrive safely in a foreign port.'

The Russian laughed, 'It would have to be the greatest information ever filched from one country to another to justify such payment. What do you have that is of such value?'

'As you will appreciate, our country has drawn up a great many plans as to what action it would take in the event of a war with Russia. How it might obtain intelligence of your preparations, our own troop dispositions and strengths. Information on scandals that might be used to bring covert pressure to bear on our politicians and commanders. All of that will be yours when I am safely on one of your vessels and halfway across the sea.'

Serov bowed his head.

'That would indeed be most valuable,' he said. 'And the information you would give when you arrive at your foreign haven?'

'A list of all the spies and agents working on England's behalf across Europe. Including a list of your own countrymen who are in our pay.'

Serov gave a quiet laugh and rubbed a finger along his moustache.

'It seems that we may become partners in such an enterprise. I will talk to my masters.'

Raikes stood.

'I will pass you tomorrow at midday on London Bridge. Slip me a note saying how you are proceeding with the preparations. I shall require half of the sum before I leave England and the rest when I disembark from your vessel. If you are not on London Bridge I will assume that your government cannot accommodate my wishes. And remember, I need to leave England within a week!'

Serov raised his glass in a toast.

'To the English Enterprise!'

Raikes frowned.

'Not the best suggestion, given that the last time someone drank such a toast was to wish God's speed to the Spanish Armada!' he said.

'Then to Holy Mother Russia!' he said, drinking the dregs of the sherry before throwing the glass against the wall.

~

It could be a lark!

It could be a lark, seeing how Wicks and his henchmen dealt with the unspeakable individuals who failed to repay their debts. Angier had never bothered much in the past with this nasty side of the money-lending enterprises, but tonight he was bored. He wanted excitement. He wanted to experience something different. He wanted... Well, he never knew for sure. But this was the only entertainment on offer this evening, without going across to Mrs Bendig's night house. And even that had become a rather dull routine. He had had all the girls at least once, so no novelty there. Besides, he could always go on to that disreputable den of iniquity afterwards.

And how does a gentleman dress to go a-debt collecting? He wasn't quite sure. So he garbed himself in his usual evening clothes, with a cape, a tall hat, and the black ebony walking cane with the silver handle. That would do. Surely that would do. Then he would be equipped for any other adventures the evening might bring along. He left his set of rooms at Albany, walked down the flight of stairs to the entrance nearest Piccadilly, then up towards Leicester Square on his way to Soho.

~

Quest had never forgotten the first time he killed a man.

It mattered not that his victim was a foul individual who had himself killed many an innocent person. A rough of the first order. Someone that the world was far better without. His name was Palmer and he was a footpad. Not that Quest generally minded footpads. But he couldn't stand those footpads who robbed the poor rather than the rich. If you have a grievance with the world, then take it out on those responsible, not their hard done by victims. That was the Quest and Monkshood philosophy.

Palmer had made three terrible mistakes.

He had tried to rob Quest in an alley in Whitechapel. He had tried to use a dagger on Quest. He had been incompetent in the use of that dagger.

And that was the last mistake Palmer ever made in the brief mortal span in which his person had polluted the world. For Quest had twisted back his assailant's knife and sent the soul of Palmer hurrying to Hell.

The experience of that first kill had shaken Quest, for although he had practised for such situations and learned in theory the tactics and techniques, nothing prepares a man for the first exercise in killing. A pointless death, he had thought, even though he had long known of Palmer's evil reputation.

And there the man lay, on the cobbled floor of a dark alley with the rain soaking down upon him. No more a part of life than the stone cobbles themselves. The cockroach that Quest had noticed crawling from wall to wall had more connection to the rest of the human race than this empty shell, once a man, now lying at his feet. Looking into the dead eyes, Quest considered that it was as though Palmer had never existed. He had seen dead men before and always considered them completely empty of whatever had once sparked the life within.

He threw the dagger on to the ground and walked on.

TWENTY-FOUR

Wicks and his two associates had begun the evening in a tavern north of Oxford Street.

It was his nature to seek out a little courage before descending on one of his victims. The two battered individuals with him considered this alcoholic priming to be part of their payment. But it was not all about financial reward. The two men, like Wicks himself, enjoyed their work. They enjoyed drinking too, and it was gone eight before they set out into Soho. They were merry and loud and didn't notice the man who followed them as they left the tavern. Nor the fat man and the thin man who joined him as he crossed Oxford Street.

'Sticks is with Mrs Jenks,' Isaac muttered, as they danced perilously through the evening horse traffic which was rushing in both directions along the busy thoroughfare.

'Then he'll have a quiet night,' said Quest.

'How so?' Josef looked puzzled.

'I intend to deal with them long before they get anywhere near the house.'

'Why so?' asked Isaac.

'We have ill thought this out,' Quest explained. 'We cannot have them attacked on Mrs Jenks' doorstep. It would implicate her in these proceedings. Perhaps put a noose around her neck, particularly if the police become aware of just why they were visiting her.'

'Sticks will be disappointed,' said Josef. 'It is a long time since he has used his fists.'

'We must tell him that he was our reserve line of defence,' Quest replied. 'He'll get a fight another day.' He hurried his pace. 'We must speed up and get ahead of them in Daws Alley. Safer that way, several streets away from Frith Court.'

~

They had drunk too much. That was the plain truth of it. Wicks looked in disgust as Moby, the tallest of his associates threw up against the alley wall. The stench of his vomit induced a further throwing up by Cazley, the bulky young prize fighter, who had faked falls and knockouts for a dozen years before quitting the ring and coming to work for Wicks.

Their employer looked on in disgust as the two retched against the filthy brickwork. After a few moments of evacuation, and a little longer as they pissed on the alley floor, the two men rallied a trifle.

'Told you to go easy on the drink,' he said. 'Now come on! We have work to do!'

They all took a deep breath, trying to ignore the surrounding stench before continuing along the wide alley, empty now but a convenient shortcut into Soho for costers and dips during more sociable hours. They had gone but a few yards before Wicks heard the voice. He might have ignored it in the ordinary course of events, but it did seem to be calling his name. And calling it in a low and mysterious tone, drawn out, something like he imagined a spectre might speak when it came a-haunting.

'Ww...ii...ii...ck...ss.'

At first he thought it was his imagination, or the wind sweeping across the distant mouth of the alley. But then it came again, more peremptorily this time.

'Wicks!'

Sharp, like the crack of a whip, echoing a little in this gap between tall buildings.

'Wicks!'

It came again. Wicks noticed that Moby and Cazley had a nervous expression, a questioning look in their eyes. They were both breathing very fast. He saw that Cazley held out his life preserver and Moby had his hand on the dagger tucked into his belt.

'Wicks!'

Now the voice was ahead of him, somewhere in the dark shadows of the alley.

'I know your errand, Wicks.'

Closer and closer.

'This is where it ends, Wicks!' said the figure that stepped out into the dim light trying to invade the alley from the gas lamp at the Soho end.

Wicks took a pace forward.

'Who the bloody hell are you?'

'Your worst nightmare, Wicks,' said Quest, walking towards the three men. 'If I thought there was any hope of your redemption I would spare you. But there isn't, is there?'

'Wotcher mean?'

'You are a foul stain on the human race, Wicks. Exploiter of the vulnerable, murderer....you don't deserve my mercy. If you are not dealt with you will go on and on...'

Wicks reached inside his jacket. He kept a weapon there, an old Navy cutlass in a leather holster. He drew it, holding it in front of him.

'Well, that makes it much easier to kill you, Wicks. You drew your weapon first. And now I shall draw mine!'

Quest pulled the blade from his walking cane.

'I don't like this,' Cazley muttered, unable to keep the fear from his voice. The young prize fighter waved his life preserver, half considering throwing it to the ground. Moby had already drawn out his dagger.

Wicks half-turned his head.

'This bastard's alone,' he yelled back at them. 'Take 'im!'

'Not quite alone,' said a voice somewhere to the rear. In a dim corner of the alley stood a bulky man, carrying a long life preserver of his own. A second figure in the distance blocked the alley.

'Get 'im! Get 'im!' Wicks shouted. 'Come on....'

And then he suddenly charged at Quest, swinging the cutlass back across his right shoulder and then bringing it across in a great sweep towards the side of Quest's neck.

Had the cutlass struck home it would have taken Quest's head. But Quest sank low, side-stepping to his left, the blade of the cutlass carving the air a bare two inches above him. The force of the swing threw Wicks off balance, the tip of the cutlass sparking against the London brick of the alley wall. Even as he evaded the cut, Quest thrust upwards with his own blade, catching Wicks in the centre of his chest, its sharp point thrusting deeper and deeper into his lungs. As he stood, Quest pulled back the blade, ready to strike again.

But there was no need.

Wicks leaned against the alley wall, dragging himself sideways towards the distant light of the gas lamp in the street beyond. His eyes rolled uncontrollably and Quest knew that his victim was done for. He had seen those first indications of coming death so often before. The spirit within starting to lose control of bodily functions. A fleck of blood shot out of the man's mouth as his lungs and heart crashed to their destruction.

Quest heard a noise and looked round to see Moby charging at him, waving a dagger. In a brief moment the tall man stood before him waving the murderous weapon in front of Quest's face. He took a pace backwards as Moby pushed the blade out towards him, moving all the time so that he might deny Quest the chance to use his own sword. Had Moby been sober he might have succeeded, but the alcohol made him unsteady on his feet.

Holding the sword stick in one hand, Quest pulled a short wooden life preserver, no longer than a fisherman's priest, from his clothing. As Moby's dagger came in again, towards his face, Quest brushed it aside with the lead-weighted stick. Even as the dagger flew through the air, even before it touched the ground, Quest's blade had penetrated his opponent's heart.

Quest looked back along the alley for the third man. But Cazley was no more. He lay on the ground, Isaac Critzman standing over him, clutching his life preserver in both hands.

'I would have let him go,' he said, 'for he was a weak creature. But he tried to attack me rather than escape. Perhaps it is better this way!'

Quest nodded.

'Your enemy still lives,' Josef called from a distance, pointing towards Wicks. 'He will be in the street in a moment.'

Quest turned and walked swiftly after the dying man.

And it was on the corner, by the gas lamp, where the alley met the street, that Wicks fell to the ground, drowning in his own blood, and giving out the most appalling rattle of death. And it was there, even at the moment he died, that Wren Angier, who had been walking the streets in the hope of joining his bullies, found their leader soaked in his own blood.

There are times in nightmares when the dreamer finds himself frozen in the terror of the moment. And just such was the moment that Angier found himself in then. And had it not been for the sight of a man with a swordstick blade coming swiftly along the alley, a sight that snapped him out of his inertia, Angier might have remained frozen to the spot, dying alongside his creature.

For a second he looked at the face of the man who approached. And then he turned and ran.

~

People in the crowds turned to watch as the hysterical individual sprinted amongst them. For a few moments Angier was oblivious as to where he was going. Just away from the bloody horror he had witnessed. He scarce saw the people or the streets. Just the hideous dying face of Wicks. And now the crowds looked at him as though he were a lunatic, drawing on to the inside of the pavements to let him pass, desperately seeking to get away from his flight. And then, at last, Angier broke his pace as sheer breathlessness overtook him.

In Piccadilly he almost folded with the pain in his lungs. He edged in towards a shop window and gasped for breath. Then a kind of relief swept through his mind. The street looked normal. Respectable people going about their business, not even noticing him now that he was still. A pair of ragamuffins swept the horse dung from the road. A clerk looked agitated, feeling his pockets for some-*thing*, then breathing a sigh of relief on the realisation that his pocket had *not* been picked. And there was nobody there who was taking the slightest interest in Angier. No sinister figure trailing him from the shadows. No drawn blade soaked in blood.

He had escaped!

And more than that, he would put a greater distance between himself and the menacing figure from the alley. He would return to Albany and pack, then take a safe cab to a railway station so that he might board a train to...?

Anywhere! Anywhere he was not known.

In his business as a money lender he had received a great many threats. Usually in the post. Menacing demands. Promises to mete out justice if he persisted in his financial trade. He had discarded them without a second thought. But now...now...Wicks was dead! His henchmen too, in all probability. And those were not deaths caused by casual street robberies. They had been on their way to exact punishment against a defaulter. That was why they had died. And if they were killed then it was inevitable that their killer would seek revenge against the man who employed them.

But who?

As he rested his head back against the window he thought of all the other recent killings and attacks in London. Against people of his class. He remembered how they had found the corpse of Henry Bartram. And the note to the press that had followed. He had known Bartram, though he had never liked him. Could there be a connection? Perhaps...perhaps. He wandered on along the street.

His breathing was completely eased by the time he reached home, nodding to the doorman as he reached the entrance to Albany. He saw nobody else as he climbed the stairs to his set. At last he felt safe. The seaside! Yes, that was where he would go, to some distant resort where he had never been. He would write a brief note to his clerk, instructing him to pursue the usual business matters whilst he was away. But he would not even tell that individual just where he was going. Clerks could be garrulous. Just that it was an urgent matter of business that took him away.

And he would pack lightly, though perhaps add a pistol to his luggage. Yes, that would do. He had a pistol, a nice one. A weapon he had never used. Just to be on the safe side of life. A pistol...

He opened the door of his set and turned up the light, walking in to the main room where the fire still burned in the grate. He loved his days in Albany, loved them so much he often wished he never had to go outside at all. He loved....

The man sat in the corner chair, dressed all in black, with a dark cape around his shoulders. He was looking up at Angier. And he had a percussion pistol pointing at Angier's heart. It was his own pistol! The one he had thought about only moments before, gone from its mounting above his desk. In the man's hand, pointing at him. His own pistol!

Angier looked into the man's eyes.

It was *him,* the threatening presence from the alley. There was no doubt about that. There could be no doubt. But how had he beaten him in that mad dash to Albany? How could it be possible? And how could he have got in? It seemed so unfair! Unfair that he was to die in the one place he had always felt safe.

~

Anders looked up and down the alley at the three corpses. A regular bloodbath, though not the first killing he had seen in this vile thoroughfare. He knew all three individuals, for they had often floated across the fringes of crime. No loss to society to see the three men removed from the world. Their killer had doubtless saved him a great deal of work in the future.

He almost felt a tiny spark of gratitude towards this assassin. But, no! That was not a road that could be journeyed. There was a judicial process and it must be followed. This man, this killer, must be brought to book and dealt with. But Anders knew he would be a trifle sad as he attended the trial at the Old Bailey and heard the clunk of the drop outside the walls of Newgate.

And who was this killer?

Was it the young William Marshall grown to an avenging manhood in the rookeries of London?

Anders could think of no other explanation but that of the poor tormented Norfolk lad, come to the city to cry havoc. This boy who had let slip his own dogs of war in a sinister revenge against the class that had murdered his father and brothers. And where was he now? Somewhere in these same streets, that would be sure. Perhaps just yards away, maybe around the next corner? Anders wondered just how often he had passed Marshall in the street, the avenging young man with a broken hand and hate in his heart? What a bloody waste of a good soul!

Anders felt tired, his eyes ached for sleep and his body felt too weary to carry on. He yawned. He would go home and rest and let Sergeant Berry arrange the removal of the bodies from Daw's Alley.

And then, at the back of his mind, hidden by the tiredness, was that feeling that there was something he should have remembered. Some connection with the past. Something Berry had said. But what the hell was it? He had nearly had it a moment before. Something he had thought.

Damn it! What was it?

Then the sergeant himself came along the alley, holding an object out in front of him. Anders didn't need to ask what it was. He knew too well that it would be a stretch of cord looped like a hangman's noose.

'Another for the collection,' Berry said. 'I know these men. They are all Wren Angier's creatures.'

Anders thumped his forehead.

'Of course! Then we must go and warn him. His enterprises are possibly the cause of all this.'

Berry looked sympathetically at the inspector. 'You look asleep on your feet, if you don't mind me mentioning it. You get some rest. I'll call on Angier and station a constable at his door.'

'That is very good of you, my dear old pal,' Anders replied.

~

'How did you get in?'

Angier looked into the man's face, seeking some hope of pity.

'No one should be able to get in here, it isn't fair!'

'Life isn't fair,' said Quest. 'It really isn't, is it? Not fair for me. Not fair for you. Not fair at all for the victims of your usury.'

Angier half fell against the hearth.

'It was just a business, the money-lending. A business inherited by me from my father.' He almost shouted. 'For God's sake it's the way the world works! Most commerce exists on credit.'

'And because of your ambitions, your desire for wealth...no, your greed, three men died tonight. Not worthy men, but villains of the first order. We won't mourn for them. But there have been others, haven't there, Angier? Innocent people. Imprisoned. Ruined. Driven to suicide. Not counting those who were murdered by your three evil followers.'

Angier breathed rapidly, unable to take his eyes off the pistol.

'It was not what I ordered,' he protested. 'Debtor's gaol, aye...that. But not the other things you accuse me of.'

Quest raised the pistol so that it was aimed clear at Angier's face.

'I will not insult you by suggesting that you have a lack of imagination,' he said, 'or that you are some half-wit, unaware of the consequences of your actions. I can see from the books on your shelves that you are an intelligent man. To expound this thesis that you were ignorant of what your creatures did...well, it compounds your own wickedness.'

'Wickedness?'

'Aye, wickedness, for wicked it is to make the lives of others a misery for the sake of your own greed. We are all born naked into the world, and naked we go out. What will happen to your wealth in a moment or two when you are dead? It will all seem rather pointless, will it not?'

Angier's hand trembled as he clutched the mantelpiece over the fire.

'Please...don't kill me...'

'Mercy? You want mercy? Why should I show you mercy? You showed little to those whom *you* destroyed. The most mercy I might be prepared to grant is a quick death.'

'I just wanted to have...'

'Have what?' asked Quest. 'Wealth? Security? Amusement? I am sure all of those you persecuted wanted the same. You have ruined lives. And why? For your own...gratification.'

'Please...I beg you...'

Angier fell forward on to his knees, just saving himself from the flames of the fire. He mumbled incoherently for several moments, tears pouring down his face. His right hand beat a tattoo on the carpet. At last he wiped his face with the back of the same hand.

'I don't want to die,' he almost shouted the words.

'Few do,' said Quest. 'But the sentence of death was passed on you a while ago.'

'Please?' The tears ran again down the man's face. 'It can all be changed. Everything I do can change. Please help me?'

'You are a pathetic individual. Why should I help you?'

Angier looked up through the blurring of his tears at Quest.

'I don't know,' he replied.

Quest lowered the pistol a trifle.

'At last,' he said. 'You have stopped trying to argue away your death sentence with excuses. Perhaps you might die redeemed.'

Angier wiped away the tears once more and pulled himself up to his feet. He breathed deeply and looked across the room at Quest. He raised his head with something approaching courage.

'If I am to die, then please do it now,' he said. 'I have no words left to plead with.'

Quest stood and raised the pistol at arm's length. He looked at Angier for a while before lowering the pistol to his side. There was a silence, broken only by the hiss of the gas light and the coals sizzling in the fireplace.

'You are not worth killing,' he said at last. 'I may spare you. And you would be the first I have ever spared. But there are matters that you would have to attend to. Changes you would have to make...'

'Anything,' Angier said quietly.

'You may not like the conditions...'

'Anything you ask...and they will be done willingly.'

Quest smiled, a smile driven more by tiredness than humour.

'Then these are they,' he said. 'You will abandon your career in money lending and cancel all the existing debts that you are owed.'

'And what more?'

'Nothing more,' said Quest. 'I did consider demanding that you give up your seat in Parliament, but perhaps not. You could do good in that dreadful place. Good for humanity. I shall keep that condition on hold.'

'That is all?'

'It is enough. For now. But if you do not abide by my conditions on the moneylending you *will* die. And in a way more painful than by a simple pistol shot. I can find a dozen different ways to execute you. You understand?'

Wren Angier nodded.

'Then I will leave you,' said Quest. 'But I will never be far away'. He looked down at the gun. 'This is a handsome pistol?'

'It was a gift,' said Angier, 'from a friend.'

'Then I will not deprive you of it,' said Quest. 'I will leave it on the stairs outside your set. You may go to collect it in five minutes.' He turned back at the door. 'And remember this, Angier. *I* have given you a gift tonight. The gift of your life. Please do not throw it back in my face.'

TWENTY-FIVE

Quest felt tired as he walked back to his lurk in Neal's Yard, all of his thoughts on Angier.

He had meant to dispatch him. He really had. Others had pleaded for mercy and been shown none. So why this particular rake? Quest didn't know.

Or rather he did, for on reflection he recognised something of himself there. How easy it would have been if he had been born with all of Angier's privileges to become such a creature. But then the same could be said for all of them. It was easy to make such excuses. He had given the man a very bad scare. Perhaps Angier would learn the lesson. There had been something in his face and voice to suggest that he would. Something that had been lacking in the other men he had dealt with.

As he wandered into the Dials, Quest snapped out of his reverie and paid more attention to his surroundings. He was still dressed as a gentlemen and this was dangerous ground for slummers who looked as though they had more than a bob in their pockets. He got some funny looks from the men who hung around the dripping walls and a couple of approaches from desperate women. But they shrank away at the threatening expression on his face and the stick in his hand.

One or two thought he looked vaguely familiar but couldn't think quite how. He reached Neal's Yard without any harassment, climbed the stairs and opened the door. He was lighting the candle when the man spoke to him. But not for a moment did he give any indication of alarm. Or halt the task. Or turn round.

'You have had a busy night, Mr Quest!'

'I have indeed,' he replied without turning. 'How skilled you must be with locks to gain entrance through my door.'

'A matter of practice,' said the man. 'I have opened a great many locks in my dubious career.'

'In the police?'

The man laughed. 'Nothing so vulgar!'

'You are a criminal then?'

'Ah,' the man sighed, 'we are all criminals when it suits us to be. Take yourself for instance? Even tonight. Three men dead in an alley. A visit to their paymaster at Albany. Did you kill Angier? And yet I think you have missed your golden prize, the one that means the most to you. And you were so close. Please turn around.'

There was a large man sitting in the battered old chair and looking up at Quest. Below his smile was a pistol aimed at Quest's heart. The irony of the situation was not lost on Quest. It was almost a replaying of the situation at Albany an hour or two earlier. Quest wondered if the man would try to make him beg for his life.

'I think you have been following me?' he said.

'Oh yes,' Wissilcraft replied, 'for days now. What an interesting expedition you had to the Inns of Court! But you didn't find any answers, did you? And then that journey from that sailors' tavern on the Thames. You knew you were being followed, didn't you? You set your crippled warrior on me! A clever tail, though not quite as skilled as you both thought. I let him have hints of my presence. A long day out for you both, and all in vain!' He laughed. 'I much admired your disguise. What a talented individual you are!'

'So tell me,' Quest asked, 'what is this golden prize I missed at Albany?'

'The man you seek. He lives there. In the set right below Wren Angier. He was there tonight, for I had him trailed back to his rooms.'

'The man I seek?'

'Oh, don't give me that look of false puzzlement, you are better than that! I know everything. I am way ahead of Scotland Yard in my investigation of you, Mr Quest. Or do you prefer William Marshall when you are in the company of friends?'

Quest sat down on the hard wooden chair to one side of the fireplace, a vision of Wren Angier spinning across his mind. Thank God the fire was not lit.

'I doubt we are friends,' he said.

'But we are!' Wissilcraft protested. 'And like all good friends who come a-calling I bring you a gift. The gift you want most in all the world. And that gift is the man you seek.' He gave an ironic laugh. 'And the amusing thing is that you were within a few yards of him tonight, at Albany. He was in his set. Just below you, there he was, that lawyer who murdered your father and brothers and put those disgusting scars on your hand. How close you came to seeing him, for he had not long been at home before you arrived to visit Angier. Did you kill Angier by the way?'

Quest shook his head.

'Why ever not? If ever there was a man surplus to the world's requirements!'

'Sometimes you have to have hope in others.'

'But not in the man you seek?'

Quest took a deep breath. 'No. Not in him. He is a man who has to die. I had planned to take his life when I caught up with him. But I fear you have other plans for me. What is it to be? Do you intend to discharge that pistol now or am I to face the drop at Newgate?'

Wissilcraft put on an expression of amused shock as he lowered the pistol ever so slightly and leaned forward.

'My dear Quest, do you imagine I treat my friends in such a way? It would be easy to get you all topped.

Your man Sticks. The Critzman brothers. Feedle. That quite dreadful actress you keep as your mistress. Your good self? You would be the centrepiece at the hangings! What tales the chapbook writers would tell of you! Your notoriety would go before you.'

'I fear my deeds would be somewhat exaggerated,' said Quest.

'My dear fellow, how could they be? You would be the hero of the hour. At least amongst the great unwashed.'

Quest sat back in the chair. 'I never quite see myself as having the materials to be a hero. Oh, pardon me my bad manners! I should offer you a drink, but I keep none here.'

'I think we might forego the social niceties. There is a man you wish to kill. I have told you where he is. Do you intend to slay him?'

Quest rubbed his fingers across his forehead in a thoughtful manner.

'You seem very enthusiastic regarding my plans to kill a lawyer? Almost as though you want me to?'

'I suspect the Bar would be better if you were to thin it out,' Wissilcraft replied. 'There are a deal too many lawyers in English public life.'

'Then you have a personal interest in this man?'

'I do.'

Quest was silent for a moment as he regarded this visitor and the weapon in his hand.

'If we are to be friends then I do think you should put away that pistol.'

Wissilcraft gave a hearty laugh, his whole frame rocking, but the pistol remaining still for a moment. Then, putting away his humour, he lowered the gun just an inch.

'That might be a fatal mistake,' he said.

'It would certainly be fatal for me if the pistol discharged,' Quest replied. 'I will not take advantage of the situation if you put the pistol down. I am your prisoner. I give you my parole.'

Wissilcraft regarded him a moment, large head tilted to one side. Then he uncocked the pistol and rested it on the arm of the chair. He folded his arms and sat back.

'That is much more comfortable,' said Quest. 'Now, you seem to know a great deal about me and my associates, but I know nothing about you, except that you say you are not crusher nor yet criminal?'

'Not either.'

'A man with a grudge then?'

'We all have grudges.'

'And is this a personal grudge or some public requirement?'

'I do believe you have the measure of me,' said Wissilcraft. 'My grudge is both personal and public. I want this man dead. My masters *require* him dead. And I want you to be his assassin.'

'And your masters would be?'

Wissilcraft shook his head. 'I cannot say.'

Quest stood suddenly, prompting Wissilcraft to move a hand slightly towards his pistol.

'Then we have no deal,' said Quest, 'and you must do your worst.'

'I would wish to be accommodating...'

'Then answer me one question. Are you here at the behest of the government?'

Wissilcraft gave a barely perceptible nod. Quest sat down again.

'I am no government lackey,' he said. 'If this man has offended the Prime Minister or Palmerston then let them do their own killing. I take it you are a government spy?'

'A word I dislike,' said Wissilcraft.

'This man? You say he is the man I seek?'

Wissilcraft leaned forward in the chair.

'I will tell you a tale of an ambitious man,' he said. 'A country lawyer with a great ambition. A man who became a ferocious advocate in the London courts. An individual who traded in favours and blackmail to elevate himself into society. And then a fool of a home secretary, a predecessor of milord Palmerston, decided that this lawyer had other gifts. A talent for subterfuge, a cunning cruelty towards all who threatened society. In a moment of madness he made him Queen Victoria's spymaster.'

Quest frowned. 'And then?'

'But that was not enough for Jacob Raikes. He wanted more. Riches beyond belief. Power without limits. Spying on and persecuting the poor was no longer enough. Seeing off the agents of foreign powers became a bore to him. You see, he has no patriotism, his only loyalty is to himself.'

'It seems a fair description of many in public life...'

Wissilcraft laughed again, 'And so it is, but Raikes has gone further. You are aware of the conflict between Turkey and Russia? It seems more than likely that we will soon go to war on the side of the Ottomans?'

'Another ruinous adventure,' said Quest. 'Another war to distract attention from the parlous state of our own nation.'

'Perhaps. But to Raikes, such a war is just another profitable enterprise. And he plans to turn traitor. Even now he has dealings with the spies of Russia. For money. For influence, perhaps. He plans to flee England within a week. He has knowledge, documents, information on our armies which might cost thousands of lives.'

'Then why not go round to Albany and bring him to book?'

'It is not so easy,' Wissilcraft smiled. 'Raikes is a man of influence. He has other documents, other knowledge. Information on men within the government, within society, within the Royal Household itself. Knowledge that he is prepared to use. This perverted man knows well the perversions of others. And that is why we want him dead. That is why we want you to kill him.'

Quest plunged his head into his hands.

'You know what he did to me?' he cried.

'Ah, yes,' said Wissilcraft. 'The country lawyer who tormented and murdered your father and brothers. Who left those scars on your hand and chased you like a hare across the countryside. You have been on his trail ever since. And now I give you the chance to take vengeance.'

'If I kill Raikes it will be for me. Not for the Queen or Palmerston or anyone else.'

'And that is fair enough,' said Wissilcraft. 'We want him dead just as you have killed the others. A hangman's knot lying nearby. Just one more assassination on a long list. Though we shall want the documents back. Not just those relating to matters of state and our own defences, but also the notebook in which Raikes keeps evidence of the doings of the more errant members of the Class.'

'And if I do this what will you do to protect my friends?'

Wissilcraft looked thoughtful for a moment.

'You have my word that none shall be arrested and that secret identities will be preserved.'

'But I only have your word for that?'

'You do,' replied Wissilcraft, 'but what more can I promise? I could have you all arrested tonight.

There is a detective, Anders of Scotland Yard, who is hard on your trail. He might arrest you anyway within days. I can cry halt to his chase. Bury any proceedings. We are not concerned with those you have slain. My personal opinion is that England is better off without them. Few will mourn their passing.'

Quest walked over to the window, looking through the blackened smears down into Neal's Yard. Both men were silent and the only noise came with the cries of the costers outside. At last Quest turned to face the fat man.

'I will go back to Albany,' he said. 'I will settle it tonight.'

'No,' said Wissilcraft. 'Not tonight. You missed your chance. He will have left Albany by now. Besides, I want him to make one last contact with his new paymasters. I will send word regarding when and how. By the way. I trust you enough to give you my name. It is Wissilcraft.'

'Unusual!'

'East Anglian, I believe. Well, now we all know one another and so we have brought some element of trust into these proceedings.'

'I do hope so,' said Quest, 'for if you betray me I will be leaving an hangman's knot alongside your own corpse.'

Wissilcraft smiled as he stood, putting the pistol away somewhere within his voluminous cloak.

'I would expect nothing less,' he said.

TWENTY-SIX

'Well, this is a deuce of a place to come,' said Sergeant Berry, as he and Anders walked through the gates of the cemetery at Kensal Green. 'I'm never happy in graveyards. Reminds me of how little time we have left. Why did they have to build the place so far out? We've been walking for hours. It's damn near in the countryside!'

'And even here the long tentacles of London are stretching,' said Anders. 'See those houses they are building over there! The last generation would have known so much of this as farmland, but the inexorable grip of the city is closing round what were once pleasant meadows and woodlands. The place'll spread over half England before it's done! Probably till it meets the expanding factory districts of your beloved Manchester. Sad really. I grew up on a farm you know? Not that we were rich. My father was only a tenant farmer...'

'Aye, so you've said.'

Anders grinned, 'Oh, I know you cherish your urban world, but remember, Berry, we need the countryside. People have to have food to eat. Not to mention the mental stimulation of rural vistas.'

'Surely that's what city parks are for,' Berry said, 'a bit of green with a view.'

Anders sighed and shrugged, 'What a philistine you are, man! When you are in some foul alley in

Whitechapel do you not yearn for a clean and open space?'

'Hyde Park'll do me!'

'I fear, my dear Berry, that there is no hope for you!'

'Perhaps not. This has been a far enough tramp for me. And I still don't know why we've come?'

'Why else would we come to a cemetery but to see a grave...'

'Yes, but whose?'

'Sometimes I despair of you,' Anders replied. 'We have come to see the grave of Josiah Quest.'

'For what purpose?' Berry asked, as they walked a gravelled path ascending a very slight hill. Anders didn't answer immediately. They were required to step out on to the grass to avoid a horse-drawn hearse and several carriages journeying up to an impressive stone chapel a little way into the grounds.

'To be honest, I really don't know,' Anders replied as the cortege moved away, the dust blowing across a huge spread of graves and chambered tombs. 'Just a feeling, an instinct. A detective's hunch, if you like. We know that Marshall, the elder, and Quest were friends, brothers in a common struggle. The beat constable in this division tells me that many poor pilgrims come to pay homage at the grave of their champion, Josiah Quest. So I thought we should do so. The constable told me where I might find the grave.'

They were approaching a steeper section of the cemetery, not far below a huge building marking the entrance to the cemetery's catacombs. The area was lined with trees that had now lost the last of their leaves. A wintry chill filled the air and Berry shivered.

'You think that Marshall will come to pay tribute?' he asked. 'We could have a long wait! And I really wouldn't care to be here after dark. What is that building up there?'

'Catacombs, where you may wander among the dead.'

Berry shivered again.

'Not for me,' he said. 'This idea of coffins being stacked in rows for every gawper to see is unseemly. The good earth wrapping round did well enough for my parents, and it will for me.'

'For a new cemetery there are a lot of graves. We must do yet more walking to find the right one,' said Anders. 'In the meantime tell me about Wren Angier?'

'He was...uncommunicative. I think he had been badly frightened by something...or someone. He told me he was off to the Continent for a few months. And insisted that police protection was quite unnecessary. He left the Albany early this morning.'

Anders took in a deep breath.

'We should perhaps have pressed him. It's a wonder he's still alive,' he said.

'Something unusual though,' Berry continued, 'I talked to Inspector Adams of the City Police just before I set out to meet you. Apparently the rumour is that Angier has suddenly dissolved his moneylending businesses and left instructions to that effect with his clerks.'

Anders halted for a moment as they walked off the gravelled track and out amongst a huge spread of graves. He rested for a moment, his back against a tree.

'That is unusual,' he said. 'I am always suspicious of damascene conversions. I suspect the man had little choice in the matter. I suspect he was coerced.'

'By Marshall?'

'None other. What a pity Angier has departed these shores. We could probably have broken him.'

'But surely Marshall would have just killed him?'

Anders plucked the last solitary dead and browning leaf from the tree.

'I believe we are hunting the most extraordinary individual,' he said. He crunched the leaf in his hand. 'But we will have him! And the answer lies here.' He looked around at the huge number of graves and tombs.

For a while they walked up and down reading inscriptions and trying to avoid the mounds of earth covering the newly buried. It took them some twenty minutes of wandering before they located the tomb that they were seeking. On a grassy level just across the path from a sprawling blackthorn. And that rang a bell with Anders. Something to do with that lost thought that had plagued him for so long. A blackthorn! It triggered something in the darkest recess of his memory. It seemed to move events on but he still could not recall why. Where had he heard the mention of a blackthorn? This reverie was interrupted by the voice of Sergeant Berry.

'Here, sir...'

Berry stood over a simple slab set into the grass. The last resting place of Josiah Quest. Even at that time of year there were a few flowers laid below the inscription. *'Beloved husband of Adelaide and father of William Quest,'* he read aloud the words on the stone. 'The wife is not buried with him?' he queried.

'I understand she died of a sudden apoplexy when Josiah Quest was speaking at a meeting in Edinburgh. She was probably buried there.'

Berry read the words again, 'Sadly it tells us nothing,' he remarked. 'And there are no messages with those flowers.'

'I did not expect the answer to be written on the grave. I just wanted to get the feel of the man. A good man by all accounts. I rather think I would have liked him.' He looked around in a vague manner. 'Is he buried with friends? Are there other Quests here?'

'Just this one,' Berry answered. He had strolled a few yards away to a long triangular tombstone, nearer to the earthen bank which rose up towards the catacombs. He knelt down and read the inscription out to the Inspector. '*William Quest, beloved son of Josiah and Adelaide Quest. Died...*'

'What!'

'*William Quest...*'

Before he could finish, Anders was kneeling beside him. 'My God, Berry! I thought the answer would be here. Something in my soul told me as much. If this is the grave of William Quest, then who is the William Quest I talked to at Hope Down?'

Berry blew out a breath.

'It is not unusual for parents to give a new child the name of a deceased brother. Not that we would hold with it where I come from...'

Anders ran his hand along the apex of the triangular stone.

'But look at the date of death, man! There could be nothing of age between the two William Quests. And those radical MPs I spoke to in Westminster. They talked of his wife and mentioned the son. *One* son. The light of his life, by all accounts!'

'I know what you are thinking,' Berry said. 'But, no, it is incredible...'

Anders grasped him by the wrist in his excitement.

'But is it?' he asked. 'What is more likely? Josiah Quest has lost his son. Another William appears, of similar age. The orphan child of his oldest and dearest friend. He adopts him, makes him his heir.

The Marshall boy takes on all aspects of the deceased William Quest. Josiah in his grief had retired from public life. Such a move would scarce be noticed.'

'But why not let him inherit as William Marshall?'

'Because William Marshall is being hunted by the Bartrams and the lawyer who broke his hand. He is at risk if he stays a Marshall. Safe if he becomes William Quest. And there is another proof, the final piece of the jigsaw. A lost memory that has been plaguing me. Now it has come back. Seeing that blackthorn! When I met William Quest he kept a hand in his pocket. The right hand. He said he had wounded it on a blackthorn. But that it didn't matter because he had grown up being able to use both hands equally well!'

Anders' infectious excitement had spread to the sergeant.

'But he kept his hand hidden because it bore the scars he received as a child?' The words tumbled out, as Berry saw the whole scene as if he had been there. 'And of course he might well grow up to be ambidextrous, given that the battered right hand would take time to heal.'

Anders stood, rubbing his chin with his own right hand.

'And so we have him,' he said at last. 'The policeman's rattle! We will lay him by the heels once and for all. He'll rattle in Newgate before the week is out. We have no need to travel to Hope Down, for he is clearly in London. He had an adventure here just the other night. We can take him at his city home and if we miss him there we'll have our man at the funeral of his father and his brothers! It is time to bring the adventures of this living William Quest to an end!'

TWENTY-SEVEN

Serov's thoughts were all of poetry as he wandered along the banks of the Thames and out on to London Bridge. He was early for his rendezvous and so he leaned on the wall and looked down at the swirling waters of the river. It was an impressive scene, no doubt about that. And this city seemed to him to be the heart of the universe.

So much more cosmopolitan than Moscow or Petersburg.

A thousand voices filled the air as Londoners crossed the bridge behind him, ordinary people, rich and poor, but so much more colourful than the Russians he had grown up amongst. He sighed and wondered what his heroes Pushkin and Lermontov would have made of this London scene. The people of Russia seemed quite insular by comparison. Serov was saddened that he would have to leave and go back to that land of long dreary winters.

And leave he would. For war was coming. It was coming to plague the earth once more, as surely as the snows of winter would be sweeping across the steppes. The Embassy would withdraw. For a while there would be no more English voices, no more London taverns with their raucous customers, no more expensive whores in Shaftesbury Avenue. And he would have to pack his books, that pleasant library he had made in his rooms in that quiet thoroughfare north of Oxford Street.

Such a shame!

He had enjoyed the society of those English authors, carefully cultivated in the literary salons of the capital. The whole new literature that had been presented to him. Not as good as the Russian authors, of course, but it did go in some interesting new directions. He patted the stonework. He could translate! Now that would be a worthwhile use of his talents during a sad exile from England. He had translated Pushkin and Lermontov into English. His works were much valued amongst the *literati* of this pleasant land. And in just such a way he might translate the best of the new English literature into Russian. It was an exciting thought. He felt quite the urge to rush back to his lodgings and begin at once. What a nuisance espionage was!

He looked around. The bridge was very busy. The bells began their twelve-times chime. It was midday. Time to encounter that odious man Raikes. God, how he hated traitors!

Serov walked slowly across, along the upstream side of the bridge. And there the man was, walking a brisk pace towards him, his cane swinging to and fro, forward and backwards, slicing the air and deterring any other pedestrian from coming too close. There was no acknowledgement as they passed one another. Their eyes never met. There was no pause in their passage across the bridge. Just a gentle brushing of coats as two gentlemen went by. Serov doubted that anyone could have seen the passing of the note. It was a technique that both men had used so many times before.

He continued across the bridge and then down the steps on the farther side until he reached the banks of the river. Serov took a brief glance back at the bridge's mighty arches and then walked, often pausing, around the church at Southwark. He sniffed with distaste at the sight of the building. A venerable old church wrecked by modern rebuilding. Would Shakespeare even recognise it now? After his first visit, Serov had written a vitriolic essay on all its modern faults, which he had had published in the artistic journal his brother edited out of St Petersburg. He walked on, vowing never to go there again. For a man of his size he paced his way quickly through the streets of Southwark on what he intended to be a roundabout route to Westminster Bridge and back to his rooms.

He was in the Borough, a few yards from the old debtor's prison of the Marshalsea, when the closed carriage drew alongside him. Its door opened and a hand gave a beckoning wave.

'Could you assist me?' said the voice of a lady. 'My driver needs instruction on the way to Newington?'

Serov leaned forward with a beaming smile. The woman was not very young, but still attractive. As he approached, he thought of all the advantages of closed carriages. He touched his hat and looked up at her. She smiled back, pointing a pistol at his head. Serov became aware of a figure behind him, a great breadth blocking out the light.

'Please get into the carriage,' said Wissilcraft, pushing his own pistol against the Russian's back. 'It would pain me to have to kill you in such a public place.'

~

'So, Angier lives,' said Isaac Critzman, 'and this man Wissilcraft knows who we all are? This is a disastrous day!'

They sat in the back room of the walking stick shop in Cheapside, a fierce fire blazing in the grate. Heavy rain had quietened the street outside.

'Simple answer,' said Sticks. 'Let's just top this Wissilcraft.'

Quest shook his head.

'No point,' he said. 'If we did I think the world would come crashing down on us. He says he has this one task for me to complete. You all know now what it is. A matter personal to me, so I have no difficulty with that. If I do his bidding he says that, within reason, we will be left alone.'

Josef nodded, 'I feel you are right, William. But how do we know that this man Wissilcraft is to be trusted? You could do the deed he requires, I can see you are longing to, but he might then close down our enterprise?'

'I shouldn't trust him a bloody inch!' Rosa added.

Quest smiled, rubbing his forehead. 'I trust few people. The majority of those I trust are sitting around this table. Wissilcraft has the power to bring pressure to bear on us. We must discover some way to hold him in thrall to the Monkshood.'

'Got an idea?' asked Jasper.

'Perhaps.'

Isaac tapped the table, 'And why did you spare Wren Angier? He has fled to France by all accounts, beyond our reach...'

'And closed down his moneylending business,' Quest countered, 'writing off all debts. I spared him because I considered him a foolish man, not a bad one. We may have saved his soul, and possibly our own, by sparing him.'

Josef smiled, 'I feel young William has done a good deed. We are not indiscriminate killers, brother. We do not punish those who may be redeemed. That is not how our fellowship works.'

'I hope we shall not have cause to regret it,' Isaac replied. 'The Fellowship of the Monkshood is under fire. People know. We have been careless. We must see what we can do to preserve our operations.' He turned to Quest. 'You are still determined to travel to Norfolk tomorrow for the funeral?'

'I am.'

'You have heard the plans we have made. You are satisfied with them?'

Quest nodded.

'They may well work,' Isaac continued, 'two plans to protect you from these policemen and the noose. But we must tread carefully, you understand?'

'I do,' said Quest. 'And as soon as the funeral is done I will labour to finish Raikes and end any threat from Wissilcraft.'

'Amen to that,' said Josef.

~

'It really is a pleasure to make your acquaintance,' said Wissilcraft. 'I very much enjoyed your translation of *A Hero of Our Time*, though I find duelling something of a bore.'

He sat, almost enveloping one of the two wooden chairs in the cellar. In the other, situated in the centre of the dank hole in the ground, was Serov. The Russian looked around at four damp walls of London brick. A pair of lanterns stood on the floor, illuminating the scene.

'You realise, of course, that I am a representative of the Tsar? I demand the privileges that the traditions of diplomacy suggest that I should have,' Serov said. 'Has my ambassador been informed of my illegal arrest?'

Wissilcraft considered for a moment, head slightly to one side, as he regarded this Russian who was almost as bulky as himself.

'Not exactly,' he said, 'besides, you have not been arrested as much as kidnapped. Nobody knows that you are here, except for myself and one or two of my associates.'

The Russian nodded, 'Ah, yes, that striking lady in the carriage. I regret not meeting her under more pleasant circumstances.'

Wissilcraft gave a humourless laugh.

'You would find my sister much more dangerous than myself. She has killed a half dozen men such as you. She has a sting like a scorpion. All matters considered, it is far better that I hold you prisoner than her. Angeline is the very devil to men who fail to be cooperative. At least I might kill you swiftly.

'And do you intend to kill me?'

Wissilcraft put on a feigned look of shock and gave a slight inclination of his head.

'Kill you? My dear chap! How could you imagine such a possibility? It would be such a tragic loss to translation and to literature.' He sat back in the chair and folded his arms. 'I find Pushkin's works quite admirable, though on the whole I prefer Goethe.'

'Goethe is a bore,' the Russian said. 'Better in his verse than his prose, I admit. But his *Sorrows*? I am quite thrilled when Werther destroys himself. Goethe is an author long past his day.'

'And what of our English authors? Mr Dickens?'

Serov gave an appreciative nod, 'Uneven, I feel. I admire some of his novels more than others. I think I prefer Scott. He had the advantage of writing poetry as well.'

'Gloomy, I always thought. And when not gloomy too coloured by romance. I much prefer Byron these days.'

Serov gave a disparaging shake of his head, 'Byron! If you are intending to kill me then please do it now, before you destroy all of my regard for your literature.'

'Ah, and I was so enjoying our little discussion.' Wissilcraft shrugged and gave a deep sigh. 'Still, if it is your wish that we return to business matters...'

Serov leaned as far forward in the chair as the hempen ropes would allow.

'I say again, I am a diplomat of the Tsar. I demand my release.'

Wissilcraft scratched the side of his face, 'Well, there you have me in a dilemma. I am sure you are aware that such protection only extends to your ambassador himself and his most senior officials. Spies don't count, do they? Much as I might wish to free you I cannot. My duty would not allow the agent of a foreign power to go free.'

'I am not a spy!'

Wissilcraft reached inside his coat and brought out a sheaf of papers.

'These are accounts of meetings you have had with Jacob Raikes. I could read the dates and times but I feel it would bore you. Only an hour or two ago you passed Raikes a document on London Bridge. Of course you are a spy!'

'I have nothing to say,' said Serov.

'You know Raikes!'

The Russian shook his head.

'Of course you do,' Wissilcraft continued, 'and you know his function as Her Majesty's Spymaster? You know of the information he was to sell you? Raikes has committed treason against the Crown. You have facilitated that treason.'

'Who are you?'

'My name is not important. Sufficient to say that *I* am our country's spymaster now. And, unlike my predecessor, I am not a traitor.'

The two men were silent for several moments. A good thing to have periods of silence in these interrogations, Wissilcraft always thought. Too much verbal sparring obscured the information that might come from a prisoner. Silence and threat were needed to increase the fear in the soul of a man being questioned. He was concerned that this Russian seemed to have no fear at all.

It was the moment to increase the pressure.

'There are three possibilities,' he said. 'I can kill you very quickly. I can call in my sister Angeline who will kill you slowly and very painfully. Or I can let you go. The choice is yours, my dear fellow.'

Serov remained silent.

'Let us consider your predicament,' Wissilcraft continued. 'You are tied captive in the cellar of a deserted house in a very unpleasant part of London. Nobody else knows you are here. Nobody will ever know you were here...'

'I demand my release!'

'You can demand what you like! Your demands will not be answered. Tell me what I want to know and you go free. As simple as that...'

'These ropes are cutting into my wrists...'

Wissilcraft sighed, 'Ah, they usually do. A minor pain, a tiny irritation compared to what you might suffer moments from now.'

He looked across to the steep flight of steps leading up to a battered yellow door. After a few seconds of consideration he stood and walked across to them, putting a foot on the first. He looked up at the door and then back at the Russian.

'Shall I call Angeline? She is up there waiting, you know! Waiting and so impatient. It is a while since she has had to demonstrate her...talents. She yearns for prey like some wild animal. I was quite scared of her when I was a boy, despite the fact that I was the elder.'

Wissilcraft noticed that Serov's eyes had followed him across the cellar. The Russian's face was pale and he was sweating with fear. His hands, tied though they were to the sides of the chair, were trembling. In Wissilcraft's experience such signs of terror and distress came not very long before cooperation.

'Think of your worst nightmares,' he said. 'Those dreams that you dread having. The ones that make you keep your eyes open and fight sleep. And then, when you have succumbed to the night, the dreams that drive you to wakefulness covered in sweat. Think of those nightmares. Then imagine a nightmare from which there is no awakening. Where the pain doesn't stop or go away. Where it just gets worse and more painful. So few of us know what real agony is. But you might. And very soon.'

He opened his mouth as though he intended to shout up the steps.

'Wait...please wait!' said the Russian.

'I am not a patient man, M'sieur Serov.'

'You offered me an alternative?'

'I offered you three,' Wissilcraft replied. 'But as you have not been immediately cooperative I have now ruled out the quick death. Two choices! You work with me or Angeline works with you. And then...when she has finished...and you have told all we want to know...just to stop the pain...your body will be found in the filthy waters of the Thames. An unpleasant end for such a brilliant scholar, as I'm sure you will agree.'

'But if I tell you my people will kill me...'

Wissilcraft smiled as he walked back across the cellar and stood above Serov.

'But they need never know,' he said. 'Raikes will be dead and it will seem that we caught him by our own good fortune. None of our success will be laid at your door. You can return to your pleasant routine. Return to Russia, if that is your desire. Or we could help you find a new home in some pleasant part of this realm, with money in your pocket. Or just reward you and let you take ship to America or anywhere. Those are the alternatives. It is up to you.'

Serov looked down at the floor in silence.

'Come!' said Wissilcraft. 'What is Russia to you? Really? Poems and prose. Folk songs spurred on by drink. A romantic vision of muzhiks labouring in the snow? Not real at all. I suspect you despise the Tsar as much as we do...'

Serov looked up into the Spymaster's eyes.

'How do I know you will keep your word?'

'I would like to say because I am an English gentleman. Only I am not a gentleman at all. You have to just accept the chance that I will. It is your *only* chance.'

The Russian took several deep breaths.

'What is it you want to know?' he asked at last.

Wissilcraft smiled once more.

TWENTY-EIGHT

Abraham Anders sat quietly in his office, eyelids half closed against the glare of the gas lamp. He wanted to go home and sleep and sleep. It had been a busy few weeks and he was tired of it all. In a few hours he would have to leave to take the late train to Norwich. To arrest a man whose motives he could understand. What a jest all life was, what a madness was existence.

Sometimes it was all too much.

He had found that as a boy in Wiltshire, working on the farm and running errands. An endless trudge of labour. All important matters. Things that had to be done. Tasks undertaken. But he had not engaged in them in the way his elder brother Arthur had. In a way it was a good job the family farm was so small that it could only ever be the inheritance of one son. And Arthur was welcome to it! It was not that Anders didn't like the land itself. He did. But it was the chain that tethered him to it that he couldn't stand. It was the principal reason that he had joined the constabulary.

Sometimes the thought of being a farmer, of being rooted to the spot, had driven him into long periods of melancholy. He had watched as itinerant labourers came and went. He knew that that would be his future. Travelling the land and working other people's farms. He recalled the day when Arthur said he was to be married, to the daughter of their neighbour. The two holdings were to be rolled into one. That was the conclusion to Abraham's youth on the farm. There was no room for him from that point on. Even with the addition of the adjoining property the farm was still small, barely a couple of hundred acres. Still not enough land to support a surplus son, in addition to his brother's wife and any forthcoming children.

So one day Anders had set off to find work, wandering miles across the Wiltshire countryside. But the agricultural depression lingered, as did his own particular bout of melancholy. He slept a chilly night on the banks of the River Avon and then wandered down into Salisbury, gazing up in awe at the great spire of the cathedral. He loitered there for a couple of days, fully intending to move on and seek work on the farms to the south.

And then he met Constable Hollis, a broad man with a great beard. There had been no formal policing in Salisbury at that time, just constables employed by the Watch Committee. There were just thirteen constables in the city and one had succumbed to a consumption.

Anders, a fit lad, had moved into the terraced house with Hollis and his wife, and within a day or two had filled that casual vacancy. And that was what had eventually brought him to this dark office in Scotland Yard. For a brief period he had worked for

New Sarum Police, then its successor, the newly-formed City of Salisbury Police, then transferred to the Wiltshire Constabulary. Then, having served a colourful period as one of the county's earliest detectives, he had moved to London and the Metropolitan Police's Detective Division.

As he looked back, he thought how long ago much of it seemed. Many of the days annoying, frustrating and a pain in the arse. But better than scraping two ends together on a tiny farm. Oh yes! Much better than that! And then, just as you thought it was all going so well, there were complications. Matters that engaged you in much extra work. Such as the note that had come down from Inspector Gurney in Norwich.

There it lay on his desk, a flimsy piece of paper containing the name of the country lawyer who had worked on the Bartram estate. The man who had carried out the murder of William Marshall and his two sons. The vile creature who had maimed the hand of William Quest. Anders wondered just how he would set about arresting Jacob Raikes? What precedent was there for a policeman to take by the heels Queen Victoria's Spymaster?

He shouted for Berry, who was napping in the adjoining room.

It was time to find out.

~

A strange party gathered at a farmhouse some little distance from the Norfolk village of Wramplingham, an agricultural holding hidden deep in the heart of long fields, wild woodlands and lonely heaths. A cold wind blew in from the east, stirring the branches of the trees that overhung the muddy track down to the house. A few cattle lowed in protest and a pair of pheasants sought shelter in the undergrowth.

'It will snow before the week is out, that is for sure,' said Josef. 'Look at those grey clouds sweeping in from the horizon – gifts from Russia.'

His brother nodded in agreement.

'Aye, we have seen such clouds so often,' Isaac said. 'Fortunately, it will not come in before the burial, though this will all be a white land before the week is done.'

Quest stood in the open doorway, Rosa at his side.

'I remember them from boyhood, these Norfolk winters,' he commented. 'Snow of such depth that it half hid the trees in the coverts. Snow that blankets the open land. And a coldness...a coldness that is beyond belief. We used to huddle around the fire in Norwich, and it scarce warmed the room. I used to think of the hut dwellers out on these heaths, struggling to gather enough twigs to keep their fires alight. Many a traveller, caught out, was found, months later, frozen on the roads.'

Jasper Feedle called them back into the room, holding a keg of brandy above his head. 'All the more reason not ter freeze with the bloody door open. Come in! Come in! There's drink fer all! We'll might die of the cold at the buryings tomorrow. Or on the journey to this Earlham place. One way or t'other. And we need warm brains for that adventure!'

They all entered the one great downstairs room of the farmhouse, shutting the door on the grey weather outside. Ambrose, the farmer, threw another log on to the fire and joined them around the table, his fingers toying with the Monkshood pendant hanging down from his neck.

'All done, like you said. Word gone out. Not just Norwich but all 'bout the district. An' there'll be fast horses nearby should the need 'rise,' he said. He looked across at Quest. 'Gran' man your father. We only held this farm thanks to'n.'

'Thank you, Ambrose,' said Isaac. He resumed his cleaning of a pair of percussion pistols. 'If the plan works there should be no trouble at all. If it goes awry, well, we all know what we have to do. The most important thing of all is that nobody gets hold of you, Will. There's little they can pursue on the rest of us, but they have enough to lag and top our young Mister Quest.'

'Ere'll be bliddy riots if they try!' Ambrose slammed his fist down on the table. 'Many a folk be there with stout Norfolk sticks. And scythes and cudgels too.'

'I bin all over the ground with Ambrose,' said Jasper. 'Our troops is drilled and ready for battle. Greatest day since Waterloo if we're driven to it. That's what it'll be!'

'Rumour has it they may call out the Yeomanry,' said Isaac. 'So let us try and avoid a conflict, shall we? If they have a suspicion who young William is then we must haste him away, not bring them to battle.'

'And that is where you come in to it, my dear Sticks,' said Josef. 'You will be the last line of defence if they try and take William.'

The old prize fighter smiled a crooked grin, looking up from his tankard of water. 'Long time since I've been in a good barney!' he said.

'No, no, no!' Quest shook his head. 'None of you are to risk your necks for me! Is that understood? I am the one putting everyone in danger by being there. It is my risk, not yours. No blood is to be spilt for me. If they take me, well, they take me. I'll find a way out, even if it is through the offices of this man Wissilcraft. But nobody else, nobody else is to play hazard.'

'We understand,' said Josef. 'Now why don't you go upstairs and rest, my boy? We all have such a busy day tomorrow.'

'I'll be up soon,' said Rosa, reaching out to touch his arm. 'I'm tired beyond belief.'

Quest nodded and climbed the steep steps.

After he had gone and the door of the upstairs room had closed, Isaac looked at the quiet assembly around the table.

'If it can be done without hazard, so be it,' he said. 'But if there is any threat to William you know what you must do. Better that any one of us is taken rather than him. But no war, Jasper! There are too few of us to form square against a cavalry charge.'

~

Anders did not wait to be announced. With Berry close behind he pushed the diminutive Barker to one side and threw open the door. And then stopped dead at the sight of the very large man occupying Raikes' chair.

'Where is Jacob Raikes?' he began. 'I...'

'Ah, the good Inspector Anders, and Sergeant Berry is it? Yes, Sergeant Berry. I wondered how long it would take you to arrive. You are swifter than I imagined...' Wissilcraft looked amused at the two near-breathless detectives. 'If you are after Raikes, well, I'm afraid the bird has flown.'

'Gone?'

'He will never grace this office again. You have a warrant for his arrest?'

'I do,' Anders sank uninvited into the great oak chair by the door.

'For the murder of William Marshall and his brats no doubt?'

'There could be other charges,' Anders replied. 'There probably will.' He glared across at Wissilcraft 'Who are you?'

'Wissilcraft. Benjamin Wissilcraft, Her Majesty's Spymaster. A more reliable replacement for the treacherous Raikes. I was recently appointed to my post by milord Palmerston.'

'So where is Raikes?'

Wissilcraft fell silent, resting his chin in his hands. He regarded the two policemen for a while before replying.

'Gone,' he said at last. 'Gone to seek out the enemies of our land. He has fled to the coast. He intends to take ship for some distant land.'

'But why?' asked Berry.

Wissilcraft smiled up at the sergeant.

'Because he is a spy and a traitor who intends to sell his mother country out to the Tsar.' He thrust a document across the table to Anders. 'Here is *my* warrant for his capture – alive or dead. Signed by Lord Palmerston a little while ago.'

'I know nothing of that...' said Anders.

'Nor is it likely that you should. Tell me, what are your intentions?'

Anders stood up and walked across to the table.

'To bring him to book for the Marshall murders. To submit him to public trial at the Old Bailey. But right now I intend to travel to Norwich to take by the heels the villain known as William Quest...'

Wissilcraft let out a deep sigh, 'Ah, you are such a problem to me, Anders.'

'Why so?'

'You have intentions that I cannot possibly let you fulfil. You see, from the point of view of the government we cannot have Raikes blabbing all in a public trial. He has information that would bring down my masters in the political world. He might make allegations that could damage the greatest family in the land. And all at a time when our country is on the verge of war.'

'I care nothing for politics...'

Wissilcraft looked up at him with a pained expression, 'Oh, but you must, you really must.' He shook his head in despair. 'These matters and the people who are the architects of these matters. They are the glue that holds our civilisation together, awful though they may be.'

Anders held out his own warrants.

'These are legitimate documents, signed by a Queen's Justice. They give me authority to take both Raikes and Quest. And it is my duty to do so. Both men are indicted for murder.'

The spymaster tapped his hands on the table.

'They are but papers,' he replied. 'I can have them revoked within the hour. What is more, I have the authority to detain both your good self and your sergeant for as long as I need, certainly until my own personal mission is accomplished.'

Anders stepped across to the window, looking down at the busy traffic in Whitehall, his mind struggling as to how he might deal with the power that this fat man seemed to yield. After a few moments consideration he turned back to face Wissilcraft.

'I can understand,' he said at last, 'how you might wish to detain Raikes for these other crimes. But what is your defence of William Quest? He is killing members of the very establishment you seem so eager to preserve.'

'William Quest is mine,' said Wissilcraft. 'He works for me and he has a commission to take Jacob Raikes. For some days now Quest has been an agent of Her Majesty and is currently above the law.'

'But that is absurd...'

'Life is absurd, my dear Anders. Haven't you grasped that yet?'

'So what do you expect me to do?'

Wissilcraft took out his watch.

'It is a trifle past five. You are taking the late train to Norwich? Very well. You can attend the Marshall funeral, just to make sure that your associate, Gurney, does nothing to impede the freedom of

William Quest. After that you may make yourself available in Norwich in case I have need of you. You can seek lodgings at the Maid's Head. I will find you there after the funeral if I do not require you before.'

'And why are you coming to Norwich? To protect Quest, no doubt?'

Wissilcraft laughed, 'Among other matters. But more important than that...' He took a pinch of snuff from a silver box engraved with Greek gods cavorting in a woodland glade. 'Oh, I beg your pardon, may I offer you some of Raikes's snuff? He did a poor line in treachery but was something of a connoisseur with powder...'

Anders shook his head.

'Pity,' Wissilcraft continued. 'You know not what you are missing. Snuff clears the head magnificently.' He took in the snuff and breathed deeply. 'Earlier today I met a Russian. A most cooperative gentleman. He came forth with information that Raikes was to take ship from the north coast of Norfolk on the day after the morrow. I intend to be there. And my companion will be William Quest.'

~

'So what do we do now?' asked Sergeant Berry.

The two detectives were in a cab on the way to the railway station. Anders muttering with frustration as the carriage fought its way both through the traffic and the thick fog that had descended on the city.

'Do?' said Anders, 'We do everything we intended to do. That odious man overlooked the revoking of our warrants. I intend to arrest William Quest if he shows his face at the funeral tomorrow. And Raikes as well if fortune allows. And if my actions bring down civilisation, then, well, so be it. Now please put out your head and urge the cabman to make more speed!'

TWENTY-NINE

They came in silence for the most part, those mourners to the funeral of William Marshall. From all points of the compass they came; from the direction of the city of Norwich, from the far villages and brecklands of the west, and the hamlets and cottages of the northern heathlands. Many worked on the land, carrying their agricultural implements with them, though there were fishermen from the coastal towns and industrial labourers from the nearby city as well.

Those travelling on foot had set out the previous day, casting their work aside to make the pilgrimage. Many a horsedrawn cart had been secretly borrowed out of stables and coach houses so that the smaller and weaker members of families might be conveyed. Gypsies had travelled from across Norfolk to be there to acknowledge the memory of a man who had long championed their cause.

Many a traveller had spent the dark hours in the woodlands and open ground between Earlham and Wramplingham, their fires burning long into the night. A number had the pendant of the Fellowship of the Monkshood around their necks. Many of the latter were armed, with pistols hidden deep in the folds of cloaks and jackets, with blades, weighted life preservers and heavy Norfolk sticks and swingels carried more obviously.

The day before the funeral, the three hundred inns of Norwich had seen a roaring trade. Much had been drunk but good order had been preserved. The city constables had shrunk away, not seeking any sort of confrontation with the multitude that filled the alleys and great green spaces. Many a justice of the peace had locked his door and shuttered his windows to give the impression that he was not at home, lest he might be called out to read the Riot Act. All that day and the night afterwards an uneasy feeling settled over the streets and courts of Norwich, a mood that was half carnival and half wake. It was as though the very city was holding its breath.

Inspector Gurney, with no smile on his face, had passed through the Erpingham Gate into the Cathedral Close, quite late in the afternoon, filling in the time before he walked down to meet Anders and Berry at the railway station. He had expected the great space in front of the cathedral and the grammar school to be full of these strangers to the town. But it was strangely empty. He wandered through the great door into the cathedral and looked around the dark interior, but there was no one in sight. He strolled around the ambulatory, and then out to the cloisters, which was his favourite place in the whole building, but not a soul did he see. The ceilings of the cloisters were covered with colourful bosses, placed there by the medieval builders of the cathedral. Many of the bosses depicted brief snaps of religious scenes, though as many were pagan, some bordering on the obscene. Any number offered glimpses of moral danger.

Studying these remnants of a lost past had given him so much pleasure over the years. But now they seemed only to echo the gathering mood outside the Close, the menace that had suddenly appeared in the streets of the city and the wilder countryside beyond. As he left the cloisters and walked back out through the Erpingham Gate, he felt something that had passed him by on nearly all of his previous adventures – a real sense of fear.

~

It was a modest church, Anders thought, set near to the turnpike in the fields above the River Yare, with the old hall at Earlham half a mile distant through the trees. Not that the fields were easy to see, nearly all their green hidden by the multitude who had come to attend the funeral of William Marshall and his two sons. The small copse of woodland to one side of the church was filled with people too, aye, to the very topmost branches of the trees. The great park surrounding the hall was filled with mourners, all standing silently, their heads bowed. The men mostly dressed in their working clothes of smocks and breeches, the women wearing bonnets and red cloaks. Many were muttering quiet prayers. Others simply looked down at the ground, their thoughts apparently far away. The feeling of grief in the air was palpable.

'Don't like the look of that!' said Berry, looking over the crowds at the fields on the far bank of the little river.

Anders looked in the same direction. Across the long slope on the edge of the wood were perhaps thirty men in red coats on horseback, the dim winter sun glinting on sabres and spurs. With them were about the same number of troops on foot, carrying either muskets or rifles.

'The local militia,' Gurney explained. 'They are not here at our request. We specifically asked the landowners not to call them out. But they refused, believing that there might be predations upon their properties.'

'I thought the militias were stood down years ago?' said Anders.

'And so they were, but one or two of the silly old buffers who own estates have resurrected them in parts of Norfolk...all these rumours of war. They are mostly house servants, gamekeepers and so forth. I doubt they'd be much use in a scrap against all these mourners.'

Berry shook his head in despair, 'Englishman fighting Englishmen! There's something not right about it! My father was in St Peter's Fields in Manchester in 'nineteen when the troops charged people just like this. He'd fought with Wellington in

Spain and at Waterloo, but that didn't stop the bastards charging him and the others in the crowd.'

'Was he hurt?' asked Gurney.

Berry shook his head, 'He was one of the lucky ones, but the anger remained with him all his life.' The sergeant looked again across the fields. 'This could be a bloodbath if we're not careful. There are thousands of people come to mourn. And look at how they are armed! Swingels, life preservers, sticks, pitchforks and what have you. And I've seen more than a few hiding a pistol!'

Anders ran his hand over the black flints lining the church, apparently lost in thought. Looking up he saw some of the people in the crowd looking suspiciously in his direction. These Norfolk people knew a policeman when they saw one.

'We may not be able to take Quest today,' he said at last, 'even if we were to find him in such a mass of people. It could trigger a massacre. I never imagined that so many would come to a country funeral.'

'Marshall was highly regarded,' said Gurney. 'Norfolk people cherish their heroes. And he was a good man. And these mourners see his murder as an attack on all their liberties.'

Anders looked across the fields.

'I'd be inclined to slay the Bartrams myself,' he said, 'if Quest had not got to them first. This is an appalling world!'

'So what are we to do?' asked Berry.

348

Anders shrugged, 'Do? I don't know! But we still have a warrant for the arrest of William Quest and I intend to do my best to execute it. At the very least we will try and identify him. We may be given an opportunity to follow him from this sad place and take hold of him when the crowds have dispersed. And Berry, look out for the man Wissilcraft. He is sure to be here.'

Berry nodded.

'Wherever Wissilcraft is, well, I suspect Mr William Quest won't be far away.'

A great silence came upon the crowd, heads bowed across the multitude. People in the churchyard looked towards the gate. Anders followed their gaze. A procession of stout men were carrying three oak coffins into the churchyard.

~

Jacob Raikes sat alone in a corner of the tiny inn, hard by the harbour at Wells. The rough weather of the night before had calmed and the waves no longer crashed against the sand and marshes of the Norfolk coast. Now, as he looked from the window, there was just a flat calm of water beyond the creek, perfect for the landing of a small boat.

Would the sea hold back its ferocity for one more day? It was a matter of deep concern for Raikes. For there was now only one way to escape the country. There could be no return, no chance of turning round. Little possibility of finding another exit. He knew how efficient Palmerston and his agents could be. One more afternoon, one long winter night, another cold Norfolk morning. All of that before the ship's boat reached the shore.

This was a desolate coastline, sparsely populated, hardly patrolled by troops or coastguard, scantily policed. But there was still every chance that he might be taken. He himself, in his role as Spymaster, had designed the very mechanisms for capturing escaping traitors. He had done the task too well. For the first time in his life, Raikes felt that stomach churning fear he had so often induced in others. He clutched even tighter the waterproof bundle containing the precious documents, and his eyes closed with exhaustion, warmed into sleep by the heat from the tavern fire.

~

'We have done well, brother,' said Isaac Critzman, as he and Josef stood by the roadside, watching as the coffins were carried along the path to the church door. 'A greater crowd than I could possibly have imagined.'

Josef nodded at the far side of the graveyard. 'Including those three detectives over there. How kind of them to come and pay tribute to our lost comrades.' He looked across to the fields beyond the river Yare. 'And those soldiers too. I do hope there will be no trouble.'

'Word has gone around,' his brother replied. 'This is to be a peaceful mourning.'

'Let us hope so! Who is that man talking to William and Rosa?'

Isaac looked across to the small glade beneath the trees.

'From the description William gave I imagine that that is Wissilcraft,' he said. 'And he is a pest! If those policemen see him talking to William then, well, so much for the disguise.'

~

'It would be helpful if you would go away,' Quest muttered under his breath. 'I am here for a funeral and I would like to see it, even if I cannot go into the church itself.'

'My apologies,' said Wissilcraft, giving a slight bow and stepping a pace or two distant.

The three watched as the coffins were led into the church by a vicar with a high-pitched voice, intoning the first words of the burial service. Even when the cortege was well within they were able to hear the words as clearly as if they were inside. Only a small number of people had been able to cram inside the building.

Then, for several minutes all went quiet, until the coffins again left the building and were carried to the far side of the graveyard. A silence had fallen over the vast crowds as the vicar's words were carried, seemingly, to the most distant corners of the surrounding fields. As the coffins were lowered into the ground the mourners surged forward, covering every inch of the churchyard and the turnpike road beyond. Quest, Rosa and Wissilcraft found themselves swept forward, to the graveside, as the vicar committed the bodies to the ground.

Quest bowed his head, fighting back the tears. For a moment he thought that he might be overcome by grief to an extent that could be dangerous. He clutched, even tighter, the thick staff he held, so that its rough bark cut into his hands. The mild pain caused his mind to focus. He looked around. Rosa was by his side, holding on to his arm, and Wissilcraft was now several yards away. On the far side of the triple grave he recognised the detectives, Anders and Berry, hemmed in by mourners. To Quest's surprise both of the policemen seemed genuinely moved by the proceedings. More importantly, they were taking no notice of him. The vicar was saying some lines from the twenty-third psalm and thousands of people in the crowd were echoing his words.

Quest looked down at the three coffins, lying side by side, trying to visualise the faces of his father and brothers, something that had grown more difficult as the years had passed. It brought back memories of those last moments of their lives. He felt himself breathing deeper and deeper, until he had to force his head back to breath at all. No! No! No! Think of the danger, think of the situation. His breathing relaxed as he calmed down. He glanced up again and saw that the detective, Anders, was looking directly at him, his head a trifle to one side as if in thought.

~

Anders always found funerals difficult. He had been to a great many in the course of his life and his problems with these strange old-fashioned ceremonies never seemed to ease. He was not a man to show his emotions in any public way. Some said he was hard, careless of feeling. But it was not true. He always tried to hide his emotions because he felt matters so very deeply.

At a very young age he had stood in a graveyard in Wiltshire as they lowered his mother into the ground. That child had thrown himself down to the earth, crying as though his heart might break. His father had lifted him away to prevent the very real danger of the boy falling on to the coffin. Everyone had looked at him, and it was the subject of conversation for weeks afterwards. People had been kind, making a special effort to be nice to the little boy who had lost his mother. But it was too much to bear. He could not deal with that much pity. It seemed to stop his heart healing. For months afterwards he had sought out the high downs and the wooded hangers as places of sanctuary. Lonely spots where there was no one to feel sorry for him.

As Anders thought back to those times he felt a tear descend his cheek. He reached up and wiped it away with the back of his hand. He looked around at the immediate crowd, many of who were weeping unrestrainedly. Since the day he had buried his mother he had never felt such raw emotion at any funeral.

He looked down at the coffins, side by side in the joint grave, feeling a real fury for the Bartram brothers, the bloody dreadful gamekeeper Walsham, the man Raikes, whom he had known only too well – the monsters who had sent these three people to an early death. All dead themselves now except for Raikes. Hopefully only a matter of time before retribution came to the man with the penetrating eyes.

And then he looked up across the graveyard. There was Wissilcraft, several yards away from the grave, trying to ease his way out through the crowds. Anders didn't know what to make of the man. Probably as cruel and ruthless as Raikes in his way, but perhaps with more of a moral compass. Hard to say on such a brief acquaintance. Undoubtedly, Wissilcraft was a man who would interfere with police business if he had to. What a damned nuisance these government puppets are! Anders remembered where he was and dismissed the swear words from his head.

How moved the people were at this ceremony. Simple people, most of them, workers on the land like his own father back in Wiltshire. Some were openly in tears, others looked in a state of shock, as though something very precious had gone out of their lives.

How pale the old field worker looked who stood almost opposite him, how white the face above the filthy and torn old smock with its embroidered collar. A man who worked hard judging by the tatterdemalion state of his breeches. He might have been any age but, judging by the weather-beaten face and grey hair, was at least fifty or sixty. He clutched a rough staff made of blackthorn, as if his very life depended on it. A young woman, perhaps his daughter, had her arm through his. She wore, as did most of the women there that day, a bonnet and a red cloak, and she was undeniably pretty. Anders wondered vaguely who they were and what lives they lived under this vast Norfolk sky.

The vicar was almost shouting out in his strange high-pitched voice the verses of the twenty-third psalm, with many in the crowd echoing the words. To Anders' surprise he found himself saying them too, so much had the mood of the day caught him.

He looked across at the field labourer but the man remained silent, though his hands held the blackthorn tighter than ever. Poor battered hands, dirty with the grime of field work. And then Anders knew from the scars on the right hand that he had found William Quest. He looked again at the man's face and, even as he studied it, the mask seemed to fall away, the old labourer, despite the grey in the hair, transforming into the younger man he had met at Hope Down.

And then Quest looked straight into the detective's eyes. He gave a slight nod of the head. Anders, absurdly he thought later, half raised an arm as if in a wave, but then he lowered it again before nodding back in the direction of his quarry. As the vicar finished the service the two men regarded each other across the open grave.

~

Raikes felt uneasy.

There were several people wandering around Wells who didn't look like locals. This was a seldom visited little port, a haunt for fishermen and those who came to shoot on the marshes. Yet these other strangers clearly didn't fit into either category. They were much too well-dressed, and, too, well, idle, hanging around on village corners and roaming along the creek to the sea. And they all seemed to be taking a great interest in the tavern where he was staying. Raikes didn't recognise any of them. But he had not the slightest doubt that these creatures were spies. Men like himself. But not as clever. By no means as clever. But there was still a puzzle if he was correct. He could not see any reason why they did not descend upon the tavern and take him into custody.

He had watched them for hours through the little window of the inn, seen their comings and goings. Noted that, when two of them passed in the street, they made no acknowledgement to each other – which in itself was suspicious behaviour between strangers in such a little place. What amateurs! If they wanted to keep up the pretence they really should engage in conversation. It was what Englishmen did when they met another outsider in a place like Wells. He looked out at a watcher who was nearly hovering on the threshold of the inn and felt contempt. Palmerston really should find more skilled recruits.

Serov must have talked. That was the only possible explanation.

The little room in the inn was empty, the landlord and his family had retreated to the back parlour. The fire was dying as the faint winter sun perished outside. Raikes sank back the last of the brandy and went outside. It was time to put his suspicions to the test. Slamming the tavern door behind him, to make sure that the watchers were in no doubt that he was leaving, he strode across the lane and down to the beach, where so many whelk and shrimp boats were moored. Standing by the headwaters of the creek, he looked back at the houses of the town, watched as lights appeared in one house after the other. The man by the inn had moved but a few yards, two more were strolling up and down the path which led to the sea. Raikes observed them for several minutes, then strode purposefully back across the lane and up the narrow streets to the parish church.

Nobody followed. Nobody needed to. Two more men were standing in the graveyard, though they drifted away as he approached. He looked up at the church tower, indistinct now as the dark fell and a slight mist wafted in from the sea. Raikes stood still for a moment or two and then walked back down the street to the tavern. The two watchers were still on the path that ran alongside the creek. The watcher by the tavern was smoking a long pipe a hundred yards further on from its door.

Raikes made his way in, climbing the ladder that led to upstairs and entering his room. He did the usual checks from habit, the items left out, a piece of straw from the thatch placed where a foot would catch it, hard by the door. No one had been in to search the room. He put the bundle of documents down on the bed and reached the knapsack out from under a grainy old cupboard. He took out from it three pistols and a powder flask. Half watching out from the tiny window, he began the task of priming the guns. He felt annoyed that he was breathing so deeply. He had been in worse situations than this and stayed calm. He was baffled at this unaccustomed trembling of fear.

~

Anders grabbed Berry by the arm and rushed around the graveside. The crowds were dispersing and Quest and the girl were heading for the churchyard gate.

'You've seen him?' the sergeant cried.

'The old peasant,' Anders replied, 'the one with the young woman. Come on!'

'It can't be,' Berry muttered breathlessly as he was led across the graveyard. 'I watched him through the service. He must be sixty if he's a day!'

'Those aren't sixty year old scars on his right hand!' Anders declared. 'That's our man. And he knows we are on to him. Hurry, he's through the gate!'

As they ran they watched Quest and his companion walk swiftly through the gate and out on to the road. To Ander's annoyance, a group of mourners got in his way and he and Berry were obliged to force their way through. By the time they came nearer to the churchyard gate, Quest was walking speedily across the road. As Anders watched a man in the crowd stopped the fugitive for a moment, spoke a few words and slipped Quest a piece of paper. The fat figure then walked smartly back to the gate. Anders knew him well. It was Wissilcraft. As the two detectives reached the gate it was pulled shut in front of them, with the Spymaster on the farther side.

'Open this bloody gate!' yelled Anders. 'Now! Come on! I'll arrest you if I have to...'

'I think not,' Wissilcraft replied.

Anders turned to Berry, 'Sergeant, remove this man from the gate. Use your billy-stick if you have to. Then cuff him.'

'The sergeant will do no such thing,' Wissilcraft said. 'If he tries he will lose his employment...and so will you!'

'You have no authority...' Anders began.

'Oh, but I do,' said Wissilcraft, reaching deep inside the pocket of his coat. He produced a letter. 'This document gives me complete authority over all members of the police, irrespective of rank. It is signed by the Home Secretary, Lord Palmerston, and your own Commissioner of Police, Sir Richard Mayne. You may read it if you wish.'

Anders snatched the paper and looked at the brief message, before passing it to Berry. He, in his turn, held it out to Inspector Gurney, who had fought his way through the last of the mourners to catch them up.

'Your credentials are impeccable!' said Anders.

'They are indeed,' said Wissilcraft. 'And you will note that my orders give me full authority to use police detectives how and where I will. I could just order your return to Norwich or London, but I have

360

too much regard for your talents to dispose of you in that way. I have a traitor to catch and I may have need of your help. You see, my agents in Norfolk lack experience. They have seldom ever been used to detain Her Majesty's enemies. I have them observing Raikes even now, but I have little confidence in their ability to take him by the heels. If Quest fails, well, I may need your help.'

'Our help?'

'I have a growler awaiting us at Earlham Hall,' said Wissilcraft. 'It will convey us to the north coast of this county where Raikes is. Quest will get there first. He will ride through the night. On horseback. This matter might be dealt with before we even arrive.'

'More likely that Quest will just decamp,' said Anders, 'given that you have provided him with a horse to escape upon.'

'Do try to remember that he wants Raikes for his own ends. He'll not decamp. He's my creature now!'

'I wouldn't bet odds on that! Quest is a man with no master, save his conscience. God help all of us if you get this wrong, Wissilcraft!'

As the three detectives followed the Spymaster across the road, Gurney asked, 'Does he really intend to let your man Quest off scot free?'

'It seems so,' said Berry, 'free to continue with all of his activities, free to take the law into his own hands whatever the consequences.'

Anders said very quietly: '*Miching mallecho!*

THIRTY

There was a strange stillness in the winter dawn that came so late to the north coast of Norfolk, as though the dark was reluctant to edge away from its marshlands and long beaches. The sun offered little heat to the early fisherman who made their way down to their boats in the creek at Wells. Then it disappeared altogether behind the stretched iron-grey cloud that hid the sky.

As the little town came to life, several men, all of them strangers, seemed to gather closer to the tavern overlooking the harbour and the long stretch of water leading to the sea. Two men stood together on the path above the creek, watching the scene from some little distance.

'You are certain he is still in there?' Quest asked a tall, sallow-faced man with dark hair. 'You have kept the place under watch?'

'Master Wissilcraft says that we should not be certain of anything where that man is concerned. But as far as we know he is. He was certainly in there last night.'

'Who else is in the tavern?'

'Nobody,' the man replied. 'No one at all. I sent a man in at midnight. He ordered the landlord and his family out.' He noticed the concern on Quest's face. 'It was done quietly and carefully. They insisted the man we want is upstairs in his room, the one at the front.'

Quest looked again at the building.

'It seems very quiet,' he said. He pulled a percussion cap pistol from out of his coat. 'In that case I shall go in now. Are your men still at the back?'

'They are, sir. But should you not wait? Master Wissilcraft said that no movement should be made until he arrived.' He looked concerned. 'Unless Raikes attempted to leave. Then, only then, should we intervene.'

'We cannot wait,' said Quest. 'If he finds the tavern empty for too long he will become suspicious. We might have to besiege the place for days.'

'I'm not sure...'

'Wissilcraft has given me full authority to act, Collins.'

Collins looked uneasy but gave a slight nod. 'It might be wise,' he said. 'We'll go down together and I'll warn my men. Do you wish me to come in with you?'

Quest shook his head.

'It is a small building,' he replied. 'No room for both of us and him, perhaps with shot flying around. Just make sure that your men are there to close any escape routes.'

They walked down to the tavern and separated, Collins making his way to the rear of the inn. Quest checked his pistol and quietly opened the door. The tap-room was empty, though filled with the clutter of the night before. Quest made his way across it to the back parlour, which bore all the signs of the hurried evacuation of the landlord and his family.

He came out into the main room and examined the near-ladder that led, through a very wide trap door, to the upstairs. If ever there was a good place for an ambush that was it, he considered. Whatever part of his body went up through the door first would be an easy target for an assassin with a pistol. Yet short of dragging out the embers from the fire and setting the inn ablaze it had to be done.

He took a deep breath and climbed the ladder. It *seemed* all quiet, that was for sure. There was only one way to find out. He sped through the trap door, pistol out ready to take a shot. If Raikes fired first at least he might get a chance to settle him as well.

But nothing happened. There was no shot. There was no one waiting for him in the short corridor that led to the three rooms of the upper storey.

Quest crouched on the floor and checked the pistol again. Everything was fine. He reached inside his coat and brought out a second pistol. He pulled back the hammer, ready to strike the percussion cap, holding both weapons in front of him. Whatever happened there was a chance that the splay of fire from a pair of guns might catch Raikes in what was obviously going to be a small room.

He came to his feet and made his way along the corridor. Three doors and Raikes was in the room at the front. Or so the landlord had said. It would be the last of the three Quest opened. He had known of men being shot in the back by going into places they were expected to search first. The first door was slightly ajar. Quest paused outside and listened. Nothing. He crouched down to ground level and almost somersaulted into a tiny bedroom. Empty. He repeated the procedure with a larger room at the back of the inn. Empty. He glanced out through the window and looked down on Collins and two of his men covering the yard to the rear of the building.

Quest stood in the doorway and looked at the closed door of the room opposite. The only one leading into the room at the front of the inn. He would not risk turning the handle. One kick and in. Somersaulting and fast. The only way. He raised his two pistols and charged against the door.

As the door flew open the air seemed to explode all around him, the noise of a pistol deafening him as he crashed inside. Quest fell to the floor, his own pistols firing in reaction as his head hit the hard wooden floorboards.

And then he knew no more.

~

'I never seen such a beach,' said Jasper Feedle, standing amidst a long line of pine trees and looking along the great stretch of sand to the distant sea. 'I never seen such a beach. Not in all the places I bin. Not with Wellington even in Portugal and Spain.'

'Nor me,' said Sticks. 'It's like deserts I've read about in books. Why, you can scarce see the water. But this is the place. Holkham Beach they calls it. Looks like the ends of the earth to me.'

The tide was well out and what they could see of the sea was iron-grey, reflecting the great cloud that lay across the Norfolk landscape. The two men stood at the end of a long line of pines that crept along the shore, separating the sands of the beach from the marshlands beyond. In the distance was a line of wooded hills. Sticks could just make out a man ploughing.

'Too much space out there,' he said. 'Hard to hide and harder to run away from. But you can see a man coming. There is that about it.'

Jasper looked concerned. 'Not in them trees. Thinner here but dense down there. There could be a score o' crushers watchin' us. An' a reg'lar army scattered in them dunes. Now, if the old Duke was here he'd say, "that's a rare place for an ambush, Feedle. Take yer skirmishers down with their rifles and have a prowl!" Got yer pistols?'

Sticks reached inside the canvas bag he carried and brought out two guns. 'Ready to fire, so mind 'em,' he said. 'This is a place to die an' all! I'm glad the others stayed in the village. This beach has a rare and dangerous air to it.'

'It is the right beach?'

'So young Will said before he took to that horse. Mind, a good job Josef can read a map or hell only knows where we'd have ended up. I fear there'll be blood on that beach afore the morning's done.'

'If it's to be an ambush, then let's be the ambushers,' Jasper replied. 'Quite like old times, that's what this is.'

~

'I thought he had you!' said Collins, helping Quest to his feet. 'The shot missed you altogether?'

'My good fortune for coming in low through the door. I felt the wind of the ball as it passed over my head. One of the oldest ruses of all, a pistol triggered by cord as the door is pulled open. I had more damage from hitting my head on these wretched boards.'

And damn fool me for falling for such a trick, thought Quest. Just the sort of ambush I would have prepared myself if the roles had been reversed. This is what comes of being so personal in this matter. It blunts common sense.

'He might have shot the landlord or any of his family,' said Collins. 'He could not know that anyone pursuing him would have come in. This man is a callous wretch.'

'He is the most dangerous enemy. He must have left the inn last night in disguise, probably when the fishermen went home.'

'Then we've lost him!' Collins replied in a voice near to despair. 'The fat man'll have our guts!'

Quest shook his head.

'We have a chance yet,' he said. 'He can't leave the beach until the boat comes for him. We have a good hour. Come on, let's get outside.'

The two men clambered down the ladder and walked to the front door of the inn, where several of Collins' men had foregathered. A group of fishermen looked curiously from the other side of the lane, wondering at the noise of the gunfire. Out on the path leading to the sea, a tall man stood by an upturned boat, something like a long telescope in his hands.

'That man has a glass,' said Collins. 'He may have seen something.'

Quest looked in the across, as the fisherman pointed the long instrument in their direction.

'Get down!' he yelled, pushing Collins to the floor. But the order was not quick enough. The rifle was discharged and one of Collin's men fell to the ground, gasping in pain and clutching his shoulder.

'Some telescope!' Quest shouted. 'I'm for him. Before he can reload. Get everyone inside and tell those fishermen to hide behind their boats.'

As it happened Quest was not quick enough. He had scarce got across the lane before the rifle barked again. But he had seen Raikes raise the gun and had time to throw himself to the ground. The ball hit the track a foot in front of his face, sending up a small cloud of chalky dust. He looked up. Raikes had gone.

Quest dashed up on to the bank dividing the creek from the marshlands in time to see Raikes mounting a horse and heading towards the sea. He turned and ran back to where a street led into the little town. Here he had left the horse provided by Wissilcraft and, in a moment, was hot in pursuit.

The high bank was topped with a very narrow path and it took all his skills as a horseman to avoid tumbling down on to the sands of the creek on one side and the uncertain surface of the marshes on the other. Looking ahead he could see that Raikes was having the same difficulties. Both riders had slowed from the first mad gallop as the path tapered as it came nearer to the sea. And then Raikes was gone, down the bank and on to a wider path running parallel to the coast. Quest saw the fugitive bring the horse to a halt and swing round to face his pursuer. He watched as Raikes unhitched the rifle from his back.

Now Quest was in peril once again, trapped on the slight path on top of the bank, silhouetted against what little light that dull morning gave. He grabbed his bag and sword stick and flung himself off the horse and down the further side of the slope, just as the rifle cracked. The shot skimmed across the cantle of the saddle, sending the animal into a panic. Somehow it managed to turn in its own length and with an hysterical cry rushed back in the direction of Wells.

Before it was even out of sight Quest had run along the bank towards the sea, desperately trying to avoid tumbling into the mud of the creek. It was steep with long grass that clung and entrapped his boots. He fought to keep his balance as he struggled along its length. If Raikes was to climb to the top of the bank Quest knew that he would have small chance of surviving the encounter. He reached into his bag, taking out a pistol. He might get a chance of a shot if Raikes' head appeared above him.

But it didn't happen. Quest reached the end of the bank, where a few spindly trees hid the great water beyond. He could hear the distant soughing of the waves. But where was Raikes? Somewhere within yards. Within feet, maybe.

Quest found out as he worked his way round to the western side of the bank. Another rifle shot rang out, the ball nearly hitting his right shoulder. And at that moment Quest charged, before Raikes could have a chance to reload. He saw the man look up in alarm as he observed his predicament. Raikes had let go of his horse's bridle as he took the shot, and the horse, hating the noise, had taken the opportunity to dash for a grassy meadow leading down to the marshes, its wild neighing echoing across the watery ground.

Before Quest had reached the broad track, Raikes had flung the rifle to the ground and fled for the trees separating the marshland from the coast. As Quest raced across the same ground a pistol barked from somewhere in the cover and he heard the ball burn through the air above his head. In a crouching run he reached the trees and threw himself down in front of an ancient pine. There was a great crashing in the undergrowth. Raikes was somewhere in front of him, fighting his way up the slope as he sought out higher ground.

Running for his life.

Quest checked his pistol and got back his breath. He adjusted the cord that held the sword stick across his back. The noise had stopped, which meant that Raikes had halted somewhere above him. Quest swore beneath his breath. He should have moved further into the wood while the hunted man was still running. Now there was only danger for him in this fixed position. But the man must be a fair way ahead and it took a good shot with a pistol to hit a man at any distance, particularly if the target was moving swiftly.

Quest stood up and ran. Up the slope towards the sea, at a right angle to the course taken by Raikes. A pistol fired from higher up in the wood, followed almost immediately by another. Where the balls went Quest could only guess for he heard nothing of their passage. As he came to a rest amidst the highest trees a third shot rang out. And there was his man! Raikes was standing a hundred yards away reloading. Quest aimed a pistol in his direction and fired, though it would have been a lucky shot to strike his prey at that distance. As he hit the ground himself, he got a glimpse of Raikes jumping sideways behind a tree.

For a few moments all was quiet except for a slight breeze through the trees and the distant splashing of the waves. Quest huddled against the roots of an old pine tree and reloaded his pistols. And then he heard Raikes, running, running for his life, crashing through the undergrowth. Quest eased himself up against the trunk of the tree and peered round in time to catch a glimpse of his quarry dashing further along the wood.

Instead of following along the same route, Quest crossed through the woodlands and out on to the edge of the sands. Then, almost at a run for several minutes, he headed parallel to the trees towards the dunes overlooking Holkham Bay.

The great beach lay beyond, vast and mysterious, its sands occasionally disturbed by the light wind that came in from the sea. So grey was the sky and the distant water that it was hard to see where one ended and the other began. Quest had visited the place once as a boy, but had forgotten the sheer scale of it. This coast, he thought, was a strange nether world, not quite of the land nor of the water. Like a place in some ancient myth where accounts are settled and men come to die. An entrance gate to Valhalla, where heroes might perish, sword in hand.

As he edged nearer to the dunes, the looser sand made running difficult and he was forced to pause for breath. In the quiet of that moment he could still hear Raikes fighting his way through the edge of the wood. It seemed that any moment he must come down on to the beach. Quest waited, holding out both pistols lest he needed to shoot in a hurry. Then, for a moment, there was complete silence. He could sense that Raikes was scanning the beach, listening for the noise of his pursuer, watching out for any possible ambush.

In the far distance, across the sweep of the beach and at the edge of the sea, a seagull swerved and caught Quest's eye. Below it a white flag was being waved, and below the signal he could just make out three or four men and a rowing boat. It seemed that Raikes's rescuers had arrived, though they were a good half mile away. The sight caused Raikes to dash out of cover and on to the beach, where he waved a hand above his head. Then, as if realising the folly of the move, he turned and looked directly along the edge of the dunes to his pursuer.

There was no cover for Quest to seek shelter. He raised both pistols and fired at Raikes, though the distance was hopeless for a good shot. Laying the guns down on the ground, he took off his satchel and, armed now only with the blade from his sword stick, walked forward towards his enemy.

When they were just a hundred feet apart Raikes held out one pistol in the manner of a duellist and fired. He was still breathing heavily from his exertions and the movement sent the shot wide. Quest vaguely noticed that the shot went into the grass of one of the dunes to his left. He saw Raikes nod his head as though acknowledging his failure. He was barely fifty feet from the man now.

A seagull gave a long mournful cry somewhere overhead and the distant waves whispered. Somewhere he heard shouting and then a distant crack of guns. He saw Raikes turn. The men on the edge of the beach were pushing the rowing boat back out into the waves and heading back towards a sailing vessel that had come within sight.

Raikes raised his second pistol and fired again. The ball caught the shoulder of Quest's jacket and then careered along the beach, creating a vivid line along the sand.

Quest walked to within a dozen feet of his prey.

Raikes turned and took one last glance at the departing rowing boat. He shrugged, before looking back at Quest, his head held slightly to one side as if out of curiosity.

'Who are you?' he said.

~

Jasper Feedle saw the rowing boat first, for Sticks was engrossed by the sight of the two duellists further along the beach. He could hardly bring himself to turn as Jasper tugged at his arm.

'What...what?'

And then he saw the boat beaching on the shore.

'Well, whatever happens we'll stop him getting away,' he said. 'Come on...'

Sticks and Jasper walked out on to the beach, oblivious to a shot that rang out from the direction of Quest and Raikes. The two men had a pair of pistols apiece. These they raised and fired in the direction of the men and the rowing boat. At that distance it would have been a fortunate shot with rifles, but the fusillade did the trick. The rowers fled back to their boat, which they pushed out into the waves. Another shot echoed along the beach. They turned and, to their relief, saw that Quest was still standing.

'Come on,' said Feedle. 'The lad may need us!'

~

'Who are you?'

Quest looked across at the man he had sought for so long. He did not reply at once, but stood still regaining his breath.

'I take it you are one of Wissilcraft's minions?' Raikes continued. 'I hear that our fat friend has replaced me as Palmerston's pet?'

'I'm not here for either of them,' Quest replied. 'Whether you are a traitor or not is none of my concern.'

'Then who are you?'

'William Marshall.'

Raikes looked across at him, puzzled. He shook his head. 'I'm afraid you have the advantage of me...' he said. 'We have met before?'

'Just once,' said Quest, holding up his hand. 'When you whipped these marks on to me with your riding crop. When you incited the Bartrams to hang my father and brothers from a tree.'

A look of understanding crossed Raikes's face.

'Of course,' he smiled, 'you are the little bastard we chased through the woods. And now you are chasing me. I take it you slaughtered the Bartrams and those other members of society? Why, yes, of course! You are the man I have been hunting. And now you've brought me to bay.'

He became aware of footsteps in the sand behind him. He half-turned and watched as Feedle and Sticks came closer, pistols still in their hands.

'And mob-handed too,' said Raikes, 'just as we were that day. So you haven't the courage to try and kill me yourself. You expect your comrades to shoot me down?'

Quest held out his arm, palm upright, to halt Feedle and Sticks. 'They will not interfere,' he said, 'and you have my word that they will let you go if you kill me.'

'So we are to duel?' asked Raikes.

'No quarter,' Quest replied, 'to the death.'

Raikes smiled again, 'You have me at a disadvantage. My pistols are discharged.'

'And so are mine,' said Quest. 'But we both have blades in our sword sticks.'

'You disappoint me,' said Raikes. 'A swordstick is hardly a suitable duelling weapon for a gentleman. They are designed for a sudden and vicious use, not for swordplay.'

'They are what we have,' Quest replied. 'We can always do this with our bare hands if you would rather. I am no duellist and I am, very fortunately, not a gentleman by your definition.'

Raikes threw the bag from his shoulder and removed the swordstick he had attached to it. He regarded the deep black ebony of the cane for a moment before withdrawing the blade. He looked across at Quest who had done the same.

'This is absurd,' he said. 'These blades have not the strength of swords. Perhaps we should reload our pistols? Is it not customary for the man challenged to have the choice of weapons?'

'I regret to say that I am out of ammunition.'

Raikes sighed.

'Then blades it is,' he said. He glanced around the sands. 'I fought a duel once before on a beach such as this. Near to Boulogne. Though in a more conventional way – with pistols.'

'And you obviously won?'

'I shot my opponent in the gut. He took an hour to die. He was in agony till the end. I stood over him and watched. One of my life's more pleasurable experiences. But I lack time to stay here and enjoy your end in quite the same manner.' He waved towards the sea. 'My transport has departed. I must hurry and find other means to leave this rotten land. That is if your guarantee is honest and your men will allow me to leave.'

Quest looked over Raikes's shoulder at Sticks and Feedle. 'I have given you my word,' he said. 'If you kill me they will let you depart in safety.'

Raikes swished the blade through the air a few times.

'Then let us not waste any more time,' he said.

And before his words were finished he dashed at Quest, thrusting the blade straight out towards his stomach. Quest took a half-step to the right and parried Raikes's blade up with his own. His opponent took a pace backwards.

'A good opener,' Raikes said. 'Now is the time to stop playing this as a game.' He swished his blade a few more times and began to advance on Quest. As he came within range he brought the blade down from on high for all the world as if it were a sabre. Quest held up his own weapon horizontally into the air and caught the blow, though its ferocity made him stagger backwards.

'That is the trouble with stabbing weapons such as these,' said Raikes. 'The point is sharp but not the edges. A sabre with its weight and cutting edge would have cut off your shoulder just then.'

'It is a poor duellist that blames his weapon,' said Quest. 'I am letting destiny decide your fate. Destiny and your skill. I could have stabbed you in some dark alley like I did Bartram.'

'I think, on reflection, you did the world a favour by killing him,' Raikes laughed. 'Did he squeal like a dying pig? That is how I imagined his end.'

'Have a care for your own,' Quest cried out, advancing swiftly on Raikes, his blade aiming at the man's throat. But he came too quickly and Raikes, pushing up the attacking blade, threw out a leg and kicked Quest in the stomach, smiling with delight as Quest rolled backwards on to the ground, gasping for breath.

'Not gentlemanly, but you failed to define any rules.' Raikes ran the few steps after the fallen Quest and, holding the handle of the blade with both hands thrust it down towards Quest's throat. Quest, seeing it coming, pulled instantly to one side, the intended fatal blow penetrating his right shoulder.

With some difficulty Raikes extracted the blade and lifted it high into the air ready to strike again. But Quest rolled again and the swordstick found only the wet sand of the beach. He switched his own blade into his left hand as he made the move and clambered to his feet as he went, the blood from the shoulder wound pouring down his chest.

'You are badly hurt,' said Raikes. 'Try and spend your last moments enjoying the pain. It will be the last sensation you get on this earth. Can you fight a blade with your left hand?'

He charged at Quest again, turning half round as he came to add force to the thrusting blow which was aimed at Quest's heart. But, even as he ran at him, Quest dropped down on to his knees. And as Raikes's blade skimmed the side of his face, Quest thrust upwards with all the force his left arm would allow, deep into the man's chest. Raikes, unable to slow his charge, took the blade further and further within himself with every step.

Quest fell backwards on to the ground, weakened by the loss of blood, but all too aware that his blade had been torn from his hand. He looked up at Raikes, standing over him, waiting for a further blow. But Raikes's own blade was lying on the sand, several feet away, and Raikes was clutching with both hands at the handle of Quest's own swordstick, which was buried deep within him.

The dying man turned a ghastly pale colour, though the twisted smile was still there. He breathed deeply, his face etched with pain.

'What a folly life is!' he shouted down at Quest.

For a second he stood still. Then he walked with uneven steps towards the place where his own blade lay. With a grunt of pain he reached down and picked it up. With the swordstick in his hand he stood and turned and faced Quest. Then, as a breath of wind came in from the east and ruffled his hair, he pitched forward on to his face.

~

'Company's coming!' said Sticks as he tore up his shirt to make bandages for Quest's arm and shoulder. He nodded towards a group of men who were fast approaching along the beach.

'Jasper has gone?' asked Quest.

'He has,' Sticks smiled, 'though he'll be watching us from the wood. He did what you wanted.' He began to wrap Quest's wound. 'Huh, a pin-prick, no more. I've had deeper gashes with my cut-throat...'

'It bloody hurts,' said Quest.

'Ah just pain on the surface, better in a week or two, though I do hope these gents what are coming don't want a fight as well!'

The four men were now recognisable as Wissilcraft, Anders, Berry and Gurney.

'The forces of law and order,' Quest muttered. 'Still they don't seem to have the darbies out. However, should they get objectionable leave me and make a run for the trees.'

'I think I'd rather stay here and top them. I've four loaded pistols in this here satchel. I was saving one for our friend there,' Sticks said nodding towards Raikes's corpse.

'I told you he was to walk away...'

'I knows what you said! But all the same. If he'd won the bout I'd have turned him off with a pistol ball in his head!'

'You are an incorrigible rogue!'

'I'm sure you all are,' said Wissilcraft, as the newcomers came up to them. 'There'd be a busy day outside Newgate if we brought you all up to the Bailey.'

'And we could still,' Anders added, turning to Wissilcraft. 'I might argue that my warrant is still valid.'

'I think not,' Wissilcraft replied. 'I'm not saying that Lord Palmerston intends anything like a full pardon. Rather that some previous occurrences are overlooked.'

Anders looked despairingly at Berry and Gurney.

'What do you think?' he asked.

They both shrugged.

Anders let out a deep breath and knelt down by Quest. 'That is a nasty wound. Best that you leave this field of battle and have it properly dressed.' He looked around the beach. 'God, this is a bleak place! I preferred the comfort of your home at Hope Down. You may go. We'll help your man carry you to the village. But I would urge you not to cross my path again, Mr Marsh...Mr Quest.'

'I'll try to keep well out of your way,' Quest replied. He looked up at the detective and smiled. 'But then I always did try to avoid the attentions of the detective force...'

'Good man Quest,' cried Wissilcraft, tumbling the documents out of Raikes's bag. 'All here...all here. Lord Palmerston will be very pleased with you.'

'Not too pleased, I fear,' whispered Quest to Anders.

'But wait!' Wissilcraft thundered. 'There is a particular notebook. Raikes's notebook. It is not here.'

Anders stood. 'What is in this notebook?' he asked.

'Quest knows what is in the notebook,' he shouted. 'It is more damning than all these documents that Raikes would have given to our enemies. Its contents could bring down the highest in the land.'

'I take it you do not now have this notebook?' Anders asked Quest.

'I do not,' he replied.

'And where is it?' Wissilcraft held out a hand almost as though Quest might throw it up to him. 'Where is the book?'

'The book is long gone,' said Quest, 'but it is safe enough. And so are the reputations of the highest in the land. I will not misuse the contents within that little volume.'

'What?' said Wissilcraft.

'What I mean to say,' Quest continued, 'is that I will not use the information in the notebook unless I have to. It will stay hidden for eternity as long as my associates and I are left alone.'

'But this is blackmail!' Wissilcraft protested.

'It is indeed,' said Quest. 'Best that you tell Lord Palmerston that it was destroyed, lest he becomes...anxious. You have my word that it will never see the light of day. So now we may all go our separate ways...'

'I know nothing about notebooks and care even less,' said Anders. 'But this man is injured and should be in the warm.' He looked up at the grey sky which was now yielding an occasional snowflake.

'Quite right,' said Sticks. 'Mr Quest needs mending so he can make his way home. And I'd remind you gentlemen that I still have several loaded pistols in my bag.'

'You won't need them,' said Anders. 'One killing is enough for a day in winter.'

~

Jasper Feedle stood high amongst the trees above the beach, watching as Sticks and the three detectives carried William Quest back to the track leading to the village. He wondered how many battlefields a man might have to see in one lifetime. He glanced down at the notebook he was clutching in his hands, wondering just what it contained.

'Ah, well,' he said aloud, 'what a place this was for a skirmish!'

As the snow began to fall he walked through the trees and then out on to the path which led back across the marshlands, his crutch swinging with every step. And as he paced the narrow track he began to hum his favourite old song: *'Where have you bin all the day, Billy boy, Billy boy? Where have you bin all the day me Billy boy?...'*

THE END
but William Quest will return...

Also available from Gaslight Crime in paperback and Kindle eBook – *A Seaside Mourning*

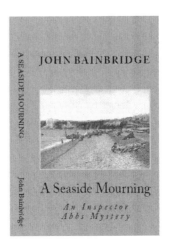

Devonshire 1873. The peaceful seaside town of Seaborough, half-forgotten on the eastern border of the county, seems an unlikely setting for a murder. When a leading resident of the town dies, the cause of death is uncertain. Inspector Abbs and Sergeant Reeve are sent to determine whether the elderly spinster was poisoned. Behind the Nottingham lace curtains and over the bone china tea cups trouble has been brewing. Seaborough is changing, new houses are going up and some leading inhabitants are ambitious for the town to become a popular resort. As one death leads to another, the detectives need to work fast to uncover the secrets beneath the surface of this respectable seaside town.

NON-FICTION BY JOHN BAINBRIDGE

THE COMPLEAT TRESPASSER

In 1932, five ramblers in England were imprisoned for daring to walk in their own countryside. The Mass Trespass on to Kinder Scout, which led to their arrests,

THE COMPLEAT
TRESPASSER
JOHN BAINBRIDGE

has since become an iconic symbol of the campaign for the freedom to roam in the British countryside.

The Compleat Trespasser – Journeys Into The Heart Of Forbidden Britain looks at just why the British were - and still are – denied responsible access to much of their own land. This ground-breaking book examines how events through history led to the countryside being the preserve of the few rather than the many.

It examines the landscapes to which access is still denied, from stretches of moorland and downland to many of our beautiful forests and woodlands. It poses the question: should we walk and trespass through these areas regardless of restrictions?

*We hope you have enjoyed reading **The Shadow of William Quest**. If you have, we would appreciate it if you would leave a positive review on this book's page on Amazon and tell your friends. You can contact us at:* <u>gaslightcrime@yahoo.co.uk</u>

The Gaslight Crime Blog

Visit the Gaslight Crime blog to keep up to date with our latest publications, news and interviews. Just Click follow at:

<u>www.gaslightcrime.wordpress.com</u>

20952683R00229

Printed in Great Britain
by Amazon